1283

GUM'S STORY

A NOVEL

GUM'S
STORY

by Rick Turnbull

HARBOR
HOUSE

This is a work of fiction. I have exercised the novelist's prerogative and created landscapes of both Vietnam and Augusta, Georgia, which, in certain aspects, reflect a much earlier era. Readers who think they see themselves or someone else in this book are mistaken.

GUM'S STORY
By Rick Turnbull
A Harbor House Book/September 2001

For information address:
    HARBOR HOUSE
    3010 STRATFORD DRIVE
    AUGUSTA, GEORGIA 30909

Jacket Illustration and Book Design by Fredna Forbes
Author Photo by Todd Lista

Publisher's Cataloging-in-Publication Data
Turnbull, Rick, 1955-
Gum's Story: a novel / by Rick Turnbull
p. cm.
ISBN 1-891799-22-3
1. Vietnamese Conflict, 1961-1975--Fiction. 2. Americans--Vietnam--Fiction. 3. Air pilots, Military--Fiction. 4. Vietnam--Fiction. I. Title

PS3620.U77 G86 2002
813'.6--dc21   2001045724

Printed in the United States of America
10 9 8 7 6 5 4 3 2 1

In memory of my father and best friend, Rod Turnbull,
who showed me that magic is accomplished
by honesty and hard work;
and to my mother, Lela Turnbull, who still believes
that magic just happens. I think both of them are right.
Thanks, Mom and Dad, I love you both!
And for Betty Cowart, you are the strongest person I have ever met.

Acknowledgements

*I want to thank Sherri and Dee Humphreys, Mark Randolph
and Paul Gonzalez for their proofreads and input. I listened to each
and every remark, and you will find your efforts reflected.*

*Elizabeth Estes, you have my never-ending gratitude.
I still have a ways to go, but I could have never gotten this far
without your patience, expertise and guidance.*

*I also want to thank my publisher and editor, E. Randall Floyd,
and my designer, Fredna Lynn Forbes, for helping make this book possible.
You guys are the best.*

*One last Thank You goes to my wife, Donna
and my daughter, Taylor. How did I ever get so lucky?*

CHAPTER ONE

Crack! Boom!

The sudden crash of thunder rolled through Phillip Turner's brain, jolting him awake. His first instinct was to duck and cover, to grab his gear and brace for incoming.

Then, rubbing his eyes, he noticed the clock on the bedside table and remembered where he was—a nondescript motel room on the outskirts of Hickory, North Carolina. He strained to make out the time—7:30 a.m., way past time to get up.

Part of the dream stayed with him, even as he tried to will himself awake. The machinegun and mortar fire, the explosions, the sound of women and children screaming and stampeding through a crowded Saigon street.

Another savage blast of thunder shook the room. Outside, the rain howled and scratched against the windowpane. Phillip pushed himself to his elbows and looked around. Yellow patches of lightning danced off the far wall, highlighting a pair of keys on the TV that danced and jangled in the mayhem.

Sweat poured from Phillip's brow, dimming his vision as tattered fragments of the dream floated through his mind.

He saw Gum riding his bike, Gum smiling and waving as he peddled hard to catch up with the big plane taxiing down the runway. He saw the approaching jeep, the glint of blue steel, the sudden puff of smoke, the frozen look of horror on Gum's face.

No!

Phillip lurched forward, grabbing empty air.

Only when he leaned back and felt the familiar warmth of his wife's body lying next to his did the dream start to fade. Half-turning, he caught a glimpse of Kassy with a pillow to shield out the noise. He fought the urge to pull her close, to wake her up so she could help him make the nightmare go away.

Phillip swung his long legs over the side of the bed and pushed up. He staggered forward, straight into a wall that wasn't supposed to be there. Once again, he remembered they were at a Holiday Inn. He and Kassy had arrived in Hickory the day before to do some furniture shopping, something they did just about every Memorial Day.

He found the bathroom, flicked on the light. The face that glared back at him from the mirror gave him a shock. It couldn't be his, no way. He leaned closer, studying the stranger staring back at him. Full-bearded and puffed, with way too much gray and more lines than should be proper for a once handsome, blue-eyed, forty-five year old. When did you get to be so old, he heard himself asking the imposter in the mirror. Phillip was always way too hard on himself. His midlife guise was more like a diamond in the rough that women found a sexual attraction to and men respected.

He brushed his teeth, then went to work on his beard with the scissors and comb. Satisfied, he toweled off and splashed on a handful of cologne.

Back in the bedroom, Phillip sat down on the corner of the bed and slipped on his clunky white Reeboks. Out of the corner of his eye he watched Kassy still fighting with her pillow. She squirmed and mumbled in her sleep. He reached down and gently stroked her strawberry blonde hair. When she flinched, he drew back. He didn't want to wake her. Not yet. It was still too early. The early morning hours belonged to him.

He stood, ready for his ritual cigarette and coffee. He blew his sleeping wife one final kiss, then opened the door and stepped into the hallway.

The restaurant was located just off the lobby. He found a table, sat down and ordered a cup of coffee. While he waited for the waitress to bring him his wake-up brew, he poured over the headlines in the local paper. Out of habit he found himself scanning the obituaries.

"Will there be anything else, sugar?" the waitress asked, brushing dangerously close as she poured a cup of coffee. The scent of cheap perfume and the sound of smacking gum made Phillip wince.

"That'll do for now," he replied. "We'll order breakfast when my wife comes down."

"Oh, you're married then," the waitress said, a trace of disappointment in her voice.

Phillip smiled. "Have been for a long time."

The waitress stopped smacking her gum long enough to heave a despondent sigh. "Some women have all the luck," she huffed. She patted her French bun hairdo, flipped her order pad shut and bustled away.

Phillip took a sip of the coffee and lit up another cigarette before turning his attention to the paper again. He flipped through the sports section, business news and editorial pages before going back to the front page. Suddenly, in the center just below the fold, he noticed a wire service photograph. It was a black and white Memorial Day shot, featuring a short, balding, sixtyish Asian male clad in a light-colored trench coat and holding a black, small-brimmed hat.

The caption read: *Retired General Chu of the South Vietnamese Army, a highly decorated hero of the Vietnam War, honors his fallen comrades with the placing of this wreath on "The Wall," the Vietnamese War Memorial in Washington, D.C. General Chu is retired and now lives in the United States.*

At that moment a brilliant burst of lightning seemed to split the room in half. The ensuing peal of thunder rattled windows and almost knocked Phillip out of his chair.

Trembling, Phillip forced himself to glance down at the photo again. *It can't be,* he heard himself saying. *It's not possible.*

Rivulets of sweat broke out across his forehead as he studied the image in the photo. An image Phillip had spent the past two decades trying to forget. His gut flipped and churned, boiled and gurgled. He felt sick, sicker than he had felt in years.

As Phillip's eyes continued to burn holes in the dreaded image before him, his mind reeled and spun, jerking him back to 1973.

CHAPTER TWO

AT AN ALTITUDE of thirty-thousand feet, the U.S. Air Force Lockheed C5a was nearing the end of a nonstop flight which had begun twenty-three hours earlier. The huge cargo jet, the world's largest aircraft, had left Travis Air Force Base the day before, headed for Bien Hoa Airbase, located several rice paddies north of Saigon in South Vietnam. The long, hot journey had required four in-flight refuelings to keep it in the air. All that extra work had exhausted the flight crew of eleven. Everyone was anxious to get on the tarmac at Bien Hoa.

Phillip Turner, the crew chief, crouched in the lower cargo bay checking gauges on the hydraulic pumps. The tall, lanky kid from Georgia had just celebrated his twentieth birthday. On that same day he had received his third stripe, making him a very young buck sergeant. His job on board the mammoth jet was to inspect and maintain the various on-board flight systems—a tall order for one so young, but one which the fresh-faced sergeant relished deeply. Ever since joining the Air Force, his goal had been to get on a flight crew. There was something about these guys that set them apart from other airmen. Maybe it was the uniforms, the olive green flight suits, or the way they carried themselves. Hell, even their "forty dash ten" regulation haircuts stood out.

Crawling and slithering, Phillip was able to squeeze past two Blue Bird troop buses, the same type used to take children to school, in order to gain access to panels on the side of the aircraft. He checked pressure readings, saw they were okay, then back-crawled toward the middle of the cargo hold. A pair of Huey helicopters caught his attention. Stripped of their rotor blades for the long, cramped ride to Vietnam, they huddled in the shadows like black, prehistoric beasts. His eyes were drawn to the stacks of gleaming aluminum caskets—"transfer cases" that reminded him where he was going.

As he gazed at the caskets, Phillip's mind drifted back to a few weeks earlier when he was home on leave. It was a Sunday morning. He and his family had gone to early Mass at Our Lady of Peace Catholic Church to allow him plenty of time to catch his flight back to Travis AFB.

They had just descended the steps when he felt his father's heavy hand on his shoulder. "Phillip, come over here for a minute," he heard his father say. "I have a few words to share with you."

His dad led him to a spot between two camellia bushes. The two men stood face-to-face on the carpet of bright green winter rye, sizing each other up. His dad sighed and said, "Your mother tells me you've volunteered to fly on cargo missions into South Vietnam," William Turner began. "You know, you don't have to really do this. Not if all you've got in mind is carrying on the Turner tradition."

Phillip felt something like a tidal wave wash over him. As the son of a son of a son of a career military man, he had always known he would follow in those footsteps. He'd just take a slightly different route, forgoing college and officer candidate school. All he wanted to do was ride those big planes, to smell the engine fuel and oil, to take to the skies and serve his country as an enlisted man.

"I've seen your face light up when your grandfather and I swap licks about our wars and battles, his in WW-1 and mine in WW-2," William Turner continued. He cleared his throat and a serious look came into his eye. "But, boy, what I want you to understand is that those were different times, different kinds of wars. God was on our side back then, and we knew we were doing the right thing." He paused long enough to wipe his glasses before continuing. "Now, this mess going on over there in Vietnam, it's different. Truth be known, I'm just not sure which side God happens to be on with this one."

The elder Turner heaved a deep sigh. He reached down and took hold of his son's right hand and gave it a firm squeeze. "You just go on and do what you have to do," he said directly. "You do the right thing with yourself. The Old Master will take care of everything else."

The plane yawed sharply to the right, jarring Phillip back to the present. He could still feel the warmth of his father's hand on his shoulders, still hear his voice rasping in his ear as he steadied himself for the plane's rapid descent.

Ping.

Instinctively, Phillip cupped his hand across his headset.

"This is Colonel Danworth," a hearty male voice boomed into his earpiece. "Just wanted to welcome you to 'the country,' Sergeant. If you want to do any sightseeing, you better get your butt up here on the double."

Phillip adjusted the boom microphone attached to his headset. He clicked on his mike.

Ping.

"Yes, sir, right away, sir."

Phillip grabbed his clipboard, finished jotting down the readings he needed, then started making his way toward the flight deck ladder. Tucking the clipboard in his belt, he hurried up the rungs leading from the cargo hold to the flight deck. Turning left, he moved toward the forward end of the aircraft.

To the rear of the cockpit on the left was the flight navigator's station, crammed with charts, weather reports and radar goodies. Captain Erin gave him a thumbs-up as he moved past toward the pilot's station.

The captain gave a good-natured grin and said, "Welcome to The Nam, Sarge."

"Ditto that," replied Captain Benson, the flight engineer. "Better take a good look."

Major Stewart, the co-pilot, leaned around, backsliding his position to the rear and said, "Come on up, rookie," he said, easing out of his chair. "You wanted to fly in here so bad. Take a seat for the big show."

Colonel Danworth, the pilot, was a big, rugged man with heroic features—strong, chiseled chin, tight blonde hair and blue, piercing eyes. He had that John Wayne "Duke" look, the one Phillip admired so much in a military man. Here's a man who could win wars single-handedly, Phillip found himself thinking. Phillip felt a kinship with the handsome colonel the second he laid eyes on him.

The colonel pointed toward the one inch thick widescreen. "Well, son, what do you think?" he asked. His voice was more like a bark than a question.

Phillip stared out the window. Down below, stretching for miles and miles, was a treeless, hilly dead zone. Some of the tops of the hills were sheared off flat. It was as if an invisible giant hand had taken a samurai sword and slashed them clean through. Peering closer, Phillip saw millions of bomb craters of all sizes.

"Looks just like the surface of the moon," Phillip muttered to himself.

"Courtesy of LBJ," the colonel retorted. "What you see down there is what happens when B-52s are turned loose."

The airplane flew over a thick jungle area. Danworth pointed down toward the western horizon. Phillip looked out and saw gentle green hills rolling in all directions. The sight reminded him of pictures of Nebraska farmland he'd seen in old magazines. Here and there the lush jungle gave way to sections of yellowish, wilted vegetation surrounded by blackened palms.

"What caused that?" Phillip asked, pointing toward the blackened palms and wilted vegetation.

"Napalm and Agent Orange," the colonel fired back. "Nasty stuff. You run into anything like that down there, boy, you remember to stay clear of it. You don't want your balls falling off one day when you're forty."

Both men continued to watch the tormented landscape float by. Phillip could only imagine the horrors unleashed by such weapons.

"War's supposed to be over down there," he heard the colonel say in his headset. "The truce was signed back in November. But let me tell you something, son. You watch yourself when we get down there. The Nam is still the most dangerous place on earth."

They had been flying on autopilot. Suddenly the colonel spotted something on the ground and switched back to manual. "Speak of the devil," he whispered, flipping controls that activated the overhead speakers.

Unknowingly, the colonel had locked onto radio transmissions from Ice Cream Truck 1, Ice Cream Truck 2, Brigand Leader and Sovereign, the main players in a search and destroy mission.

"Watch this, son," Danworth snorted. "You're fixing to see some serious rock-and-roll down there at about two-o'clock. See that patch of jungle running along that hillside? Keep your eyes peeled for a couple of Huey gunships. They'll be flying zigzag pattern right about tree-top level."

Phillip had no trouble finding the pair of helicopters. They resembled two black dots, almost like shadows, roaring near the tree line. He leaned forward and yelled, "I see 'em, sir!"

The colonel craned his neck for a better view. "Those will be the ice cream trucks. What those cats are doing is decoying. They fly around like that trying to draw any type of enemy small arms fire."

Just then, the radio blurted: "Roger, Ice Cream Truck 1, I confirm you have customers. Brigand Leader, this is Sovereign. You are to deliver extra popsickles to zone 846. Do I have a copy?"

"Roger that, Sovereign, zone 846. Brigand2, Brigand3, on my command, form up on me and drop down to the hard deck. We got some goodies to deliver. Watch your ass for Triple A now. Brigand2, Brigand3, click your mikes two tones for confirmation."

Pong, pong.

Pong, pong.

"We are confirmed. Go! Go! I repeat, go, go!"

The excitement was contagious. As Danworth and Phillip listened in and followed the line of Hueys, Benson and Erin surged forward to get in on the action.

"Looks like Charlie's fallen for the oldest trick in the book again," Danworth cracked. "Now watch this shit. This is where it gets good."

Phillip couldn't tear his eyes away. He watched the pair of Hueys peel off in opposite directions, disappearing from view. A few seconds later three North American F-100 Super Sabre fighter-bombers screamed onto the scene. The trio of jets rose straight up. Then, with afterburners full lit, they swooped back down and went into corkscrew barrel rolls as the jungle floor below them ignited. Huge clumps of yellow and red fire erupted over the forest.

Phillip was blown away. He had just witnessed his first napalm attack.

The silence in the cockpit was heavy, almost mystical. It was Colonel Danworth who broke the silence. "Show's over, boys," he said, flipping off the overhead speaker. "We got work to do."

As Phillip got up to go, the colonel cued his mike. "Sergeant Toomes? Sergeant Reynolds? You boys alive back there or what?" He waited a second, then said, "Come on, guys, pick up the damn mike. We're about five minutes to touchdown, ain't got all day here. You need to secure and prepare to land."

When no answer came, the colonel turned to Phillip and said, "Okay, Turner, get your butt back there to the troop carrier compartment and see what the hell's going on."

"Right away, sir," Phillip replied, scurrying out of the cockpit.

He made it through the maze of cargo to the rear of the plane. At the back was another set of metal stairs he had to climb before entering the troop carrier compartment. Once there, he felt the plane bank hard to the left. He peered down the narrow aisle just as an empty gallon bottle of Jack Daniel's whiskey rolled out from under one seat across the aisle to under another seat.

Three steps down the aisle he almost tripped over Sergeant Toomes. The burly noncom had passed out, his head resting in Sergeant Reynolds' lap and deck of playing cards still clasped in his right hand.

"Rough night, huh, dudes?" Phillip asked.

No response.

He leaned down and flipped the seat lock, flinging both drunks forward.

Toomes rolled onto the floor, then staggered to his feet. "What the hell'd you do that for, Turner?"

Phillip steadied Toomes with both hands. "Look, guys, the old man's been trying to raise you on the PA. We're getting ready to land."

"Hot damn," Reynolds snarled. "We're in deep shit now."

Ping.

The overhead speaker flashed on. It was Colonel Danworth. "Turner, you back there yet, son? What's the story?"

Toomes and Reynolds staggered into their seats and plopped their headgear into position. Phillip grabbed another headset. "Everything's A-OK back here, sir," he lied. "We had a little problem with the PA. Shorted wire, I think. But, we've got the problem up and running."

"Fine. Just strap yourselves in back there. We land in sixty seconds."

The second the PA went silent, Toomes and Reynolds rolled their blood-shot eyes toward Phillip. "We owe you, man," Reynolds blurted.

"Yeah, man, we owe you big," Toomes agreed.

Phillip shrugged. "No problem. Let's clean this mess up before the old man decides to lead a tour back here."

The big plane took a steep dive. Toomes gagged, swallowing hard to keep from throwing up. "Anybody got an aspirin?" he moaned.

Ping.

The intercom came on. It was the colonel again.

"Good morning, girls. It's 0-138 hours ZULU time. That will make it 0-838 hours here in beautiful South Vietnam. The temperature is a steamy 84 degrees and the skies are partly cloudy, as always, with a threat of a thunderstorm. I want to welcome you girls back to The Nam. You may depart the aircraft as soon as Sergeant Turner gets his butt back up to the side cargo hatch and opens up. Oh, and thank you for flying USAF airlines today. We hope you will enjoy your stay."

CHAPTER THREE

PHILLIP CRACKED THE HATCH and felt the Nam's tropic heat burst into his soul. The air had a feeling about it, a choking, mud-baked feeling that conjured up images of dirt and light and dripping green foliage. It also created a curious sense of desperation, especially among fresh arrivals from The World.

From where he stood near the hatch opening, Phillip had a clear view of the flight line. Before him sprawled a chaotic tapestry stitched with killing machines—aircraft, mostly, but there were tanks and anti-aircraft guns and helicopters of all shapes and sizes in shades of green and brown. It was a wonder that any enemy could stand up to so much might, let alone a puny, backwater clump of dank earth like North Vietnam.

Scanning the horizon, Phillip saw in the distance a green and yellow rice paddy stretching toward the base of a small, blue-tinted mountain. In the center of the paddy a lone peasant clad in black pajama bottoms and a white straw coolie hat stood working a team of oxen in the saturated muck. The farmer, a frail, elderly man with leathery-brown skin, seemed lost in his own world of gentle rhythms and cyclical tasks, utterly oblivious to the waltz of war swirling all around him.

Phillip spied a shadow coming toward him. He turned to see Colonel Danworth crawling down the ladder from the flight deck. Out of the corner of his eye he spotted a small spiral notebook falling onto the seal of the hatch plate. Phillip bent down and picked it up.

"You dropped something, sir," Phillip said, handing the colonel his notepad.

The colonel gave an odd look, then snatched the notebook out of Phillip's hands. "Must have fallen out of my pocket," he snapped before hurrying down the ladder toward a parked jeep.

Phillip watched the colonel hop into the jeep where a fancy-dressed South Vietnamese Army officer awaited him behind the wheel. Both men exchanged warm greetings before driving off, leaving Phillip shaking his head.

The air base of Bien Hoa had a temporary permanence about it. In most respects it looked as if it had been thrown together only a few days before and would, in all likelihood, be torn down and moved tomorrow.

Phillip surveyed his new home away from home—a congested village of tin roofs and tin walls. Tin doors that hid tin interiors. Tin fences and tin barriers. Everywhere, the glint of tin.

After debriefing at squadron headquaters, Phillip wandered across the base, conscious of the burning smell of asphalt and the ever-present scent of rain. Behind him came the sounds of many small feet pattering closer. Phillip stopped and turned around. He found himself staring into the faces of six little Vietnamese kids. They were barefooted and dressed in rags.

As he eyeballed the group of giggling youngsters, he couldn't help remembering something a buddy had said years earlier: "Those little dink bastards are a dime a dozen, Turner, old buddy. But, don't turn your back on 'em, pal. They'll steal you blind or maybe drop a grenade down your pants."

Phillip stared deeply into each child's face. His friend couldn't have been more wrong, he told himself as he studied these dark-eyed angels with bowl-shaped haircuts. Phillip bent down and smiled at the kids. He was rewarded with shy grins and a round of gracious bows. They began chanting in broken English: "USA number one! USA number one!"

Phillip's heart continued to warm at the sight of this little band of beggars. He knew they had targeted him for a mark, but what the hell, they were only kids. He dropped his duffel bag, reached inside and pulled out a small wrinkled brown bag.

"Maybe this is what you want," he laughed, opening up the bag and tossing out candy.

The children jumped with glee, pushing and shoving their way closer with outstretched hands. Only one little boy stood back, a sad-eyed little tyke too shy or proud to accept a gift from the big American.

Phillip noticed the boy and said, "Ah, let's see if I have something left for you, little buddy." He dug deep into the paper bag and grabbed a pile of candy and bubble gum. He held out his open hand and said, "Here you go, just for you."

The boy tiptoed closer, studying the contents of Phillip's outstretched hand. Then, to Phillip's surprise, the boy picked through the different types of candy until he found two pieces of Bazooka bubble gum.

He snatched the gum and unfolded the inner wrapper. Smiling, he folded the wax paper comic into a tightly packed triangle, then carefully placed it in a cigar box he had been carrying under his left arm. Phillip saw that the box was full of bubble gum wrapper triangles.

The sound of an approaching jeep sent the youngsters scurrying away. Two Security Policemen hopped out and sauntered over to Phillip.

"Hey, Sarge," one of them asked, "you seen any dink kids running around here? The little linoleum lizards sneak on base scavenging, and we thought they were in this sector."

"Nope," Phillip replied. "Just got here myself."

The burly SP shrugged and said, "Well, if you see any, detain and report them to security." Before turning to go, he added, "Whatever you do, don't give them anything, especially candy. That only encourages them to keep coming back."

Phillip tapped the bill of his cap with his finger as if to say, "I got you, General."

The two SPs jumped back into the jeep and sped away. They hadn't been gone ten seconds when Phillip felt a tug on the back of his flight suit.

"Where you want to go, GI?" a small voice asked. "You looking for bed?"

Phillip spun around and saw the sad-eyed little kid with the cigar box full of bubble gum wrappers. The boy clutched the box as if it were full of gold nuggets instead of paper.

"What are you trying to tell me, boy?"

"You want place to sleep?" the boy asked. "Come with me," he added, pointing back with a dirty finger. "I take you to where you need go."

Phillip stared in the direction he had been walking and could just make out a sign that read Mess Hall. Turning in the opposite direction he saw the NCO flight crew barracks. Phillip scratched his head, wondering how this little fellow came to know where the NCO barracks were located.

"How'd you know what I was looking for?" Phillip asked his new friend.

The boy grinned and said, "You new. You green. You still got duffel bag on your back."

Suppressing a smile, Phillip reached in his pocket and pulled out two pieces of bubble gum. "Here," he said, tossing the gum to the boy. "Thanks for steering me straight."

The boy unwrapped the gum. He stuffed both pieces in his mouth before folding the paper and placing them in the cigar box. "You number one, GI," he said.

"What's your name, kid?"

The boy bowed. He tapped his chest, and in a polite voice said, "I Dung Choc Pang Sue."

At least that's what Phillip thought he heard the boy say. He returned the bow. "Well, I'm very pleased to meet you, Dung Choc—uh, whatever," he sputtered. "Tell you what, I'm going to make this a little easier. What do you say if I call you Gum? OK? That's fitting, seeing as that's what you like so much." He stuck out his hand. "So, Gum, nice to meet you. My name's Phillip Turner."

The little boy smiled a toothless smile, gums blackened with decay, as if he knew exactly what Phillip had meant. Phillip reached down to pick up his bag and started to say something else.

He looked back up and his new friend, Gum, was nowhere to be found.

CHAPTER FOUR

WHEN PHILLIP ARRIVED at the NCO barracks, he found Toomes and Reynolds lounging around the pool table.

"How'd you guys beat me here?" he asked.

"Easy," Reynolds replied. "We bribed the crew on Balls 17 to do our off load. So tonight when we hit the big city, it will be payback time."

Balls 17 was the C-5 parked next to Balls 12. It had arrived just before Balls 12. Balls was the nickname for the number double zero or 00. These were the numbers given to the C-5's because there were so few of them in the brand new fleet.

"Big city?"

"Yeah, man," Toomes piped in. He chalked down his stick and said, "we get to party hearty. Tonight we do the Saigon shuffle."

Phillip was confused. He didn't think they were that close to Saigon.

Toomes eyed down the stick, focusing on the eight-ball. "Want to go a round soon's I finish trashing this dirt bag?" he asked.

"Maybe later," Phillip sighed. "Right now all I want's a long, cold shower. Then I'm gonna put on some clean duds, chow down and take a nice, long nap. What time you guys heading into town?"

"Meet us here at seven," Reynolds said.

Down at the other end of the flight line, back behind the motor pool, unbeknownst to Phillip and the rest of the crew members, Colonel Danworth and the fancy-dressed South Vietnamese officer huddled in a warehouse just behind the out-processing morgue. It was a grim, forbidding place, full of spiders and dank smells. All the windows were painted black. "Contaminated Material" stickers were plastered all over the walls, as were "Keep Out—Authorized Personnel Only" signs. If the stickers and signs weren't enough, extra bolts and locks on doors and windows were enough to discourage anyone from snooping around.

Not that many outsiders found their way to this bleak, run-down section of the base anyway. The only regulars were the "bag boys"—personnel who ran the morgue. Their job was to identify, tag and bag bodies, then get them ready for their last ride home. The "bag boys" were a pretty weird bunch. For the most part, they kept to themselves. Their unwritten rule was not to associate with anyone outside their team. That made it easier not to have to bag a friend.

The two officers watched as three South Vietnamese peasants carefully loaded burlap packages, each the size of a baseball base,

two-foot by two-foot square by four inches thick. The packages
were placed inside aluminum caskets stacked high in the warehouse. Once the bottom of each casket was lined with tightly
packed bundles, black plastic sheeting was laid over the top of the
cargo and tucked in along the sides. A body bag would then be
taken out from the shipping crate, laid out on top of the black
plastic sheeting and unzipped.

Working quickly, the peasants rolled up a big, 55-gallon barrel and lifted the top off. Colonel Danworth and his South
Vietnamese counterpart, also a colonel, covered their noses and
mouths with handkerchiefs to keep out the stench. One worker
then dug into the barrel with his hands until he found what he was
looking for—bloody, decomposing water buffalo parts which he
slung into the body bag.

The Vietnamese colonel turned to Danworth and said, "Four
more of these bad boys to go, and we'll be ready to ship."

"Wait a minute, Chu," Danworth replied. "Last time we were
hauling hash bricks. This time we got black opium. The dogs can
smell this shit a lot better."

The colonel named Chu said, "No problem. All we do is add
some more lime to throw the dogs' noses off."

"You know, we shouldn't get too greedy here, Chu. Hell, we'll
clear a hundred grand for each box anyway."

"Ah, keep in mind, Colonel, the war is over. We may not have
much more time left."

"Well, Chu, I almost wish you were right. But I know how
these things work. Trust me, there will be plenty more body bags
to fill with that stinking crap you got."

Chu reluctantly agreed. Colonel Danworth took his little notebook out and jotted down a couple of lines of figures, then turned
back to Chu and said, "I'll meet back up with you tonight at the
club in town. I better not stay here too long or the general will
want to know where the hell I've been."

Chu nodded. "Take the jeep outside," he said, as the American colonel headed for the door. "I have another around back. See you about 2200 hours then?"

Danworth gave a wave of acknowledgement then slipped out the door.

As darkness fell over the air base, the NCO barracks came alive. Reynolds broke out his eight-track tape player and set the two parts up so that the speakers were aiming at the center of the room. Turning the volume up to max, he popped in an Eagles tape. The guitar crash at the beginning of the song caught the underwear-clad group's attention.

As *Take it Easy* started, the guys broke into a sing-a-long.

Not one of them could carry a tune or knew the words. But nobody cared. The stale, musty scent of Thai Weed was enough to take care of all inhibitions. Clouds of smoke wafted over the room as Reynolds and Toomes passed the toke around.

Suddenly, Reynolds raised each armpit and sniffed. "Turner," he yelled, "you got any Old Spice, man? Canoe or anything, man? My pits are killer."

Phillip rummaged around inside his kit, found a bottle of Hai Karate. "How about a little of this? Three drops, guaranteed to take the stink off an Arkansas mama-pig in heat."

He tossed the bottle to Reynolds, watched him splash lotion under his arms, around his neck and face. "Hey, man, aren't you gonna shower up first?"

"No, man, if I take a shower now I might knock off some of the buzz I got going," Reynolds replied. "Here, take a toke."

"Maybe later," Phillip replied.

Choking and retching, Reynolds said, "Come on, man. This is some good shit. What's the matter with you, don't you partake? Hope to God you ain't one of those holier than thou preppy freaks."

Phillip sighed. "I partake, man," he said. "I'm cool. I just want to keep my head a little longer tonight for my first trip to town. That's all."

Phillip thought back to the summer before the twelfth grade. He and two buddies had gone to Atlanta for a Three Dog Night concert. They had been drinking beer and jamming to some tunes on the dash-mounted eight-track tape player in Jerry O'Conner's mom's Chevrolet Caprice station wagon. The entire 134-mile drive to Atlanta from Augusta had been a blast of a party.

When they finally got to Fulton County Stadium, they were totally awed by all the cool-looking people. Augusta was hip, but Atlanta was the "big time." They were feeling right, feeling good, parading around the packed outer concourse of the stadium like the three finest, most awesome studs ever unleashed. Phillip sported shoulder-length brown hair, a tie-dyed muscle T-shirt and the tightest bell-bottom blue jeans he could find. He even had his mom split the bottom of the bells and sew American flags into the flares.

Then the absolute coolest of the cool dudes with the most boss-looking chick in tow approached them. "Window pane," the dude crooned. "I got your window pane."

All Phillip could see as he heard this chant was the dude's chick. His 17-year-old hormones kicked in, tying his brain in knots and his balls in a sling. His eyes floated over the girl, past slender ankles and tan calves and tight thighs. His stare rested at the point where the girl's black mini-skirt came in contact with a little brown mole nestled on what he figured to be the softest part of her body, the spot where both thighs made contact. She wore the tiniest of tank tops that did little to hide the secrets within. Her hair was long and blonde and clean, splashing over her shoulders like a golden waterfall.

This was it, the finest girl in town. Phillip was in love. There'd never be a lovelier chick, a more desirable babe in all the world than this vision of beauty and raw sexual appeal. She was swaying so close to him he could smell her lust and heat.

The girl's beauty tantalized Phillip and his pals long enough for her boyfriend to make a sale. Then, sale done, she vanished like a dream into the crowd, her laughter and long blonde hair trailing behind her like the stream of some whooshing supersonic jetliner.

"What a babe," Phillip heard one of his friends mutter.

The girl was gone but they still had the drugs. Midway through the concert, Phillip was in the parking lot retching and hurling. Jerry and Jimmy got scared and dumped him at the emergency room door at Grady Memorial Hospital. All Phillip remembered the rest of that night was getting his stomach pumped and knowing he was going to die any second.

He hitch-hiked back to Augusta the next day, and on the way vowed never to screw with drugs of any kind again.

From the window Phillip saw the shuttle jeeps pulling up outside, then heard their horns beeping. The front doors to the barracks burst open, and a mad dash broke out to see who got the coveted shotgun seat.

Each jeep was built to carry four, no more than five passengers. So much for regulations. When all was said and done, no fewer than ten guys piled into each jeep for the ten-mile trip to Saigon, the city of sin.

CHAPTER FIVE

THE JEEP roared into Saigon with soldiers and airmen dangling on all sides. Phillip held on tight as the driver careened around fruit stands and kiosks, honking his horn and beating on the side of taxis and bicycles to get out of the way. Threading his way through swarms of pedestrians and bikers, the driver turned down a smaller side street before roaring to a halt in front of a crowded sidewalk café.

"Welcome to Sin City, gentlemen," the driver announced. He was a young, crook-nosed sergeant with a slight Southern accent. "You got two choices. There's the USO down thataway with foosball and coffee and the latest issue of *Boys' Life*. But if you're looking for some high life, some hot action, then let me suggest B Street."

The driver kicked back and lit up a smoke before continuing. "For the benefit of you new turkeys, let me clue you in about B Street. The rules are as follows: You start at one end of the street and work your way down to the other end. If, by some miracle of God you're still alive and in one piece when you get to the other end, you'll be begging somebody to put you out of your misery. Believe me, gentlemen, you won't know what hurts the most—the head on your shoulders or the head on the little soldier in your pants."

Ten minutes later Phillip and the guys were tooling down B Street on their mission to hell. It was a night thick with humidity and full of expectation. Music rocked the street, blasting in from dirty little bars and the maze of outdoor cafes where drunk GI's cavorted with B girls. Mosquitoes swarmed and buzzed, but nobody noticed. They were too excited or drunk or stoned to care.

The threesome didn't waste any time. They hit one bar after another as they worked their way down the infamous B Street. By the time they reached their destination, they were feeling no pain.

"Here it is, buddy—Mecca," Toomes said, gazing toward a brightly lit doorway. The concrete block building was dark and sagging and smelled like piss. Swarms of GI's and bar girls staggered in and out, laughing and cursing and clutching each other like there was no tomorrow. "You know that song, *Alice's Restaurant*? Just change the name from *Alice* to *Sally's*. *You can get anything you want, at Sally's Restaurant...*"

They made their way through the narrow door, pushing and weaving through the crowd of inebriated and stoned revelers. Rock music blasted the smoke-filled room, rattling windows and dirty glasses hanging on the walls. There must have been a million smells in that room, Phillip mused, as he wandered deeper into the pit of writhing, sweating bodies, most notably hash, pot and opium.

Sally's was like something out of the Old Wild West.

South Vietnamese B girls scooted and twisted among the customers, clad only in hot-shorts and fluorescent bikinis. Sally's was known to employ only the best girls Saigon had to offer. Some of the long-haired beauties danced on tabletops made out of empty cable spools and from cages hung from the ceiling. Others sat on the laps of soldiers and airmen, promising them a night of heaven in exchange for a smoke and few bucks.

Phillip figured there must have been at least two-hundred airmen and soldiers in that room, not one of them over twenty-two years of age. For some, this would be their last night on earth. The bush awaited them in the morning, so they were hell-bent to make the most of what might be their last chance to party.

Craning his neck, Phillip noticed a balcony railing encircling the entire two-story open room. The balcony ended in a steep spiral staircase made of crudely welded steel. About every four feet along the balcony walk, filthy red curtains indicated doorways to darkened rooms where war stories were going on that no one would be writing home to Mama about.

Midway along the catwalk stood a huge American with long, greasy, black hair and a Fu-Man-Chu mustache. Phillip figured he was an AWOL Marine working as a bouncer. Every now and then the greasy hulk would lumber behind one of the curtains, retrieve a drunk GI and toss him out the door. Sometimes a hysterical B girl, clad only in panties and bra, would race along behind the GI, screaming, "You no pay enough for that, you American pig! Next time you bring more money."

Phillip suddenly became aware of small hands tugging at his pant's leg.

"Hey, Turner," a tiny voice shrieked. "Hello, Turner."

Phillip looked down and saw a small, black-haired Vietnamese kid in ragged shorts. It was the same kid he had given the bubble gum to earlier.

"Gum," Phillip said as soon as he recognized the boy. He

looked around, searching for some clue that might explain what the boy was doing in such a worldly place. "What the heck are you doing here, little buddy?"

Gum motioned for Phillip to follow him, which he did, to a darkened corner on the far side of the room. There the boy pointed to a curious display of bubble gum paper triangles sprawled on the filthy floor in a mosaic-like pattern.

Phillip looked at the odd art form and said, "I wondered why you folded the comics. Now I understand." He pointed to one display. "What's that supposed to be?"

Gum shrugged his tiny shoulders. "Got any more, Turner?" he asked.

"Sorry, pal. I'm fresh out of bubble gum tonight."

The boy gave a disappointed stare. "S'ok, Turner. Next time, yes?"

Phillip nodded. "Yeah, pal, next time. See you."

At the bar he found Toomes and Reynolds already hooked up with some of Saigon's finest.

Toomes said, "Here, ace, we saved one for you." He placed one of the B girl's hands on Phillip's crotch. "This is Honey. Honey, meet Turner. He is the stud with the ten-incher I told you about."

Reynolds mumbled under his breath, "More like ten millimeters."

Honey giggled and squeezed a broad smile across Phillip's face.

"Actually, Honey's real name is Pang Yang," Toomes went on. "And these two ladies," he began, circling his arms around two other girls, "are Flame and Sugar."

Phillip nodded politely. He was mindful of Honey's hand still on his crotch.

The group moved to a table closer to the back of the room. Phillip reached inside his flight suit and took out his Kodak

Instamatic camera and said, "I have got to get some pictures of this." He tapped a soldier on the shoulder and said, "Hey, pal, you mind taking a couple of shots of us with our new girlfriends?"

The soldier took the camera. "No problemo, dude," he said, focusing. "Okay, everybody smile real pretty now and say, Ho Chi Minh sucks."

Flash.

Then an idea popped into Phillip's mind. He turned and motioned for Gum to come over. "How about taking one of me and my new little buddy here, too," he said.

"You want a picture of a little dink?" the soldier asked incredulously.

"Just this one," Phillip explained.

The soldier shook his head and sighed, "It's your film, man."

Phillip pulled Gum in front of him and struck a pose. The flash went off, just as Gum cut loose with one of the biggest smiles Phillip had ever seen.

At that moment a red curtain hanging behind Phillip yanked open and a pretty Vietnamese woman stepped out. Clearly visible in the room behind her was Colonel Danworth. He sat at a table talking to Colonel Chu, the same Vietnamese officer Phillip had seen him with earlier. They appeared to be going through Danworth's little notebook.

"Wonder what the colonel is doing down here?" Toomes asked.

The pretty Vietnamese woman snapped her fingers at a waitress and said, "Send in more vodka. Two more bottles!"

The waitress bowed. "Yes, Miss Sally, right away, ma'am."

Miss Sally glanced around the room, then turned around and went back inside the room, jerking the curtains shut behind her.

"Damn," Reynolds said in a low breath. "There really is a Saigon Sally. I'll just be screwed."

Toomes piped up and said, "Speaking of screwing, you ladies

ready to go upstairs for some fun in the sun?"

The girls giggled and nodded. One of them, it could have been Flame, squeaked, "Not so fast, big, strong GI. You want fucky sucky, we want five bucky."

"Five dollars for just three of you? You got to be kidding, girl."

"Three, shit. You crazy, GI. Five dollar each girl. You know that cheap price. All of us virgins."

Reynolds roared with laughter. "Virgins? Well, hell, why didn't you say so? Deal."

The party of six struggled to their feet, leaning on each other for support. Placing their hands on each other's hips, they formed a Congo line as they bobbed and weaved toward the stairs. Just then a small, familiar voice piped up. "No, Turner, you must not go!" Phillip looked down and saw Gum, an urgent look on his round, little face.

"Say what?"

Gum yanked at Phillip's pants. "I say you no go with girl," he pleaded. "She no good for you."

"What are you talking about, little buddy?"

"VD, VD girls. Bad for you, Turner."

At first Phillip thought Gum was saying VC—short for Viet Cong. He had heard stories about VC who disguised themselves as bar girls, only to take GI's off and whack them in some side street or back alley. His mind drifted back to a training film about "Shoe Shine Boy." It showed an innocent looking Vietnamese boy about Gum's age gleefully shining a GI's boots. The boy was all smiles as he worked, then told the GI he had to go get something, would be right back. He then reached inside his shoeshine box, fumbled around, stood up and ran away. Before the GI could react—*Blam!*—the whole world blew up in his face.

Another segment was called "Flower Girl." Here a pretty young Vietnamese girl was riding her bike, a basket full of fresh flowers mounted between the handlebars. She rode along, smiling and waving, until she came across several GI's standing on a street corner. She reached into the bunch of flowers, dug out a hand grenade, pulled the pin and held it until the last possible second, then lobbed it into the crowd of GI's. *Boom!* Movie over.

Again, Gum said: "Turner, girls VD. They sick. Sick, got VD." He grabbed his crotch and pretended to grimace.

A warning light suddenly came on inside Phillips's head. "Oh, you mean VD, little buddy."

"VD! VD!"

Phillip couldn't help smiling. He pointed up the stairs to a series yellow index cards taped on the wall next to each red curtain. The cards were part of a U.S. government program to help stamp out venereal disease among the military. Each card indicated that the girl had been checked out and cleared by a medical doctor to work as a prostitute. GI's jokingly referred to the yellow-carded girls as USDA, Grade A-Number-One-Prime-Beef Whores.

"No, Turner, card mean nothing," Gum persisted. "My sister real sick now, and she get new card. She just pay Miss Sally one American dollar and she get new card."

"Okay, okay," Phillip replied, trying to calm the boy down. "I get your point, little buddy." He looked at his friends and said, "Hey, guys, I don't think this is such a hot idea."

Reynolds glared back uncomprehendingly. "You gone crazy or something?" he snapped. "Come on, man, these gals ain't got all night."

"I got information that says they might have the clap," Phillip said.

"Clap, crap," Toomes fired back. "These bitches got Uncle Sugar's stamp of approval. They're USDA. Now, get your ass in gear, man, and let's get it on. We're keeping these lovely girls waiting." He squeezed one of the girls and plopped a loud, wet kiss on her cheek.

Phillip shook his head. "Go ahead. But don't say I didn't warn you."

Toomes and Reynolds lumbered up the stairs with their arms wrapped around the girls. VD or no VD, an earthquake wouldn't have stopped those guys from their appointed rounds that night.

Phillip sighed. "Oh, well, we tried, didn't we, Gum?"

He looked down, but Gum was gone.

It was time to go anyway. B Street had left him with enough memories to fill a scrapbook.

Stepping outside, Phillip felt a strong hand on his right shoulder.

CHAPTER SIX

"NEED A RIDE, SERGEANT?"

Phillip looked over his right shoulder and saw Colonel Danworth smiling back at him.

"Colonel! Sure do, Sir! I was just fixing to wonder about how I was going to get back to base."

"Well, hop in. This is my stallion right here."

The jeep eased its way down B Street, weaving back and forth through the throng of mindless people, turned right and headed out of town. The lights of Saigon faded behind the speeding jeep. The jeep hit a pothole in the road and Phillip let out a long gurgling, bubbling belch.

"S'cuse me, Sir. I guess I have had more than my share to drink tonight." Another belch followed.

Chuckling, Danworth replied, "That's alright son. For a

minute there I thought you were fixing to start selling Buicks. Can't say I've never been there before myself."

"Sir, mind if I ask you a question?"

"No, I don't mind, sergeant. What would you like to know?"

"Well, Sir, I was just curious, Sir. What you were doing in a place like Sally's back there?"

Chuckling, Danworth said, "Well, we'll just say I had a little private business to tend to at Sally's. Besides, a friend of mine is part owner of the joint."

The jeep pulled up to the guard station at the main gate. The SP peered into the cab. Danworth and Phillip held out their ID cards. The SP snapped to attention and saluted the Colonel.

"Good evening, Sir. Go right ahead, Sir. Have a good evening, Sir."

The guardrail was raised and the jeep allowed to pass.

"Okie-Dokie, Sergeant Turner, here we are."

The jeep brakes squealed to a stop in front of the NCO barracks.

"Oh, by the way, we depart at ten-hundred-hours instead of thirteen-hundred-hours. That's Nam time and not Zulu. Pass the word to Sergeants Toomes and Reynolds when you see them."

"Yes, Sir. I will, Sir." Phillip replied as he exited the jeep. "Sir, thanks for the lift."

"No problem, son. See you soon." Danworth waved and sped away.

At 0600 hours Nam time Phillip's alarm clock began screaming in his ear. He rolled over and slapped it across the room.

He sat up, rubbing the top of his head, then did a free-fall backwards onto his bunk. He again attempted to rise. This time he managed to stay halfway erect and dropped his head into his hands. It felt like his brain forgot to stop and was crashing into his forehead.

He rubbed his eyes with a fury, trying in vain to rub away the agony he was feeling. With no hope of deliverance from the pain, Phillip grabbed his towel and shower kit and stumbled to the latrine. Toomes and Reynolds were already there, shaving, brushing their teeth and cracking jokes.

Phillip looked into one of the small-framed mirrors hung on the wall just above each of the six sinks. As he picked at his teeth, he remarked, "Geeez guys, I don't know how you do it. I mean I feel like crap, man!"

Toomes and Reynolds continued talking among themselves and completely ignored Phillip.

"Man, you guys still mad about last night or what?"

No response. Toomes and Reynolds finished cleaning up and left. Phillip got in the shower. When he got out, he spied a message fingered on the steamed up mirror: "DICKLESS DADDY" and "FAG BOY." He wiped the spew from the mirror in disgust.

After getting dressed Phillip left the barracks in search of relief for his hangover. He made it to the mess hall and slurped down as much coffee as he could hold. It was all he dared attempt to keep down. He spied a LIMA truck passing by as he left the mess hall and hitched a lucky free ride to the flight line.

It was now 0800 hours. He had two hours to get his preflight inspection and fuel-up done. If no problems cropped up, this normally took one and a quarter hours. He took his time, working down his check-lists. When he got to the rear of the aircraft, the clamshell cargo doors were swung wide open and the loading ramp was still down. He looked up inside the cargo hold and saw Toomes strapping down a pallet of transfer cases (caskets).

"Is that it, Sergeant?" Phillip hollered up to Toomes.

"Yep, that's all that I know of coming on board, Sergeant. Oh, did you get our little message?" Toomes yelled back coldly.

"Yeah, very funny. Hurry up and finish what you're doing and lock these doors down. I need to unkneel the aircraft," Phillip said in cold response.

As Toomes hit the button to close the cargo doors and the doors started to cycle close, a beep, beep, beep, was heard as a late forklift carrying a pallet with just three transfer cases on it zoomed up. Phillip stepped back out of the way to give the fork-lift clearance to get by.

Reynolds stuck his head out the door. "Where'd you come from?" he questioned the driver.

The driver said, "Sorry, man, we forgot to ship these body-part caskets earlier today. Hell, didn't even know we had them till I just turned around in the morgue and, there they were, along with this special manifest. Here, Sergeant, could you sign right here on the next to last line?"

The driver handed Reynolds the clipboard. Reynolds scrawled his name on the manifest, tore his copy out, and handed the clipboard back.

"You could have kept them damn body parts for the next flight! I don't know why, but those particular boxes just down-right give me the willys, man."

"Yeah, me too!" Toomes added.

"Just doing a job, fellows, just doing my time. Thanks. Later dudes."

The driver dropped the forklift in gear, gunned the motor, and took off doing a drag-strip wheel stand. Reynolds pushed the pal-let of caskets onto the floor rollers and up snug against the rest of the pallets. Toomes cycled the doors closed.

Phillip resumed the exterior checklists and unkneeled the air-craft. It was now 0915 hours, and Colonel Danworth and the rest of the operational fight crew had arrived. The fuel trucks pulled up, and Phillip placed his headset on and adjusted his boom mike. Holding about two hundred feet of headset cord in his left hand, he signaled the fuel truck with his right hand. The driver backed the truck in and stopped on Phillip's signal. He got out and plugged the four-inch fuel hose into the side of the aircraft. Phillip keyed his mike.

Ping.

"Captain Benson, good morning, Sir. Do you have a copy, Sir? We are ready to start sending you fuel."

Ping.

"Roger that. Good morning, Sergeant Turner. Did you and the guys have a big time last night? The fuel panel is fired up and ready to receive; all main valves are open."

The fueling process began and took about twenty minutes. Colonel Danworth did his final walk around and started to climb the stairs to the flight deck. He stopped his climb when he reached the cargo bay. He turned and wound his way through the strapped-down pallets to the rear of the aircraft. The cargo hold was loaded with only the aluminum transfer cases. This was really an eerie sight: all those caskets lined up and stacked four high. Danworth paused as he reached the aft end of the aircraft and found what he was looking for. He smiled, took his index finger on his right hand and rubbed at the turned-up edges of a bright yellow sticker on one of the three aluminum caskets on the last pallet, making sure the human body fragment stickers he and Colonel Chu had affixed earlier didn't come off. As Danworth turned back to the front of the aircraft, Toomes stuck his head out and hollered down from the troop carrier compartment. "Morning, Sir! Everything OK down there?"

"Yes, Sergeant, everything looks fine, just fine. Why would you ask that?" Danworth questioned.

"Just don't get the pleasure of your presence back here much, Sir. Are we going to be departing soon, Sir?" Toomes answered back.

"We will be leaving on schedule, Sergeant. Have a good flight."

"You do the same, Sir."

It was now 0935 hours. All inspections and preparations were complete. The aircraft was ready to fly. Phillip was on the ground with his headset draped around his neck. He paced back and forth killing time until engine run-up. The flight crew took their seats and the back up crew headed to the sleeping quarters behind the galley.

Ping.

"This is flight three-niner-zero, Balls 12, C5a, heavy. Colonel Danworth in command. We are requesting early departure. Tower, do you read?"

Ping.

"This is Bien Hoa control tower; we will clear you as soon as the Viet customs OK's you. Viet customs are enroute to you now and should clear you as soon as they get there. Over."

Ping.

"This is three-niner-zero. Roger that. Over."

Colonel Danworth surveyed the vast flight line and could see the Vietnamese Customs jeep with two white capped officers in the front and a German shepherd drug-sniffing dog riding in the back, heading his way. The Colonel wanted no part of that dog on his aircraft. Not today. *Ping.*

"OK, Sergeant Turner, let's get the chocks out and prepare for engine run up." A pause. *Ping, Ping, Ping.* "Turner, you hear me down there?"

"Yes, Sir! Sorry, Sir, got my headset stuck for a minute," Phillip fired back. He signaled the ground crew to take the chocks out and ran up the throttle on the APU unit so he would have enough air volume to start the massive turbo-fan engines.

Ping.

"Sir, ready for engine start. Air to engine one, turbo-fan is turning and ignition firing. Number one engine up and running, Sir."

Colonel Chu appeared out of nowhere in his jeep and flashed his headlights twice. He spun the jeep around and sped away. At the same time that Chu flashed his lights, Phillip felt some concrete chips stinging into his face.

"Damn, what the hell was that?" Phillip blurted, his mike still keyed open.

Ping.

"What the hell was what?" Danworth questioned back.

One of the ground crew team members fell to the ground. He was belly crawling as fast as he could to the protection of the LIMA truck. At the same time he was pointing to the tree-line about 500 feet behind the aircraft.

Ping.

"Shit, Sir, I think we have a situation down here! Wait, I think I can see now. Ah, shit, Sir. We got us a shovel-faced sniper in the trees just behind the plane, Sir!" Phillip's heart was racing out of control.

The other ground crew member got up and ran to the LIMA truck and dove inside.

Ping, ping, ping.

"Bien Hoa tower, this is three-niner-zero. We have an emergency! Repeat, we have an emergency! Sniper fire! Sniper fire!" Danworth alerted the tower.

Ping.

"Three-niner-zero, we copy and are responding; security is being dispatched!" The tower flight controller went into emergency mode. *Ping.* "Three-niner-zero, if you have engines running, you are cleared for emergency taxi and take off. Get the hell out of there if you can, three-niner-zero!"

Phillip heard the info from the tower on his headset, and nervously pinged in.

Ping.

"Sir, I think I can get the other engines going. We can start all three at once and save some time, Sir!" Phillip crouched behind the APU to shield himself.

Danworth responded. *Ping.* "OK, sergeant, you're the mechanical whiz. If you say it will work, we will give it a shot. Just don't get yourself killed down there, son!"

Ping.

"OK, Sir, I am running up to full power on the ground APU. Sir, run engine one to quarter power. Then shoot air to engines two, three, and four at the same time. This should do it, Sir!"

Ping.

"OK, Turner, here we go! Engine one up one quarter, air going to engine two, turbo fan reading, engine three is coming on, and now there goes four. Great! You did it, boy! We have power on all four of these suckers! Now get your ass aboard!"

Ping.

"Yes, Sir! On my way, Sir!"

Phillip jerked the power cord and air nozzle from the aircraft leading to the APU and let them drop to the ground. He crouched down and ran under the nose of the aircraft and headed for the stairs. He could see the Vietnamese Customs jeep turn away just as another shot rang out and hit close to the jeep. This time he got a bead on where the shots were coming from. Kill or be killed instincts took over. He crouched down behind the stairs. He took out his military issue 45 caliber Colt automatic from its holster.

He called up to Danworth. *Ping.* "Sir, I believe I have a shot at that shovel-faced son of a bitch.

Ping.

"Say what? What in Sam's hell are you talking about, boy? You secure your side arm and get your stupid ass up here now!" Danworth screamed out and throttled up the aircraft, causing it to lurch forward.

Phillip had no choice but to grab hold of the ladder and climb up. He got to the top of the stairs and hit the retract stair button, coiled his cord in, and dropped his headset onto the floor. He located a jump seat in the cargo hold, sat down, and fastened his seat belt.

Flight 390 rolled onto the taxiway. It braked and stopped when it got to the end of the runway. Danworth pushed all four throttles forward. The four jets screamed to life and the aircraft turned onto the runway. Brakes on, full throttle, brakes off, and Balls12 began its takeoff roll. The aircraft began to grind and growl as it picked up speed, and then smoothed out as it lifted off the ground.

Belted in back in the troop carrier compartment, Reynolds turned to Toomes and said, "Glad that's over with. You know it seems like every time we're doing one of these casket hauls back to the States we get a sniper attack."

Toomes shrugged. "Ah, probably just a coincidence. You want to play some cards?"

Ping.

"This is Bien Hoa tower. Everyone OK up there? Flight three-niner-zero, heavy you are cleared to three-eight-zero feet, heading two-eight-zero. Oh, and sorry for the little inconvenience, Sir. We do hope to have you back with us soon. Have a good flight, Colonel! Bien Hoa Tower out."

Ping.

"This is flight three-niner-zero. Roger, heading two-eight-zero climbing to three-eight-zero feet. And very funny guys! Catch you on the flip-flop. Three-niner-zero out," Danworth signed off with the tower. *Ping.* "Turner, where are you? Want to come up here for a minute, son?"

Ping.

"Right away, Sir," Phillip responded.

Upon entering the flight deck, Phillip was surprised by all present as they started to applaud. Danworth switched on the Auto Pilot, slid back in his chair and stood. Holding out his right hand to shake Phillip's, he said, "That was one hell of a job you did down there, son, and I for one won't forget it."

"Yeah, way to go, man."

"Good one, Turner."

"Super, dude, just super."

The rest of the crew chimed in their gratitude.

The rest of the flight home was smooth as silk, long as usual, but everything worked well. Phillip spent a lot of his flight time down in the cargo hold reading the death reports on each victim resting in his individual transfer case. All the paperwork for each body was located in a clear plastic pouch attached to the side of the aluminum casket. To Phillip's surprise about fifty percent of the causes of death were "friendly fire," meaning a soldier was killed by his own military, be it rifle shot, misplaced land mine, or air drop. Toomes and Reynolds were still not talking to Phillip so he had plenty of time to read the reports and take naps.

Flight 390 broke over the California coastline just before sunset. Phillip had come up on the flight deck and was able to take in the view. 390 flew dead over San Francisco and straight east along interstate 80. She made a 180-degree turn to line up on the main runway at Travis AFB. As soon as 390 faced due west, the purple rays of the setting sun flooded the flight deck. With the coastal mountains in the foreground and the ocean reflecting the drowning sun behind, it was truly a sight to see.

Colonel Danworth looked back at Phillip and remarked, "Pretty, isn't it?"

Phillip nodded and said. "Don't mean to sound too corny here, but when you see a sight like this you kinda know what the author of "America the Beautiful" was talking about. The purple mountains' majesty and sea to shining sea."

The Colonel smiled and nodded. The aircraft made a flawless touchdown and Flight 390 aboard Balls12 mission came to a close.

*

A week had passed. Phillip entered the latrine located inside the squadron headquarters building. Both Toomes and Reynolds were standing side by side trying to use the wall-mounted urinals. Toomes moaned out.

"Geezzz, Louise, that burns. I can't take much more of this crap!"

Reynolds squeezed hold of the chrome flushing-handle until his knuckles turned white. He let out an agonizing groan of pain.

"Man, this stuff is for real. I ain't never messing with another broad as long as I live. They're evil, man! When did the Doc say this was going to ease off?"

Toomes squealed in agony. "After that double shot of penicillin we got this morning, I think Doc said the Saigon drip will start to dry up in about three more days. Problem is I don't think I want to live that long."

Phillip quietly moved over to the mirrors located above the two sinks. Huffing his breath in order to fog each mirror up. He took his index finger and wrote "DICKLESS DADDYS" on one mirror and "FAG BOYS" on the other. He turned and slowly walked out the door.

"Hey, guys, I left you a message back there." he said. Still smiling, he said under his breath, "Thanks, Gum. I owe you one."

CHAPTER SEVEN

PHILLIP STOPPED by the commissary on the way home. It did-n't take him long to fill up a small grocery cart with a fresh sup-ply of candy and Bazooka bubble gum for his next trip to Vietnam. He was standing in line at the checkout counter when he heard a seductive female voice behind him whisper, "Getting ready for Halloween a little early, aren't you cowboy?"

Phillip spun around and found himself staring into the most beautiful pair of green eyes he had ever seen. Key lime green. Gulf of Mexico green. The kind of green that makes a guy think of cool waterfalls and shimmering tropical paradises.

For a moment Phillip had the odd sensation that he was star-ing at a goddess, a real, honest-to-gosh goddess with strawberry blonde hair, lilting voice and a body that belonged in a museum. A real work of art.

"I'm sorry," he stammered, "Were you talking to me?"

Catching himself quickly, he pointed to the assorted packages of candy and gum sprawled across the counter. "Oh, you mean this stuff." He grinned sheepishly. "It's for some special little friends overseas."

The woman stuck out her hand. "Hi," she said in that same seductive voice. "I'm Kassandra Walker."

Phillip stared at the hand in awe. He was struck by what he saw--long, slender, ivory-white fingers with perfectly-painted red nails. The hand of a goddess. There was also something vaguely familiar about this woman with the key lime eyes and ivory-sculpted fingers.

"I'm Phillip Turner. Sergeant Phillip Turner. Don't I know you?"

"That's possible. I work over at the hospital. I'm a nurse."

The cashier rang up the charges and started bagging the goodies. "Twenty-five dollars even, " she barked.

Phillip reached into his pocket and pulled out two tens and a five. "Thanks, " he said, tossing the bills onto the counter and reaching for his bag. "Well, it was nice to meet you Kassandra Walker. Or is it Captain Kassandra Walker?"

"Lieutenant will do just fine," she replied. "Although the promotion would be nice."

Phillip gave another sheepish grin. "Well, Ma'am, Lieutenant Kassandra Walker, it sure was nice to meet you."

"Same here."

He turned to go, then stopped in his tracks. Clearing his throat, he spun around and said, "Ma'am, if you're not doing anything tonight, would you like to meet me for a drink off base? Just a thought."

He was way out on a limb and knew it. Officers don't date enlisted men. Goddesses don't cavort with mortals. But, what the hell, it was worth a shot. Besides, it wasn't every day that an airman in the United States Air Force got to meet the woman of his dreams.

Kassandra smiled. "I think that can be arranged. As long as you stop calling me Ma'am."

Phillip's heart did a loop-de-loop. Grinning broadly, he babbled, "Thank you, Ma'am, I mean, Miss Walker, Kassandra. Whatever."

"Kassy will do just fine."

"Kassy," he gushed. "That's a great name. Ever been to Zack's, Kassy? It's a cool little place with…"

"I know Zack's," Kassy interrupted. "Why don't I meet you there at eight?"

"Eight. That's great." Phillip took a deep breath, drew his shoulders back. He felt like shouting to the world. Instead, he grinned again and said, "See you at Zack's."

The moment Phillip danced away from the counter, the clerk smiled at Kassy and said, "Lieutenant, if I didn't know better, I'd say that airman's in love with you."

Phillip arrived at Zack's early at 6:45. He didn't want to be late for his goddess. The place was almost empty, so he headed straight for the bar and struck up a conversation with Pete, the barkeep. Pete listened patiently to Phillip's long, drawn-out story about how he had just met the most beautiful girl in the world.

"They're all beautiful, mate," the burly keep said in his Australian accent. "At least in the beginning."

"No, Pete, this one's special. I've known a few ladies in my time, but I gotta tell you, this woman is different. If you want to know the truth, I'm scared to death."

He was also worried. Worried that his new-found dream girl

wouldn't show up. What made him think the most beautiful woman in the world would be seen in a joint like Zack's?

His fears eased at exactly eight o'clock when Pete glanced past his shoulder and saw Kassandra. "That must be your babe now," Pete said, nodding toward the door. "You were right, mate. She's a real looker."

Phillip whirled around. He almost fell off the stool when he saw her, dressed in tight jeans and a western-style shirt. Her strawberry blonde hair spilled over her shoulder in curly strands that made him think of a rippling waterfall.

He jumped up and hurried over. "Kassy," he said, staring hard.

"Hello, Sergeant Turner," she replied. She waited for a moment, then said, "Well, are we just going to stand here, or do we get to sit down?"

Phillip laughed. "Right this way," he said, escorting her back to the bar where they took a seat. "I'm just glad you could make it."

Pete sauntered over and ran his eyes over Phillip's date. Flinging a towel over his shoulder, he leaned forward and quipped, "What'll it be, Ma'am?

"I'll have one of those," she replied, pointing to Phillip's open can of Miller.

Phillip and Pete exchanged glances. "One Miller coming up," Pete replied. "Need a glass with that, Ma'am?"

"Nope. The can will be just fine."

Pete popped an icy can, wiped it down with a cloth and handed it to Kassy.

"Thanks," she said. Kassy took a long slug and saw Phillip staring at her. "What's the matter? Never seen a girl drink a can of beer before?"

Phillip hesitated. "No, it wasn't that. I just didn't figure you for a beer girl."

Kassy turned the can up for another drink. "I've been drinking Miller since college. Do you mind?"

"No, not at all, don't mind a bit. I just can't believe my lucky stars. Not only have I found a girl who likes to drink beer, she drinks my brand, too."

Several rounds later, Phillip leaned close and asked, "Mind if I ask you a personal question?"

Kassy studied his expression for a moment, then said, "Depends. Why don't you ask, and we'll see."

"Fair enough." Phillip knocked back another swig to boost his courage. "I just want to know why a beautiful girl like you, a lieutenant and all, would bother going out with a low-rank klutz like me to a low-rank hole like this."

Kassy smiled. "So that's it." She sighed. "Well, if you want to know the truth, I felt sorry for you. Not back there at the commissary. Before, when you and your buddies were at sick call getting checked for the Saigon drip."

Phillip paled. *Oh, Christ, not that.* "You were on duty?"

Kassy nodded."Relax," she said, then reached out to give him a reassuring pat on the hand. "I see that kind of stuff all the time. Not as bad now as it used to be, what with the war winding down and all."

"You didn't think that I...that I had..."

Kassy cut him off with a wave of her hand. "Oh, no, not at all. I knew you were only suffering from the Alcohol Flu and your hangover would go away. Not so with your pals. They're going to have unpleasant memories of Saigon for a long, long time."

Relief washed over Phillip. He got the waitress's attention and ordered another round and asked for a fresh basket of nuts. Desperate now to change the subject, he asked, "So, where you from?"

"New York. Born and raised in Woodstock. But, before you ask, the answer is no, I did not go to the festival."

"That was some show."

"Made some mess, too."

Phillip leaned back and smiled. "You know, Kassy, from now on I'll believe anything you tell me. Want to know why? You and I are the only two people our age who'll actually admit they didn't go to that concert."

The waitress brought the new rounds and bowl of nuts. Phillip plopped a handful of salty cashews in his mouth and said, "Well, aren't you least bit curious where I'm from?"

"No, not really."

"No?"

Kassy gave a lop-sided grin. "That accent tells me you can only be from Georgia."

"What's that supposed to mean?"

"Nothing. I love it, I love it. I think it's the cutest thing I've ever heard."

"Yeah, I bet you tell that to all the guys."

Kassy smiles mischievously. "Only those from the Deep South," she cooed. "Also, remember, I've had access to all your medical records. I know everything about you, Sergeant Phillip Turner."

Phillip almost spat out his beer. "Hey, that's not fair," he protested.

"All's fair in love and war, Sergeant. Didn't they teach you that in boot camp?"

The night raced on. Phillip soon found out that Kassy's father was a small town newspaper publisher, her mother was a nurse and Kassy had gotten her undergraduate and nursing degrees from New York State University. She also had her tonsils taken out when she was twelve and had broken her arm when she was six or seven.

Phillip clung to Kassy's every word, and she to his. The conversation flowed smoothly and wondrously, magical for the next couple of hours as they knocked back more Millers, laughing and joking as they exchanged more details about each other's past. There seemed to be something special about this new relationship, something fresh and original, almost predestined. It was almost as if fate had sent Phillip to the hospital with his buddies.

It was shortly past midnight when they decided to call it a night. Phillip stood and guided Kassy toward the bar. "How much do I owe you, Pete?" Phillip asked.

Pete snatched the tab off a spike and slapped it down on the bar.

"That'll be thirty bucks and change."

"My treat," Kassy said, reaching into her purse.

Phillip stopped her in her tracks. "No way, this is mine. Besides, we don't let the women pay down where I come from." He reached into pocket and pulled out two twenties and a ten.

Kassy suppressed a giggle. "Oh, I see. This is some male ritual chauvinistic thing."

It's just the way it is," Phillip said firmly--more firmly than he had intended. He dropped a five-spot on the counter for a tip. "For you, Pete."

The big Aussie eyeballed the five note. "Oh, thank you, kind sir. Your generosity exceeds your kindness." He slapped Phillip hard on the back. "You can bring your lovely friend back here anytime."

"Thanks, Pete. See you next time."

Outside, Phillip turned to Kassy and asked, "Want to grab some coffee and a bite to eat? There's an Awful Waffle just up the road."

"Sure, why not? Sleep's out of the question for tonight anyhow."

"There's just one problem," Phillip said. "I don't have wheels."

"No problem," Kassy replied. She looped her arm in his and steered him across the street toward a bright red MGB convertible. She went around to the driver's side and hopped in. "Up where I come from, we don't wait for menfolk to open our doors."

Phillip cut loose a loud guffaw, then opened the passenger door and slid into the small bucket seat.

"Better buckle up," Kassy warned.

"Buckle up? Why?"

Without answering, Kassy slammed the gearshift into first and gunned the little sports car into the street.

After breakfast Kassy drove Phillip home. While the engine idled, Kassy reached across and pressed his hand. "Thanks for a wonderful night," she said softly. She leaned forward and kissed him on the cheek. "I've had a great time."

Instead of kissing her back and risk making a fool of himself, Phillip opened the door and crawled out. "Maybe we can do it again sometime." It was more of a question than a statement.

"Maybe."

Phillip slammed the door shut and waved goodbye. Kassy blew him a kiss, then put the gear in first and pulled away from the curb. Later, roaring down the highway at seventy miles per hour, she peered into the rear-view mirror and whispered to herself: Someday I'm going to marry that boy.

Four hours of sleep really weren't enough, Kassy admitted later that morning as she strolled into the waiting room with a clipboard in her hand. The shower had helped, along with a crisp, clean uniform and several cups of coffee. She pledged never to stay out so late on a work night again.

When she got to sick call she called out: "Sergeant Turner,

Sergeant Turner, this way please."

Oh, my God, she thought as she looked up and read the name of the patient again. When she saw Phillip stroll into the room, tall, handsome and clean in a fresh-pressed uniform, she let out a little gasp. She led him into the examination room and pushed the door shut.

"Phillip, what on earth are you doing here? Are you sick?"

"No," he smiled. "Thanks to you I've never felt better in my life." He pulled her close to him. "I just had see you again, make sure you're for real and not something I dreamed up."

Still shocked, Kassy said, "You shouldn't be here. We should-n't be doing this. Not here." She gave him a gentle push toward the door. "Now go. And don't forget to call me tonight. She reached into her pocket, pulled out a card and pressed it into his palm. "My number. Forgot to give it to you last night."

"I'll call you tonight," Phillip stammered.

"Tonight," Kassy agreed, reaching for the doorknob. Suddenly she placed her palms on Phillip's face, drew him down to her level and kissed him on the lips. She surrendered fully to Phillip's warm mouth and strong arms that circled her waist. Shock waves rippled through her body, causing her to swoon.

In that moment Kassy Walker knew she was in love.

The mood was broken only by a sharp rap on the door. Suddenly the door swung open and a tall, fuzzy-haired doctor sporting a handlebar mustache walked in.

"Good morning, I'm Major Jorworski," he beamed, reaching down to scoop up Phillip's record which was lying on the desk. "Don't worry, you won't be asked to spell it or pronounce it."

Raising the glasses hanging around his neck, he scanned the report and asked, "So, Sergeant Turner, what seems to be ailing you this morning?"

Phillip swallowed hard. "Well, actually, Sir, it's nothing. I feel a lot better now."

The major looked up. "Oh?"

"Yes, Sir. I think it must of been a bug or something. You know, one of those twenty-four-hour bugs that just ran its course."

"I see."

"Yes, Sir. Thank goodness I'm feeling all better now. With your permission, Sir, I better be getting on back to work."

"By all means, Sergeant. Don't let a quack like me stand between an airman and his duty."

Phillip grabbed his headgear, winked at Kassy and hurried out of the room. After he left, the major turned to Kassy as if to get an explanation.

She shrugged her shoulders and said, "Guess he was one of those guys looking for free aspirin."

Phillip and Kassy hit it off. Not a day passed that they didn't find a way to see each other or at least talk for hours on the phone like teenagers. The only time they were separated was when Phillip had a mission to fly.

The next few supply missions to the Nam were flawless and uneventful. Toomes and Reynolds had made up with Phillip, and they had become tight once again. Phillip, however, had lost interest in going down to B-Street partying with the boys, and they did rasp him about that. They ran around singing, "Love is a many splendor'd thing." They even made up a few tunes of their own, like "baby got a chain round his neck" and any other thing they could come up with to torment him.

Phillip did go down to Saigon Sally's when he was looking for Gum. He could always find him there, sitting in a corner with his folded triangle-shaped comic wrappers, arranging them into their different mosaic patterns. The collection had grown in size since Gum and Phillip had become such good friends.

"Hiya, Gum, looks like you're going to have to get another cigar box soon."

Gum looked up and smiled the toothless smile. "Turner. Good to see you, Turner. You have good fight?"

"Flight, Gum not fight. With an 'L'. Yeah, the flight was fine as frog hair."

"Frogs have hair in America, Turner?"

Phillip laughed. "Never mind. It was a good flight. So, how have you been?" Phillip squatted down beside his friend. A dark blue knit stocking cap rolled up with a pair of black leather gloves with rabbit fur lining fell from the back pocket of his flight suit. Gum reached over and picked up the cap and gloves.

"Turner, these things fall out. What these things for?"

"Thanks, I had forgot I even had those back there. They are warm gloves and a warm hat. You see, it was cold where we were yesterday; in fact I even saw some snow flurries in the morning."

"I see this snow fury thing before, Turner. Sue Ling has glass jar with snow fury in it. You shake jar up, and this white snow fury stuff go all around this upside down white spike in middle of jar."

Phillip scratched his head and pondered awhile. Then it hit him. Gum was talking about one of those glass globes with a snow scene in it, and the upside down white spike probably was the Washington Monument. He figured some GI must had given it to Gum's friend Sue Ling as a keepsake. He chuckled. "Flurry, Gum, remember your "L's."

"You have to put these things on when it cold? What you mean cold? Never felt cold before. It cold all over place like on the outside and all? Cold like ice Miss Sally keep over there in cooler? How does this cold feel, Turner, when it all over the place?"

Phillip pondered the question awhile. He rocked back on his heels and let his butt hit the floor. Wrapping his arms around his knees he licked his bottom lip. "That's a tough question, Gum ol' buddy. Let's see. Cold is when you're feeling kinda sleepy and you walk outside and the cold air wakes you up real fast. Cold is maybe like when you take a bath and you feel all clean and refreshed. Does any of that make any sense to you?"

"No. I just wait, Turner, maybe I feel cold one day for myself. Then I tell you how it feels. Yes?"

"Yeah, Gum, that's a good idea. But I don't think you'll feel cold here any time soon. I think the coldest I've seen that it gets here is in the seventies at night. Tell you what, you keep the gloves and cap just in case, though."

"You mean it? Thanks, Turner!" Gum immediately put the gloves and cap on. Sweat began to pour down from his forehead. But Gum wasn't about to take off his new treasure.

Phillip spent all of his free time when in the Nam talking to Gum and his friends. He was learning quite a lot about the Vietnamese culture and way of life there. By observation, he had decided that Vietnam had been occupied by so many countries, and the Vietnamese people had been so dominated that they had become complacent in nature. They kept things simple and to the bare minimum with a purpose. They knew that families would get ripped apart each time a new occupation took place, so each individual was a member of the whole family of Vietnam. All they truly held dear in the fight for survival was one another.

But the one thing that really hit Phillip was that children were the same no matter where they were in the world. They were giving, honest, loving, and just wanted to have a little fun and to be loved back. He had become kind of the Pied Piper to these kids, and he loved his role. It was a role of reversals: that by spending so much time with the kids he was filling the long-term loss he felt from not having had enough time with his own father.

As soon as Phillip would arrive home at Travis, he would call Kassy and spend hours describing some little something the kids had done. Kassy would just sit there and listen to his stories. She had assumed the role of a doting godmother being told tales of her godchildren's adventures.

Phillip told Kassy of the time he took a kite with him. It was one of the new types of kites, a black and yellow delta-wing design that really looked cool to Phillip. He thought it would impress Gum and the rest of the kids. Little did he know, that these kids were masters of kite design, and they had a lot to teach him about kites and flight. They could take scraps of rice paper and glue, a few skinny bamboo shoots for struts and, *presto*, a kite would appear, complete with a stabilizing tail made from stripped banana leaves. With just a couple of running steps in the right direction the kite would become air-borne. Gum would study the kite's flight path in the breeze, tug on the string this way and that. The kite would respond and gently gain elevation. Phillip said he just sat there cross-legged on the warm grassy mound and watched in true amazement.

The high point of the kite episode came when Gum noticed that Phillip kept sniffing the vinyl fabric of his kite. Phillip tried to mimic Gum's voice, "Turner, Turner, you put your nose in kite. Why, Turner? What you smell?"

He laughed when he realized what he was doing and said, "Well, Gum, the smell of this kite reminds me of the smell of a new car back home."

Gum, confused, took a whiff. "Umm, smell like new car, Turner? Don't know much about car. Hey, Yung Pak, you come here and smell this. Turner say it smell like new car in United States."

After that, every kid in town had to have a sniff. By the time all the smelling and sniffing had been done, there wasn't much left of that kite. Phillip summed up the story by saying he guessed more fun was had with a kite he couldn't get to fly than if he had got it up in the wind. Then, there wouldn't have been any sniffing going on. He learned how to make kites, and they learned what a new car smelled like.

"It was a good day, Kassy." Phillip finished his memory fondly.

CHAPTER EIGHT

PHILLIP WAS DUE to be discharged in two weeks, so he knew this was going to be his last flight to the Nam. Before taking off, however, he had one last stop to make--the base commissary to stock up on more candy and gum.

Near the checkout, he saw a stock boy putting some candy in various racks and called out: "Hey, what do I have to do to buy a whole case of bubble gum?"

The stock boy look confused. "Bubble gum?"

"Yeah, you know. Bazooka bubble gum. I want to buy a whole case. Can I do that?"

The boy mulled the question over for a moment. "Sure, I don't see why not," he replied. "Let me go see what we've got in the back."

He was back in a flash, clutching a 1,000-count box of Bazooka bubble gum wrapped in cellophane. "Here you are. Sure this what you wanted?"

"You got it, man, perfect. Thanks." Phillip took the big box of gum and placed it with the other candy on the counter.

When the cashier spotted the large amount of candy and gum, she said, "That's a lot of candy and gum. You got a sweet tooth or something like that?"

"Something like that," Phillip replied.

The cashier shook her head as she rang up the sale. "Each to his own, I guess."

The flight into Bien Hoa was long as usual, but no problems cropped up. Upon arrival, Phillip debriefed and stowed his gear in the barracks, and set out to find Gum. He found his friend sitting on the curb in front of Sally's place. Gum's head was hanging down between his legs. He was doodling in the dirt with a stick and did not see Phillip arrive. He nudged Gum's dirty little sandal-clad foot with his shiny-toe jungle boot.

"Hey, how you been?"

Gum leaped straight up into the air and shouted with glee.

"Turner, you back, you back! Good, good! Glad to see you, Turner. You been good, good?"

Phillip laughed. "Fine, Gum. I'm just fine. Here, let's sit here awhile and talk, OK?" The two sat down Indian style on the curb.

"Gum, I have met a girl back in the United States and I like her a lot. I want you to take me to Market Street and help me buy her something."

"Sure, Turner, we do that. Is girl pretty? You marry her?"

"Not so fast, Gum," Phillip chuckled.

"Tell you what, Turner. You marry her and take me back to States with you. I be your number one shoe-shine boy, and I be her number one house boy, yes?"

"Gum, if only I could." He paused and his eyes became misty. "I would take you back to the States as my number one son in a heartbeat, but unfortunately that can't be."

"I know Turner. You good man. I wish I really did belong to you, Turner. You be good father one day."

Phillip took a deep breath and thought to himself: *how can one seven-year-old kid possess so much wisdom?*

"Well, now, let me tell you about my lady. Her name is Kassy, and she's a nurse."

"Lassy?"

"No, Ka-Ka-Kassy. Kassy short for Kassandra with a K, Gum." Phillip tried to straighten out confused little Gum.

"Ka, Ka, Kassy. I see now, Turner. Come, Turner, we go to market. Want to get there early or all good deals be gone."

"OK, lead the way, my main man, Gum!"

They both stood and walked side by side down the dirty street. Gum reached up to grab hold of Phillip's right hand with his left one. Phillip gave the grungy, frail little hand a gentle squeeze. Gum had never shown such affection or trust in public before, and Phillip, knowing this, beamed with pride as they walked along hand-in-hand.

Arriving at Market Street, Phillip analyzed the sight before his eyes. The scene reminded him of one of the Tarzan movies he used to watch as a kid. He pictured Johnny Weismuller as Tarzan, decked out in his brown loincloth. Tarzan would be strolling down the middle of the dirt boulevard with Cheetah, his trusty chimpanzee, riding high on his shoulders. Although the show was shot entirely in black and white, his childish imagination had no trouble seeing all the colors of the Turkish bazaar Tarzan found himself in the middle of. The golds, the purples, the silvers, with belly dancers and beggars running amok. The two separate scenes intermixed in Phillip's mind; Market Street was packed with people of all sorts: GIs, peasants, prostitutes, just name it, they were there. Each side of the wide boulevard was lined with battered wooden or tin portals. The doors varied in size from two feet to six feet in width. Each postern pivoted out like an older style garage door back home would. Once in the open position, they served several purposes. The overhang was used as a shade to protect from the burning rays of the sun or a shelter to keep away the monsoon rains. They also served as an excellent support on which the merchant could hang his wares. Some of the doors had faded tattered booths set up in front.

On Market Street one was sure to find anything from A to Z and back to A. Smoke and steam billowed up from behind some of the booths, giving off the smells of cooking. Some of the aromas were wonderful to breathe in, and some brought a gag of disgust. Food took top priority here, as well as it did everywhere in-country. Dozens of little old peasant ladies wearing white straw coolie hats squatted in random clumps in the blistering sun. From Phillip's six-foot-two-inch view, their cliquish formations looked as though a handful of white poker chips had been tossed on the table to ante up. In front of each of the old ladies, one would be greeted by a flat, round straw basket filled with her wares. It was a potpourri of color and a sight to behold. Some baskets had apples, jackfruits, guavas, or durians. Others had garlic, chili, watermelon or custard for sale. Clumps of butchered raw meat sat baking to a blackened rot from the heat of the noonday sun in another basket.

Phillip and Gum continued their walk. A basket full of colorful live Gecko lizards sold by the slithering kilo caught Phillip's attention. Gum explained that these were dipped live and whole in batter and pan-fried, "kind of like what you call fish-sticks," he said. Beside the lizard basket was one full of sandworms. And just when Phillip didn't think it could get any worse, an old lady smiled up at him. Her dried-out, sunken-in, sun-baked red cheeks wanted to crack open. She reached into her basket and fished out a light green frog. With a couple of swift snips from her rusty scissors she skinned the frog. She laid the frog, still squirming around, on top of the basket for Phillip to purchase. He looked to Gum for help.

"And just what am I supposed to do with that?" He pointed to the frog. Gum rubbed his tummy and licked his lips. "Never mind, never mind, I don't even want to know. Let's move on."

The two made their way past the poultry section. They passed several monkeys in very cramped chicken-wire cages. "I'm thirsty, Gum. Let's find something to drink," Phillip said.

Gum motioned for him to follow and stopped where a small man was holding a siphon tube that disappeared into a black plastic barrel. "One beer." Gum held up one finger.

"GI want special drink? Make you have happy happy, love life. Make you strong and sexy." The small man with one eye knew his spin well.

"No. One beer," Gum persisted.

"Wait, Gum, what is the special drink?" Phillip stepped into this one. "You no want, Turner."

"I might." Phillip sounded insistent.

Gum shrugged his shoulders. The small man with one eye took this as an order for the special drink. Behind him was a basket. He turned and carefully opened the lid. He used his one eye to peer inside and thrust his hand in. Gritting his teeth, he yanked out a wildly whipping green snake about three feet long. He grinned, his one good eye about to pop out of his head. He took out his knife and split the snake right down the middle from one end to the other. Digging around inside the snake, he removed its gut string. He then bit the entrails, tugging and yanking until they broke. Over a dirty shot glass he squeezed the blood from the snake, making sure every last drop had fallen into the glass. He poured a trickle of rice alcohol on top of the blood. Turning to Phillip he bowed and offered the drink. "Special drink, GI. One dollar. American."

Phillip rolled his eyes at Gum. "I'm not going to drink that shit!"

Gum was laughing himself into a fever. "Don't matter, Turner, you still owe him one dollar." Gum tried to control his choking laughter. "Just pay him dollar. He sell special drink to someone else at discount."

Phillip gratefully handed the one-eyed man a dollar. "Geez, Gum. You people will eat or drink anything, won't you?" The two turned and trekked on, Gum still in his fit of laughter, Phillip shaking his head in disgust.

They finally pushed and shoved their way to the merchandise part of Market Street. Here they found a booth full of beautiful hand-carved teak sculptures. Another nook featured carvings made of water buffalo horns. Phillip paused to pick up one of the modelings. He held it close to his eyes, slowly turning it to all angles. He was fascinated by the complex micro details and the skilled artistry that had gone into bringing the piece to life. They entered a cramped cubicle that offered the finest silk gowns, all hand-sewn. Phillip had found the gift he was looking for. It was a pale blue tea dress with ornate silk multi-colored embroidering on it. Gum bartered a good price for the dress. Phillip paid the clerk and the pair ducked under the cloth doorway to leave.

"Ah, very, very nice, Turner. You will make your lady very happy, I sure."

"Thanks, Gum."

Further down the street Phillip spotted a bike for sale. He stopped in front of the bike. He put his hand on the right side of the handle bar and gave the rusty bell a ring with his thumb. Jangle, jangle.

"Hey, Gum, have you ever had a bike before?"

"No, Turner. They cost too much. I been saving up my comics."

"Saving comics?" Phillip was confused.

Gum dug into his torn front pocket and produced a special comic he had wrapped up in rice paper. Phillip carefully unwrapped it and looked at the advertisement printed in small print. There he saw a picture of a brand new red Schwinn bicycle equipped with a basket and a bell. The ad read that if one saved up 15,000 comics and sent them in, a bike just like the one in the picture could be redeemed as a premium.

Phillip thought to himself, *That's what all the arranging of the folded comic triangles was about. Gum must have been counting the comics. He wasn't trying to make some kind of mosaic picture at all. He was simply adding his comics up. I wonder how many he has now?*

Phillip smiled. "Well, Gum, I have brought you a present to help you on your mission to save comics. I got you a case of the stuff back at the barracks, and I will give it to you tomorrow."

"A case? How many case make, Turner? Thanks, Turner! I have ridden a bike before so I be ready when I save enough, yes?"

"Oh yeah? OK, Mr. Gum bike rider, let's see you ride this one." Phillip turned to the bike seller, an ancient relic of a man with long, dirty yellow white hair and beard with long, yellow fingernails to match. He asked, "OK he try?" The age-old bearded peasant nodded approval.

Gum hopped aboard and peddled off like a pro, weaving in and out of people and grinning from ear to ear. He pulled the bike up right where he started, got off, and patted the seat like he would a good horse.

Phillip clapped. "Good job, Gum!" Turning to the merchant, he asked, "How much for the bike?"

"Ten dollars American." The old man held up both hands, fingers spread wide open.

"Hmm," Phillip pondered, thinking of the bike pictured in the comic ad. "And a basket to go with it?"

"Seventy-five more cents," the old man spouted.

"Tell you what, old fellow, I will give you seven dollars and fifty cents American money for bike and basket. The front wheel is bent, you know."

The haggard man threw his hands up in the air, shaking his

head in dislike as though he had just given away his first born male child and exclaimed, "Sold!" The old man started to take the bell off the handlebars with a rusty screwdriver.

Phillip stepped in. "NO, NO, all of the bike!"

The old man released his grip on the bike and Phillip paid him. He turned to Gum and shouted, "There you go, my main man, she's all yours."

Gum started to cry tears of joy. "Oh, Turner, thank you, Turner. You so good to me, Turner. Thank you, Turner."

"OK, OK. Stop it, Gum, enough already. You are so very welcome. Now go enjoy!"

Gum hopped aboard his bike and again took off, careening through the crowd. Bobbing and weaving, he freed both hands from the handlebars and stretched his arms out like wings. He shouted, "Turner, look at me. I fly, just like you do, Turner! Look at me fly! *Wheee!*"

The look on Gum's face, the sheer glee and contentment was worth a million bucks to Phillip. He was so very proud and happy for his friend.

Moments later a military police jeep wheeled around the corner and skidded to a stop in front of Phillip. Gum peddled his bike over to see what was going on.

"You Sergeant Turner?" The driver called out.

"You got him," Phillip replied.

"Sergeant, you are to return to base with us, per Colonel Danworth's orders. Your plane is on emergency priority. It will take off as soon as the crew is assembled. Your gear has already been stowed on your aircraft."

"So, what's the scoop, guys?"

"I think it has something to do with the typhoon due in here. Anyway, let's get a move on!"

"OK, OK. Just give me a minute with the boy." He pointed to Gum.

"Make it fast, Sergeant."

Phillip stepped over to his friend and put his hands on his shoulders. He knelt down on one knee, looking up. "Gum, I didn't think I would have to leave you this way, but I have to go now."

The glee was still smeared from ear to ear on Gum's face.

"That's OK, Turner, I wait and see you next time. I show you how good I learn to ride bike."

"No, Gum, you don't understand. There won't be a next time." Phillip's eyes began to tear up. He shook Gum's shoulders lightly to enforce the finality of the situation.

"You not come back here, ever?" Gum realized what Phillip was trying to say. The glee left his face and was replaced with sorrow and confusion.

"No, Gum, I not come back here ever. I can't, Gum. I'm sorry."

Gum pulled away, letting his new bike fall to the ground. He ran off into the crowd, crying, not understanding why his friend would not be coming back.

"Gum!" Phillip shouted into the anonymous crowd. "Gum, please! Please come back!"

"Look, Sergeant, I'm sorry but we got to get a move on!" The driver urged.

Phillip stood up and wiped the tears out of his eyes. "Yeah, OK," he said.

He climbed into the jeep over the tailgate and hopped over the back of the bench seat. He draped his right arm over the back of the seat. Resting his chin on his shoulder, he looked back at the crowd as the jeep pulled away. He couldn't see Gum anywhere, but he waved his hand goodbye to the nameless throng just in case Gum could see him. Phillip felt a loss deep in his heart, a void causing an emptiness he had never felt before. It sent aches and chills up his spine. For the first time in a long time, he felt all alone in the world. He missed his friend already.

CHAPTER NINE

THE DRIVE BACK to the base and on to the flight line took only a few minutes but seemed an eternity to Phillip as he worried about Gum. *What will he do? How will he get along without me or, worse yet, how in the hell am I going to get along without him?*

As the jeep raced down the taxiway, Phillip noticed the noise of all the planes fired up and ready to go. There were people everywhere: maintenance personal running around doing last minute jobs, LIMA trucks running from one plane to the next, dropping off various crews and equipment, tow-tractors zooming in and out. A real three-ring circus was going on. He had never seen this much commotion on the flight line before.

The jeep arrived at Balls 12 and screeched to a halt. Phillip jumped out the rear of the vehicle and headed to the stairs.

At the foot of the stairs he stopped to look around and take in the situation again. He noticed the air changing pressure as his ears popped. The steady, hot, moist breeze was being overridden by cool swirling gusts, blowing dirt and dust into his eyes. He lowered his head to shield his eyes from the flying debris and trotted up the stairs. Reynolds met him at the hatch opening, and handed him his headset.

"Greetings, Lover boy, we got a bad one moving in." He pointed to the western horizon. "That, Sergeant Turner, is the start of Typhoon Julia. We don't want any part of that bad bitch. They're trying to get as many of us out of here before it rolls in. Captain Erin said it's packing 180 mph sustained winds and will probably hang around here for a couple of days. So here's your brief. The aircraft is fully fueled, all pre-flights are done, and we got a light load, more of them damn coffins full of body parts. Fuck, man! I thought the war was over! So all you need to do is stand by the APU and wait on Major Stewart and Captain Benson to arrive. Do your engine start-up thing and we're history. Copy?"

"Affirmative, Roger that! Thanks, Reynolds!"

As Phillip turned to start down the stairs, he paused and looked out at the approaching storm. The clouds were boiling in hues of black, gray-blue, with flecks of white swirling around. The sight brought to mind a witch's cauldron from some fairy tale of long ago. But this was now, and it sure as hell wasn't a fairy tale. Phillip shook his head and thought, *What a mother of a storm! I hope Gum will be alright.* Once in position, he cued his mike.

Ping.

"Good afternoon, Sir. This is Sergeant Turner standing by, waiting your orders, Sir. Looks like we're in for quite a blow today."

Ping.

"Roger that, Sergeant. Hold tight and I'll give you the word shortly. Just as soon as my last two crew members get their butts here. Colonel Danworth. Out."

Phillip thought, *the Colonel seemed a little edgy. Must be the damn storm.* About twenty minutes went by. Finally a LIMA truck pulled up with Captain Benson and Major Stewart. They started up the stairs.

Ping.

"Sergeant Turner, let's fire these babies up and head home!"

Ping.

"Sir! Yes, Sir! Running the throttle up on the APU. Putting air to number one turbine now. Ready, start engine one, Sir!"

Ping.

"Copy. Engine one coming on, engine one up and running. Next, Sergeant?"

Ping.

"Sir, ready start engine two."

Ping.

"Copy, engine two coming on, engine two up and running. Sergeant?"

Ping.

"Sir, ready start engine three."

Ping.

"Copy. Engine three coming on, engine three up and running. Sergeant?"

Ping.

"Sergeant?"

Ping. Ping.

"Sergeant?"

Phillip noticed Colonel Chu pulling up to the side of the aircraft in his jeep. Chu flashed his headlights two times and sped away. While following the path of Colonel Chu's jeep, he spotted not one, but two of the Vietnamese Inspections jeeps heading in their direction.

Ping.

"Sorry, Sir, I got distracted. Ready on engine four run up, Sir!"

Ping.

"About time! Copy. Engine four coming on, engine four up and running. OK, Sergeant, signal chocks out and come on aboard."

Phillip stared intently at the approaching jeeps. At a hundred and fifty yards out and to the left of the jeeps, he could just make out a small figure riding a bike and waving one arm in the air as the other arm fought to stay in control of a wobbly front wheel. *Oh no, it can't be! If it is, how in the hell did he get out here on the flight line?*

Phillip climbed up on top of the five foot high APU to get a better look. He clasped both hands over his eyes to form a visor to keep the blowing dust and dirt out. He had to shuffle his feet to stay in balance against the whipping wind. His flight suit flapped wildly and the back bellowed out. He was now able to confirm that it was Gum out there.

Ping.

"Colonel Danworth? Sir, we have a problem down here, Sir!"

Ping.

"I see you down there on top of the APU. Didn't I just give you a direct order? You want to tell me what that's all about, Sergeant?"

Ping.

"Sir, can you see at about 12 o'clock that little boy riding the bike heading in our direction?"

Ping.

"Yes, Sergeant, I see the civilian." Colonel Danworth's voice was impatient.

Ping.

"Sir, I think he is trying to get to see me, Sir."

Ping.

"Hogan's Goat! Sergeant, we don't have time for this kid! Wave the boy off and get your ass up here now! I repeat, that's an order!" Danworth's voice was at a fever pitch, almost to the point of panic. His eyes bore down on the Vietnamese inspection team rolling ever closer, now already half way across the tarmac.

Phillip tried to signal Gum to go back, but Gum kept on pedding as hard as he could.

Ping.

"Shit, Sergeant, do something down there! Wave the boy off!" Danworth's voice demanded action. He was about to explode.

POP ZING!

Phillip looked down. He knew what had just happened. A bullet had ripped a hole in the top of the APU sheet metal.

Ping.

"Sir, now we have another problem Sir. That sniper is back, Sir! He just hit the top of this APU!"

Phillip was jumping up and down in frantic jumping jacks for Gum to turn around and go back. Gum kept pace toward the aircraft. About 500 feet out Chu's jeep reappeared. He pulled alongside Gum and motioned for him to turn around. Gum ignored Chu's motions. Chu positioned his vehicle between the bike and the aircraft and slowed to Gum's rate. He pointed for Gum to retreat. At 200 feet out from the aircraft, Chu had had enough. With his 45 caliber automatic pistol cocked and resting in his lap, he took hold of the weapon, aimed it sideways at Gum. Chu pulled the trigger and let go one round.

The bullet hit Gum point blank in his side, lifting him clear off his bike and throwing his small body into the air. The bike continued to roll another ten or fifteen feet before spinning itself flat on the concrete. Gum's frail, lifeless body hit the tarmac hard, rolling over and away from the aircraft.

The scene had frozen Phillip. He couldn't move, couldn't utter a sound. Everything was spinning in slow motion, distorted and oddly colorless. The whole world had turned black, without depth or meaning. Phillip knew only one thing. Gum had been hurt. He had to get to his little friend's side, had to get there in a hurry.

Screaming at the top of his lungs, he jumped from the APU and charged across the tarmac toward his fallen friend. Halfway there his eyes met Colonel Chu's and they locked. Chu glared back for a moment, then turned quickly away.

Gum lay still, face down on the oil-stained tarmac. Phillip stood over the lifeless little boy for a moment, then dropped to his knees.

"No, please, God, no," he wailed.

Just then Phillip heard a loud crack, then felt a sharp pain in his left leg. He tumbled forward, across Gum's body.

Ignoring the pain in his leg, Phillip sobbed, "Here I am, Gum. You're gonna be all right, little buddy. I'm gonna get you a doctor. Everything's gonna be okay, you'll see."

Even as he spoke, Phillip knew things were not going to be all right. Little Gum was dead and nothing would ever be right again.

He raised Gum's tiny head and gently cradled it against his chest. He wrapped his arms around the boy and began to rock back and forth, the way a mother or father would soothe a crying baby. Another bolt of pain flashed through Phillip's leg. But that pain was nothing compared to the ache he felt in his heart for this little boy.

"I'm sorry, Gum," he whispered. "So very sorry, little buddy." With tears streaming down his face, Phillip lifted his gaze toward heaven. "Why, God? Why this little boy? He's only seven. Why him?" Why not me? Why not that bastard who did this?" Stroking Gum's raven black bangs back from his brow, Phillip leaned in and ever so gently kissed his friend goodbye. "I'll get him for this, Gum, I promise. Don't you worry, if it takes the rest of my life, I'll hunt that son-of-a-bitch down and take him straight to hell."

At that moment a heavy hand fell across his shoulder. "You okay, Turner?" Toomes asked, squatting down next to him.

"He's dead, Toomes," Phillip said softly. "Gum's dead."

Toomes bent over and saw the blood pouring out of Gum's side. "Jesus, man. I'm sorry." Instinctively, Toomes knew Phillip was one heartbeat away from going into shock. He slowly removed his headset, strapped them over his ear and keyed the mike.

Ping.

"Sir? Colonel Danworth? Sir, we've got a real mess down here, Sir. The little boy is dead, and I am not sure what is wrong with Turner. Sir? Help, Sir?"

Ping.

"Toomes, is that you?"

Ping.

"Yes, Colonel, this is Toomes. Help, Sir."

The Colonel did a quick survey, checking for the inspection team. They must have seen the boy go down and changed course, heading toward Gum. The Colonel wanted to take advantage of the time this had bought.

Ping.

"OK, Toomes, check Turner. If he is not hurt physically, then I think he is real shook up right now. You and Reynolds get him back to the plane as fast as you can. I can see an ambulance headed your way about 1500 feet out. They'll take care of the boy. We have been given emergency clearance by the tower. So let's get on with it and put this whole thing behind us! We need to go now. Copy, Sergeant?"

Ping.

"Yes, Colonel. I understand, Sir."

Toomes looked over at Reynolds. "Hey, Reynolds, think we can get Turner up and back to the plane?"

Toomes tossed the headset to the ground. Reynolds nodded.

Both men stood and placed Phillip, who was now in a zombie state, between them. They draped his arms over their shoulders and headed back to the plane.

Reynolds noticed Colonel Chu's jeep parked behind the aircraft and Chu bracing and shielding himself on the hood. Chu's arm recoiled and a puff of blue smoke issued from his pistol. Then Reynolds saw a body fall from a palm tree on the other side of the fence-line where Chu had been aiming. Chu jumped back in the jeep and took off.

Toomes turned back in time to see a C-130 cargo plane taxi down the runway. The prop wash caught Gum's cherished treasure box full of triangle shaped gum wrappers and spun it into the air. The lid popped open, spilling Gum's life's work to the winds.

As soon as Reynolds and Toomes got Phillip on board, they retracted the stairs and locked the hatch. Balls12's engines roared up to power and she began her taxi roll.

Reynolds and Toomes dragged Phillip back to the troop carrier compartment where he could rest. After take-off, Reynolds flipped his seat belt loose.

"Give me a hand and let's see if we can get Turner cleaned up and a new flight suit on. It might make him feel better. Oh shit! Look at this. I think he must have took one down there."

Ping.

"Sir, we have a problem back here. We were cleaning Turner up and, well, he's been shot in the left leg, Sir!"

Ping.

"How bad is it, Sergeant?" Danworth asked anxiously, thinking of his precious cargo. *Ping. Ping.* "How bad is it? Can we go on, or do we have to divert?"

Ping.

"Sir, it does appear to be just a flesh wound. I was in para-rescue before I transferred to loadmaster. I think what we have on board in the first aid kits should get us by."

Ping.

"Good boy, Sergeant Reynolds!" A sigh of relief took over Danworth's voice. "If you need to, load him up with morphine from the first aid kits. Let the poor boy sleep for the next twenty-three hours, and when he wakes up, we will be home sweet home. Oh, and if you need more drugs, we have a couple more kits up front here."

Ping.

"Copy. I will keep you informed, Sir. Reynolds out."

Balls12 touched down at Travis AFB and rolled to a stop in its parking grid. Kassy was waiting nervously in the ambulance with the trauma crew. She had overheard the crew getting ready in the emergency room at the hospital and had insisted on going along.

As soon as the engines were shut down, the hatch opened and the stairs started to extend. Before the stairs fully dropped, Kassy leaped up and pulled herself onto the stairs and raced up. Toomes and Reynolds had brought Phillip to the hatch opening and had him sitting on a crate by the door. Kassy shrieked when she first saw him.

"Oh my God! Phillip, what happened to you, baby?"

The look on Phillip's face sent chills right through to Kassy's soul. It scared her like no sight had before. His face was gaunt with a gray tone of death to it. His eyes were glazed over. The crystal blue irises that she had fallen in love with just a short time ago had turned to a demonic black. She felt him looking through her and not at her, as if he was staring into an underworld of some type. What she was now looking at made it hard to trust her inner feelings of love and compassion. Hate, disgust, and fear almost won the battle of emotions racing through her mind. She reached down deep and came up swinging for the man she loved.

"Ma'am, I think that look on his face is from the morphine we gave him," Reynolds said, trying to calm Kassy.

"Bullshit! I have seen morphine states before. What the hell happened to him?"

Reynolds filled Kassy in on the loss of Phillip's friend and how it had happened. As Kassy listened she stroked Phillip's hair. When Reynolds finished, Kassy began to cry.

"No! Not the bubble gum boy, not him. But why? How?"

Kassy was still totally confused after the explanation. Phillip was rushed to the hospital and admitted. His leg would heal in a couple of days, and he was awarded the purple heart. But his heart and soul wounds would remain open and unhealed forever. For this, the Air Force did not have a medal to give.

On Phillip's last day in the Air Force, he had finished all of the out-processing and found himself killing time in the Squadron break-room. Colonel Danworth knew this was to be his last day and had been looking for him. He walked into the break-room and took a seat next to Phillip on the top of a picnic table. Danworth gently patted Phillip's knee.

"So, how's the leg, son?"

"Fine, Sir," Phillip replied.

"You can just call me Ben from now on. And no more of that sir stuff for you, my boy. You're a civilian now!"

Danworth reached around to his back pocket and took out a bulging envelope, slapped it a couple of times in his hand and offered it to Phillip. "Here, Phillip. It is Phillip, right? Take this.

It might help you get started in your new life and help you forget some of your old bad memories. I know how much that little boy meant to you. Here, just take it."

This was a half-hearted attempt on the Colonel's part to atone for some of the remorse he felt in the death of Gum. At the same time, he hoped the large sum of money would work to his advantage. He figured Phillip would be so busy living it up that the murder would become a faded memory and soon disappear altogether.

Phillip took the envelope and stole a peek inside; it was full of what appeared to be one-hundred-dollar bills.

Hoping to head off any questioning on Phillip's part, the Colonel offered up another explanation. "Oh. By the way, I had your accusations of Colonel Chu's involvement in the incident with the boy checked out. The authorities in Nam have him in custody, and he won't be seeing the light of day for a very long time, if ever!"

Foolishly and completely trusting in Danworth, Phillip replied, "I am glad to hear that, Sir. Did the little boy have any family back there?" Phillip had an idea of what he might do with the money Danworth just gave him.

"No family except 'Saigon Sally.' She was supposed to be his aunt or something, and cut the sir stuff out already." Danworth hopped off the picnic table, thinking that the "fix" was in. He turned and shook Phillip's hand. "Well, take care, and if you're ever in Kentucky, look me up." Danworth left.

Phillip gave a wave to Danworth and walked over to the Coke machine. He took a quarter out of his pocket and spun it into the coin slot. He knocked the Coke button with his fist and looked down at the drink slot. Out fell a Nehi Grape. Phillip smirked and thought to himself, *Damn. Nothing ever changes around here.*

As he paced down the hall, he kept rehashing in his mind what had just taken place. *Why would the Colonel give me this money? What did he want in return for it? He did say he thought it would help me forget. Well, I don't want to forget.* He looked to the ceiling and said out loud. "I will never forget you, Gum."

He entered the locker room, finished his drink, and crushed the can in his palm before flipping it into the garbage can. Phillip located Colonel Danworth's locker. He took out his pen and scribbled on the bulging envelope of money, "THANKS ANYWAY." He then stuffed it into the vent slot on the locker and heard it hit the bottom. For some reason Phillip felt that accepting the money wouldn't be right. The money seemed tainted and gave him a funny kind of sick feeling. He couldn't put his finger on it, but something was just not kosher.

CHAPTER TEN

JUST AS QUICKLY as that bolt of lighting had flashed onto the picture of Colonel Chu in the paper in Hickory, North Carolina, and had sent Phillip Turner back to 1973, Kassy was able to draw him once more to the present.

"Phillip? Are you alright? Phillip?" Kassy had found him sitting contorted from an invisible pain at his table in the restaurant. He had drool dripping from each side of his mouth, oozing past tightly clenched teeth. The cigarette had burnt completely down and out, scorching his fingers. Kassy removed the burnt out butt. "I hate these damn things." She dropped what was left of the butt into the ashtray. "Phillip, please, you're scaring me. Snap out of it, baby. What got you this way? Phillip?"

The nurse in her took over, and she began to assess Phillip's condition from a medical standpoint. She feared this was maybe a cerebral hemorrhage or a cardiac arrest. She took his left wrist, feeling for a pulse. His pulse was racing wildly. Kassy was now getting frantic as she looked around the room for some help. She shook Phillip hard; she took her right hand and propped up his chin so he was staring straight into her eyes. She gasped as she saw once again those demonic black irises staring through her soul. Her heart sank. She had seen this look a couple of times before, but so very long ago.

"Phillip, what is it?" Kassy shouted. The restaurant patrons took notice.

Phillip was now beginning to come around; he blinked his eyes and shook his head. The blue started to slowly return to his eyes. "Kassy? When did you get here?"

"No, I think the question is: Phillip Turner, where in the hell did you go? You scared the crap out of me! I haven't seen that look on your face since they brought you back from South Vietnam, the day you got shot!"

"That's just it, Kassy. I was just there."

"You were just where, Phillip? You're scaring me again."

"I was just remembering. It was so real. So real, Kassy!" Phillip's trembling hand reached for his now cold cup of coffee. He took a sip and realized he must have been out awhile. "What time is it anyway, and how did my fingers get burned? Shit, that hurts!" Phillip dunked his burnt fingers into the glass of melted down ice water.

Kassy replied, "Around ten. I overslept. You know how I like to sleep late in rainstorms. We better get a move on if we are going to make all the stores today!" Kassy was trying to fluff over what had just happened and get Phillip to move on as quickly as possible.

Phillip groped for words. "Kassy, I just don't feel like furniture shopping today. I just want to go home now. Really, can we just load up and go home?"

"Phillip, what's happened to you? Why this sudden change? We've come all this way. P.T. will be so disappointed if we don't bring him back the 'Big Boy' bedroom suit we promised." P.T. was Phillip's and Kassy's seven-year old son, Phillip Turner, junior.

Phillip became insistent, "I'll make it up to P.T. He'll get over it. Now let's go! I want to go home! I just really need to get back home!"

Kassy knew not to press further. She could tell that something had gone terribly wrong in Phillip's mind. As Phillip stood, he picked up the paper, folded it, and placed it under his left arm as he reached around his back with his right arm to take out his wallet to pay.

The waitress passing by noticed Phillip's gestures. She held up both hands, snapped her chewing gum, and said, "No, please sir, the coffee is on the house. I am just glad to see you have returned to the world. I was worried you had a stroke there for a minute!"

Kassy smiled warmly at the waitress. "That makes two of us. Thank you."

Phillip packed up their late model Chevy Suburban. Fifteen minutes later the Turners rolled out of the wet motel parking lot, pulling the empty U-haul rental trailer behind. Phillip drove as if he was on a mission. His eyes never left the road as he steered his vehicle ever closer to his goal: home to south Georgia. He felt safe and at peace there. He needed his safety and peace now more than ever.

The drive home through the North Carolina mountains should have been a beautiful, relaxing journey. The dark, stormy skies of the morning had given way to a sunny bright cobalt blue palette. The wild flowers dotting the green hillsides were crisp from their predawn watering. There was not a cloud in the sky. The golden sunshine streaming into the cab of the truck flashed in a strobe-light effect as the truck wound beneath the towering oaks and pines. The air was sweet, cool, and clean with not one drop of humidity, a rare early summer's treat this far south. The silence between the two occupants in the cab was stark and tense. Neither noticed the wonderful day slipping away from them and passing into evening. Each time Kassy thought she might try to say something she would stop herself, thinking it would be the wrong thing. She decided to wait until Phillip was ready to talk about what was bothering him.

Dusk had set in, and P.T. was standing guard up in his tree house. At seven, P.T. was tall and lanky, just like his Dad. He also sported Dad's deep blue eyes, but Mom won out when it came to hair color. The curly strawberry blond locks were a dead match. He crouched down as he heard the familiar sound of his Mom and Dad's Suburban approaching. Zeke, P.T.'s dog, began to bark and raced down the driveway to meet the oncoming truck. Excitement overtook P.T. He reached for and dropped his trusty walkie-talkie three times before he was able to bring it under control and up to his ear.

Click.

"Red Leader, Red Leader. This is Mad Dog. Do you read me? Over. Come in, command post. This is Mad Dog. Over."

Click.

"P.T., is that you?" P.T.'s grandma answered. "Glad you called, P.T. It's getting dark out and you need to come inside."

Click.

"Grandma! This is Mad Dog. Remember? You're supposed to be Red Leader. I have some important info for Red Leader!

Over."

Click.

"Uh? Oh. Sorry. Go ahead, Mad Dog. This is Red Rover. Oh, yes, sorry again. Over."

Click.

"Grandma! You're supposed to be Red Leader, not Red Rover! Shoot. Over."

Click.

"Red Leader, I have spotted an enemy vehicle approaching. No, wait, Red Leader. It's a friendly. Confirm, confirm, it is a friendly, Red Leader."

Click.

"P.T., what are you talking about? Sorry. Mad Dog, please tell Red Rover more details?" *Click.* "Sorry again. Over or out or wilco or Roger that."

Click.

"Red Leader! Red Leader! Not Red Rover! It's Mom and Dad. They're home! Over and out!"

P.T. threw his walkie-talkie to the floor of the tree house and climbed through the trap door.

As soon as Phillip caught sight of his home from around the corner of the long dirt driveway, he felt a little more at ease. This place of his was one of the things he was most proud of pulling off in his life. He bought the ten acres twenty years ago. Kassy protested, saying she didn't want to live full-time out of town. The sticks, she called it, even though it was just twenty-five minutes to downtown Augusta.

Phillip bought a small used travel trailer and conned Kassy into thinking this was just going to be a vacation home or maybe some place to retire. He told her to give him a year to get it started and they would move back to town, and he would go back to work at the airport where he was employed as a FAA licensed airframe and power-plant mechanic. He said he needed to stay out there if he was ever going to get any work done on it. Kassy gave in. Phillip went to work hauling river stones up from Horse Creek. He would stack and cement the stones he hauled each day until late into the night. When he had finished the stone walls, he started felling pines on the property and hewing them into beams. After he got the roof up and the rest dried in, he started wiring and plumbing. He knew his year was just about up, and he'd better come up with something good. So when Kassy went back to Woodstock, New York, for a two-week visit with her parents, he put his plan in motion.

When Kassy arrived back home as scheduled, she found the dinky travel trailer gone. Phillip's Blazer was nowhere in sight. When she got out of her car, she noticed smoke coming from the chimney. She was startled seeing this, for it was mid-July and it had to be at least one hundred degrees that day. She approached the door and found it unlocked. Carefully she opened the door; just barely she poked her head inside and sheepishly called out, "Phillip? Are you in there? Is everything OK?"

"HO, HO, HO, Merry Christmas! Come right into Santa's workshop, little girl," Phillip bellowed forth.

Kassy pushed the door wide open. There, to her amazement, Phillip was standing in a Santa suit complete with white beard and red cap. He had taken all the Christmas decorations out of storage and put them up. He had the stockings hung on the fireplace mantle and had gone out and cut a fresh balsam. The job he did on decorating the tree was better than Kassy had ever done. Kassy, with mouth gaped wide open, scanned the room. As she peered in the direction of the master bedroom through the maze of two-by-four studs, she saw what was left of the travel trailer. Phillip had taken all the bedding and made a make-shift bedroom for them. He went so far as to hang towels up for curtains.

"Phillip, you want to tell me just what is going on here or what?"

"HO, HO, HO! Why, haven't you ever heard of Christmas in July, little girl? Well, maybe not, since you come from the wrong side of the Mason Dixon line."

"Alright, Phillip, cut to the chase."

"HO, HO, HO, Merry Christmas and welcome to your new home!"

"I knew it, I knew it, I knew it! We aren't moving back to town, are we? Well lucky for you, buddy boy, I kinda like living in the sticks, too." In the short year there Kassy had fallen in love with the place.

"HO, HO, HO, why don't you come over here and sit on Santa's lap and we can talk about whatever pops up." Santa gave an evil wink.

"Why, Santa, you are so naughty, aren't you?"

The house really was something to see. It sat nestled safely between two towering, massive Georgia short needle pines. They stood like sentinels on each side of the house. The covered porch ran around the entire house. It greeted you with open arms as it beckoned you to come on up and sit for a spell in one of several handmade rockers Phillip had fashioned out of thick, wild wisteria vines. From its ten-foot high outer hand-stacked stone walls, to its twelve-twelve steep pitched cedar shake roof, one could tell immediately this house was built by someone who cared for craftsmanship and had a feeling for the land the house would be sharing. It was big and rustic, but Kassy had brought to it intimate charm with her decorative touches. Phillip's main regret about the house was that his father never saw it. He was so proud of it but could never get his dad to come out and look it over. When he did finally convince his dad to come to Sunday dinner one day, Dad pulled a fast one and died of a heart attack the Saturday before the Sunday dinner. Phillip somehow felt responsible for that too.

The Suburban with empty trailer in tow circled around the drive and came to a stop. P.T. and Zeke began to fight for a position at the driver's side door of the truck. Phillip stepped out and turned to P.T.

"Hey, buddy, how ya doing?" He reached down, rubbed P.T. on the head, and petted Zeke once.

"Hi, Dad. Dad, Grandma won't play right. She is supposed to be Red Leader and she keeps saying she is Red Rover!"

Phillip said nothing more as he disappeared inside his house. P.T., puzzled, raced around to the other side of the truck. Kassy was waiting for him with outstretched arms. P.T. leaped into his mom's grasp.

"Mom! Did you hear what I told Dad about Grandma? You guys came back early. Good! What'd we get? Bunk beds, I hope. What's wrong with Dad? When are we going to unload my bedroom? How much did it cost? Did I get new sheets, too?"

"Whoa! Hold on there a sec. One question at a time, and I hope you're not going to be too disappointed."

"Disappointed? Why?"

"The reason we got home early is," Kassy said as she tried to come up with an excuse a seven-year-old could accept, "Your Dad got to feeling sick so we had to leave early. We didn't get your furniture yet. But wait, before you go flying off at the handle. I promise you that first thing in the morning you and I will go shopping. This time I will let you do the picking out. You can choose whatever bedroom furniture you want even if it doesn't match. Okay?" Kassy thought to herself, *Lord, help me on this one.*

"Okay, Mom. That'll be cool. I can't wait till tomorrow. I hope Dad's not too sick; maybe he will come with us."

Kassy softly patted P.T.'s head. "He'll be okay, sweetie. Just give him a couple of days."

Several days passed and Phillip seemed to be withdrawing more and more. He had to make himself go to work every day at the mom and pop convenience store they had started right after the house was finished. Phillip never did return to his position at the airport. Instead, he found a shack for a good price just down the road on Highway 30. He started selling what he could afford to buy: some RC colas, moon-pies, and boxes of red wiggler worms. He stayed at it day and night seven days a week. Slowly, *Turner's* grew to become quite a success. They had three types of gasoline at the pumps, sixteen brands of beer in the cooler, every kind of cigarette known to man behind the counter. *Turner's* had pizza cooking in the back and videos to rent up front. If you looked real hard, you might even find a belt for your vacuum cleaner. Not to mention you could still get a RC cola, a moon-pie, and a box of red wiggler worms.

Phillip ran the store with a passion. But when P.T. came along seven years ago, he knew something was going to have to give. He wanted to spend more time at home watching his son grow up. He remembered what it felt like not to have his Dad around. As luck would have it, he met Jack and Cindy, a semi-retired, transplanted Yankee couple Phillip knew he could trust. They had been co-managing *Turner's* for Phillip ever since.

All the kidding and clowning around with his customers and friends at the store had stopped. Kassy noticed that his night sweats were back, along with some disturbing mumbling and teeth grinding. She feared that all the work she and the psychiatrist at the VA did so many years ago was quickly melting away. She wondered if maybe she should call the VA and tell them what was going on. *Well,* she thought, *I would call if I knew exactly what was happening myself. Last time, time did more healing than the doctors did.* She felt so alone and helpless.

One night at dinner P.T. asked, "Hey, Dad, there are lots of stars out tonight. Can we do some gazing?"

"No, not tonight, son, maybe some other time," Phillip answered coldly.

"But, Dad. Please, Dad?"

"No, damnit all. Now leave me alone!"

P.T. pushed his chair back and ran to the front door. The chair rocked back and slammed to the floor. Crying, P.T. looked back at his Dad. "I hate you!" he screamed and ran out, slamming the door.

Phillip jumped to his feet. Rage filled his eyes. "I'll give you something to hate, you little shit!"

Kassy's hand on his shoulder restrained and pressed him back down to his chair. She patted him gently. It was the only thing she knew to do.

CHAPTER ELEVEN

PHILLIP LOOKED UP to see the motor pool mechanic at Bien Hoa AFB grinning back at him, tapping him on his shoulder.

"Just remember, Sergeant Turner, have the jeep back by dark or it's my ass. Enjoy your sightseeing and stay on the main roads. There's still a lot of shit going on around here."

"Will do, airman, and thanks again for letting me get the jeep."

"Hey, you paid for it, Sarge." The airman smiled and snapped the twenty spot at Phillip.

After clearing the check-point gate, Phillip turned right, heading for Saigon. It was a nice day out--low humidity with puffy white clouds in a sailing regatta in the deep Asian blue sky. After motoring about five klicks from the base check-point, Phillip eyeballed a small figure on the other side of the road limping towards the jeep. Immediately Phillip recognized Gum. He muttered to himself, "I would know those bony little knees from a hundred miles away." Just as the jeep passed by Gum, Phillip locked the brakes down, cut a doughnut in the middle of the road, squealed the tires, and came to a dead stop right beside Gum.

"Looks like you had a blowout there, pal," Phillip said, referring to Gum carrying his left sandal in his left hand while the cigar box full of Bazooka wrappers, as always, was secure under his right arm.

"Turner! Good to see you, Turner! I broke shoe week ago. Need to get fixed, I guess."

"A week ago? You've been carrying that sandal around for a week?" Phillip chuckled, "Gum, what am I ever going to do with you? Hop in. Where're you heading?"

"Heading?"

"Going, Gum, going. Where are you going?"

Grinning, Gum replied, "Oh, I see. I heading to see Sue Ling. She got hurt. That's when I broke shoe. I got some medicine for her. See?" Gum, now seated beside Phillip in the jeep, opened the lid on his cigar box.

Phillip looked over to see a dirty glass tube of Alka-Seltzer tablets and chuckled. "I don't think that medicine is going to help Sue Ling unless she has a tummy ache or a hangover, Gum. So just what happened to her? And where do we go?" Phillip put the jeep in gear and zoomed off in the direction Gum had been walking.

"I tell you when to turn; it way past base. We were playing at Sue Ling's. It's a game of chase and tag, I think you call it. We all sit in a circle. The one that is the chosen one walks around the circle. When chosen one tag kid in circle, kid have to chase and catch chosen one."

"Duck duck goose," Phillip replied.

Gum turned his head puzzled. "Luck Luck Loose?"

"No, duck duck goose. That's the name of the game you were playing. I used to play that same game when I was a kid."

"You know this game, Turner? Wow! Sue Ling was chosen one. She tag on Dung Pak; he get up and chase Sue Ling to edge of rice paddy. Big explosion happen. Dung Pak blown clear. He no hurt. Sue Ling no more have leg. This leg gone." Gum slapped his right leg, showing Phillip. "Sue Ling Papa-san say it land mine."

The placing of land mines in the DMZ (demilitarized zone, strictly civilian areas) was a diabolical trick the Viet Cong used. Their sole goal was to maim and kill the innocent locals and fire up distrust and hatred toward Americans. They would spread the rumor that Americans were responsible, they were the ones who planted the mines.

Phillip's happy-go-lucky expression had changed to deep concern. He pictured Sue Ling in his mind. She was around twelve, the prettiest of all the children he had seen in Vietnam. Her parents had never cut her long raven-black hair since she was born. She managed to keep all her teeth in perfect shape, and when she smiled at you, your heart would light up. Phillip's heart now ached for Sue Ling.

"So, what did the doctors say, Gum? Is she going to be alright?"

"No doctor, Turner. Sue Ling's Papa-san say she be ok, I think."

"How much further, Gum?" Phillip grew anxious.

"You make turn this way at next road." Gum held out his right hand.

The jeep slowed and made the turn. Phillip gunned the engine and down the dirt road they flew. The jeep teetered precariously on top of the narrow levy road that threaded the needle between the rich, green rice paddies. He braked sharply each time he came to a deep trough in the road. The troughs were irrigation ditches between the paddies, and acted kind of like speed bumps in reverse. The jeep fishtailed from side to side each time they took off again, just missing sliding off the edge into the soft, rice-paddy mud. Phillip spotted a hootch at the end of the road.

"We here, Turner. Sue Ling in there." Gum pointed at the hootch.

The jeep skidded to a stop. Phillip jumped out, and noticed a bomb crater on the edge of the rice paddy. He figured that was where it must have happened. The grass-thatched shack had a piece of rusty tin propped up in front that served as the front door. Phillip ducked down and between the tin and entered behind Gum. There were sticks of incense smoldering all around the one-room hootch. The thick smell of the incense was no match to cover the odor of infection and decaying flesh. Sue Ling was lying on a mat made out of elephant grass. Her Mama-san was kneeling beside her fanning her and chanting what sounded like a Vietnamese prayer. Mama-san gasped and turned her head away in fear when she saw Phillip enter. Phillip noticed the frightened Mama-san.

"Gum, does she speak English?" he asked, gesturing to the woman.

"No, Turner. I can tell her what you say."

"Tell her I will not hurt her or Sue Ling. I have come here to help."

Gum did what he was told. The woman forced a timid smile and offered Sue Ling to be examined. The closer Phillip got to Sue Ling the more overwhelming the stench grew. He knew it was going to be bad, real bad. He cautiously bent down on one knee beside Sue ling and smiled. Sue Ling weakly managed to get both sides of her pretty mouth to turn up in response. Phillip held up one finger to signify he wished to unwrap the bloody, dirty rag bound around Sue Ling's stump at the knee. Sue Ling nodded OK and closed her eyes tight, getting ready for the pain that was going to hit her. As carefully as he could, Phillip raised what was left of her leg and began to unwrap it. The fumes gushed forth, causing Phillip's eyes to burn and water. With the wound exposed, it was worse than he could have ever imagined. Phillip gagged in horror as he saw several leeches squirming around in the yellowish black goo. He was sickened by the practice of leeching wounds. He did not realize the placing of these leeches to Sue Ling's wound had probably been all that had kept the infection from killing her already. He reached with his clean hand to Sue Ling's neck and placed two fingers against her carotid artery. The gangrene had taken firm hold; he could barely feel a pulse.

"Gum, come here, son. I have to get Sue Ling to the base hospital now. She is very, very sick. Tell Mama-san."

Gum relayed the message to Mama-san. She muttered back and shook her head no.

"She say no. No take Sue Ling. She say Sue Ling's older sister come to see her tomorrow. She say she want Sue Ling here."

"Damn it, Gum! Tell her that sister will see Sue Ling tomorrow on this floor dead. Sue Ling will die if I don't get her some help. Now! Do you understand me, Gum? Help me, please!" Phillip's teeth were clenched and his lips were quivering.

Gum turned back to Mama-san, pleading with her. Mama-san looked into Gum's eyes and saw that this had to be done. She motioned to go and take Sue Ling. She kissed Sue Ling on the forehead and stroked her hair as Phillip gently picked her up.

Phillip kicked the tin door aside. He quick-stepped to the jeep and placed Sue Ling in the passenger seat. Off in the distance he heard a Vietnamese male voice screaming. It was getting closer and closer. Phillip looked to see a man slashing madly towards him, knee deep in the rice paddy mud.

"Shit, Gum. Who is that?"

"That Sue Ling's Papa-san, Turner. You go. I handle him. You go fast and help Sue Ling now."

Phillip cranked the jeep, slammed his foot on the gas peddle, and took off, spewing mud in a rooster tail. He made it to the main road back to the base. Barreling down the road, he had the jeep wound out as fast as it would go. He passed another jeep like it was standing still. Phillip's eyes darted from front to side, checking the road and Sue Ling every second. He skidded to a stop at the barricade checkpoint to the base. His bumper was touching the red and white pole that blocked the road. Phillip pounded his fist on the horn. *Beep! Beep! Beeeeeep!*

A cocky Airman First Class SP sauntered out from the guard shack. "What seems to be the rush, here, sarge? I mean, you going to a fire or what?"

"Look, airman. See this little girl I got over here? She's sick, man. She's hurt real bad! I need to get her to the hospital ASAP!"

"Now, sarge, you know better than that. I can't let you bring no dink kid on base without the proper authorization. I mean, we'll have to make calls and fill out the papers and all. So why don't you just turn this jeep around and take the little zipper head back to where you found her."

A helpless feeling filled Phillip. He looked down at Sue Ling. Her breathing had become more shallow, barely visible. As he turned back to the SP, he got a crazed look on his face. He reached up with the speed of a cobra strike, grabbed the muzzle of the SP's M-16, and planted it firmly on his own forehead midway between his eyes.

"Look here, you sassy mouth prick, look what you just did."

The SP was startled.

"Now you may not give a goodie Goddamn if this little girl lives or dies. But I care so much so, that if she is to die, then I will die with her. So, now you have to make your choice. Either back off and raise that fucking pole or pull the fucking trigger and end this right now."

The SP was so rattled he was shaking. He remained frozen

with his weapon digging into Phillip's forehead. He was trained to kill the enemy but never dreamed he would be facing one of his own in a situation like this. Like an archangel sent from above, another hand snatched the barrel upward, pointing it towards the sky.

"Safety your weapon, soldier!" a commanding voice barked. "Calm down, son. I'll take it from here." The same command voice was speaking to Phillip. The stand-off was over.

Phillip snapped his head back to see Colonel Danworth standing beside the jeep. "Colonel? Where'd you come from?"

"Hell, Turner, you just about ran me off the road back there. I chased you down to see who I was going to get to court-martial. You get the little girl to the hospital now." Danworth turned back to the SP. "You want to raise the pole now? I will take care of the authorizations. And, airman, this never happened, did it?"

"No, Sir. It never did, Sir." The relieved SP moved over to raise the barricade.

"Thank you, Colonel!" Phillip restarted the jeep.

"Go, son, go! No time to lose!" The Colonel patted Phillip on the shoulder.

CHAPTER TWELVE

"PHILLIP? PHILLIP?" Kassy was patting his shoulder.

"What?" Phillip answered from a stupor.

"You did it again. You had another one of those blackouts, didn't you?"

"She never cried, Kassy. She never cried. Not once. P.T. is out in front yard crying his eyes out for no reason, and she never even shed a tear."

"Phillip, what are you talking about? Who never cried?"

"Sue Ling. Never mind. Just leave me alone, please. Just leave me alone, Kassy."

"OK, Phillip Turner. I have had all of this I can stand! What has got all this started up again? Tell me so we can start to work this out! You have got to tell me! For P.T.'s sake, for God's sake, for my sake. Please, Phillip, we're falling apart here!" Kassy began to weep.

Phillip propped his elbows on the table and cradled his head in his hands. He looked over at his beloved Kassy seated beside him. She rubbed her watery eyes, then patted him on his knee.

"Phillip, talk to me! We have always been able to talk, baby. It seems like ever since that morning I found you in that restaurant in Hickory things have gone haywire."

"You're right, Kassy. I know you're right."

Phillip stood and walked away toward the master bedroom. Kassy wiped some more tears from her cheeks and waited, bewildered. He went to his closet and reached up behind some shoe boxes and pulled down his old green flight bag from the Air Force. He brought the bag back to the table and set it down. He unzipped it and took out The *Charlotte Observer* from the Hickory trip. He opened it to the front-page picture. He then reached to the bottom of the bag and retrieved the small case of Bazooka bubble gum he had bought 25 years ago. He placed the bubble gum beside the newspaper.

Kassy was perplexed. "What, Phillip? What?"

"Don't you see, Kassy? That son of a bitch right there on the front damn page is the same bastard that murdered little Gum."

Kassy picked up the paper and reached for her reading glasses. She looked over the photograph of Chu at The Wall.

"Oh, my Lord, Phillip, are you saying that's a picture of that Vietnamese Colonel who shot your friend? Are you sure? Oh, baby, I am so sorry you had to see that!" Kassy dropped the paper. She put her arms around Phillip and held him tight.

Sobbing onto her shoulder, Phillip said, "I have killed that bastard in my mind a million times. I always thought he had died in some prison over there for what he had done. And now, *wham!* The bastard is living in my country as some kind of retired war hero. I don't get it. Did Colonel Danworth lie to me about him? I always had a funny feeling about what Danworth told me about

Colonel Chu."

"Oh, Phillip, I am just so sorry. You must try and put this behind you and just go on. We live in a whole different world now. You have to do it for P.T."

"I can't let this be. P.T. is part of the reason I can't let it lie. I am unable to look P.T. in his eyes without seeing Gum's eyes and that bastard mowing him down like he did!"

"What are you planning to do then?"

"I don't know yet. Hell, I don't know what to do. I just know I need to do something." Phillip broke down and began sobbing more.

"Let me tell you this, Phillip Turner. You have a wife that thinks the world of you and loves you more than anything else. She will stand by you in whatever you decide to do. And secondly, Mr. Turner, that little boy you just ran outside idolizes you. He thinks you walk on water. And he had every right to cry. I see more and more of your father creeping into you. Don't you dare waste these precious years with P.T."

"My Dad? What's my Dad got to with this? I loved my father and I respected him."

"You two had your ways, that's for sure. But you hardened yourself to where you didn't need him anymore. I don't want P.T. to get that kind of hard, do you?"

"No, I want P.T. to know he can always count on me no matter what. I always knew I could count on my Dad."

"Maybe so, but the needing was gone."

"Just what are you trying to say, Kassy?"

"Okay, let me put it to you this way. When your father died you went to his funeral. That you had to do for outward appearances."

"No, I went because I loved him, and I wanted to go."

"Well, tell me this then. Why haven't we ever gone back to his gravesite? And just wait, better yet, answer this." Kassy paused and took a deep breath. "When you are all alone and looking for some answers, when no one can see you, have you once ever stopped by the cemetery?"

"No." Phillip dropped his head.

"Keep that need alive in P.T, Phillip. He needs you now and you need him. I think he may hold your answers. Now pull yourself together and get out there and see if you can smooth things over with him!"

Kassy pulled Phillip to his feet, wrapped her arms around him and squeezed him tight. She kissed him as if this was the last time she would ever see him again and sent him on his way.

Phillip found P.T. sitting in the grass in the middle of the front yard. He was sitting Indian-style, legs crossed, head bowed, and still sniffling. Sitting down beside him, Phillip patted P.T.'s leg.

"How ya doing, little buddy?"

P.T. looked over at his dad then, jerked his look back away. "You hate me, don't you?"

"Oh, no, P.T.. I love you, son, more than all the stars in the sky tonight. Clear up to the moon and back." Phillip pointed to the crystal-clear, dark sky. "Look, I didn't mean to yell at you, but I have just got a lot on my mind. Forgive me?"

P.T. turned away, reached down and started to pick blades of grass one at a time, slamming each one to the ground.

"Please, P.T., let's make up. Look, there's the big dipper up there, see? Wow, look at that, a falling star!"

P.T. took interest and looked up for the falling star, "Where, Dad, where?"

"You must have missed that one. Maybe we can see another. Let's get set!" They both stretched out flat on their backs, head top touching head top on the lush, cool centipede grass carpet. They stared straight up at the heavens. That time of year the sweet fragrance of wisteria and honeysuckle blooms hung thick in the air and would leave a too sweet saccharine taste on the tip of your tongue. The tree frogs, locusts, crickets, katydids, and bullfrogs started their summer-night sonata. Out of the woods, P.T.'s dog, Zeke, wandered up and gave each face a good licking. Both jerked away from the foaming slobber and banged their heads together.

"Yuk! Ouch!" both exclaimed in unison and the laughter began. Giggling and wiping the dog slobber from their faces, the father-son bond took hold. All was forgiven. They gazed up into the night, watching the fireflies mingle with the stars. P.T. especially liked the rare green ones. He called them his lucky flies.

"Dad?" P.T. questioned.

"Yes, son?"

"Dad, I was wondering, what happens to you when you die? I mean do you get to go up there in the stars and play in the clouds with Pepper, our dog that died? Is that what heaven is like?"

"That's a nice thought. Yeah, I think that's part of it." Phillip reached back above his head and found P.T.'s outstretched hands waiting. They grabbed hold of each other's wrists in a blood-brother greeting.

"Hey, Dad, today in school we had a police officer come talk to us. He told us that drugs are a very bad thing and to never try them. He said if you do bad things like drugs and hurt people, then he has to come and take you to jail. He said that jail is a very bad place for bad people. Oh, and he showed us his police car. We got to turn on the flashing lights and blow the siren! It was real cool!"

"That sounds real neat, P.T. The police officer is a very smart man. You can't go around doing bad things and hurting people or you will have to pay the price!"

"Price, Dad?"

"Price is just another way of saying go to jail."

"Oh, I see. If someone does something bad to me, will you make them pay the price, Dad?"

Phillip rolled around to P.T.'s side and cuddled him close. "Oh, sweet son of mine, I will never let anyone bring harm to you!" Phillip kissed P.T.'s cheek. "Come on, my main man, let's go inside. It's bath time and if we hurry, I'll finish that story I was reading to you about the boy and his magic box."

"Great! I thought we were never going to get back to that story."

Phillip climbed to his feet, reached down and hoisted P.T. up into his arms. "Geez, boy, you get any bigger and old pops here won't be able to carry you around anymore."

Phillip hiked P.T. up and adjusted his grip. He turned and walked towards the house with P.T.'s feet dangling just above the ground. Phillip thought to himself, *I will be Gum's police officer! I will see to it that Chu, that son of a bitch, pays the full price! There well be no blue-light specials for you, Colonel Chu!*

After P.T.'s bath and story, Kassy and Phillip tucked him in bed and kissed him goodnight. Kassy turned out the light. On the way down the hall Kassy put her arm around Phillip and patted his side.

"You seem some better," Kassy said.

"That depends," Phillip replied.

"Depends? Depends on what?"

"Kassy." He took a deep here-it-comes breath. "I want to make Chu pay for what he did and Colonel Danworth too if he had any part of it. I just need to know if you are alright with this decision."

"I can only remember how long it took you to get over Gum the first time. I remember how low and despondent you were, how scared I was that I might never get the same Phillip Turner I fell in love with back. Now I see this dark cloud coming back into our lives. If going after Chu and getting your answers or dues will keep that from happening again, then I want you to do it! But, Phillip, promise me this: Whatever you do and wherever you go, you will stay safe. And that you will return to P.T. and me as soon as you can."

Phillip stopped at the doorway to their bedroom, turned to face Kassy. He reached out and placed his hands on her shoulders and slowly slid his firm hands down her arms and took hold of both of her hands. With a gentle squeeze he pulled her closer, sending the chills of love and passion up the back of her neck.

"I promise I love you and P.T. I promise I will do the right thing. I promise to make Gum proud. I promise I won't get hurt, and I won't stay away one second more than I have to." Phillip embraced his best and truest friend. They both teared as they realized the gravity of what the uncertain future might bring.

"Come on, Sergeant, it's past your bedtime!" Kassy winked as she wiped the last tear from Phillip's cheek with her thumb. Kassy led the way inside the bedroom, closed the door, and turned out the light. That night Phillip and Kassy Turner made love like two eighteen-year-old newlyweds!

At 4 a.m. Phillip awoke, drenched in a cold sweat. The dream was back. He got up and went into the bathroom for a drink of water. He wiped the sweat from his brow as he peered into the mirror. He squeezed his eyes tight as he conjured the dream back up. It was the same dream he had night after night so many years prior. Phillip would find himself in the moonless dark of night walking a lonely set of railroad tracks. The fog was rolling in and he was cold. He could hear off in the distance in front of him some sort of crying. The closer to the cries he would get, the harder it was for him to walk. Behind him he could feel a presence of doom. When he forced himself to turn and see what threatened him, his legs would freeze. A bright light was blinding him, and bursts from a blaring air horn caused his ears to ache. He realized a freight train was bearing down on him and he needed to get off the tracks. At the same instant he remembered the cries. He turned. The pulsating light now illuminated a small figure just down the tracks where it curved to the right. He cupped his hands around his mouth to scream out and warn the figure. He was screaming as loud as he could but no sound was coming forth. He tried to free his legs in vain. Just at the instant the train was to run over Phillip, he found himself free to move. He jumped to safety and watched helplessly as the speeding train continued to bear down on the trapped figure in the curve of the tracks. At this point in the dream he always jerked awake, sweating and shaking. He never found out who or even what the figure was on the tracks but he was always overcome with guilt at the end of the dream.

He remembered back to his psychiatric sessions when he and his doctor were trying to purge this dream. Phillip had many different types of nightmares, some related to actual events in his life and some that never happened. But his psychiatrist determined that the train dream held the key. The doctor explained that the figure most probably represented his friend Gum. The freight train represented Colonel Chu and was an unstoppable force which Phillip had no control over. When he saved himself time after time in the dream, it was to bring on the guilty feelings when he woke up, this being his burden to bear of blaming himself for Gum's murder. The doc put a tag on it for Phillip and called it survivor's guilt, a very common syndrome.

Phillip remembered what his remark was to the doctor. "Yeah, right, Doc. Makes sense to me, so how do I stop blaming myself?"

The doc replied, "Sergeant Turner, you didn't kill that boy. As you say, that Vietnamese Colonel did the shooting. You had nothing to do with it at all."

"It's like this, Doc. If I hadn't bought that boy that bicycle that day, there would have been no way he could have made it onto the flight line looking for me. It's all my fault. You know it. And I know it!"

Somehow each time the session got to this point, the doctor

would check his watch and conveniently end the session, saying that next time he hoped they would have more time to explore the different possible meanings of Phillip's dream.

Knowing sleep was over, Phillip quietly slipped into his bathrobe. He noticed Kassy had placed his flight bag beside the closet door. He figured he must had left it out on the dining room table. He flipped the light on in the walk-in closet and reached up to the top shelf to replace the bag. Beside where the bag sat, he saw an old Florshiem shoe box he had kept. He opened the lid, pulled back some old letters he had written to find pictures from the war. The very top picture was the one he had the soldier take of him and Gum in Saigon Sally's bar. Phillip smiled, took the picture out, and returned the shoe box to the top shelf. He headed for the study, sat down in front of his computer, and turned it on. The monitor flickered and the computer beeped. He propped the picture up against the small right speaker beside the monitor. With mouse in hand, he maneuvered the little arrow-shaped cursor until it came to rest over the icon he wanted. He left clicked the button on the mouse to his internet connection. He wanted to kill some time surfing the web. After bouncing around to a couple of Vietnam sites, he surfed over to some of his favorite sites.

He looked up at the picture of Gum. He moved his head closer and squinted his eyes into focus. This time he noticed in the background Colonel Danworth and Colonel Chu seated in the room behind Gum and himself. That gave Phillip an idea. *I wonder if I can find ol' Mr. Chu on this thing?* He then typed in http://www.four11.com. His internet browser took him to the four11 directory site. If you were listed in the phone book anywhere in the United States this search engine would find you. Pausing, Phillip pushed his chair back, stretched his legs. He leaned back, arching his back to relieve some of the muscle tightening. He typed in Chu, no first name, because he never knew it. He clicked his cursor arrow on *enter search*. After a couple of seconds the search responded. A message popped up on the screen: "Found over ten thousand matches for last name Chu. Please narrow your search." Straining his eyes and rubbing his chin as he read the message, Phillip whispered out loud, "Damn. I knew that would be too easy."

He then typed in the last name: Danworth; first name: Ben; state: Kentucky. He clicked *enter search*, then *wham, bam*. Search results message flashed up one listing, Ben Danworth, US Air Force ret. Col. Lexington, Kentucky. Phillip thought, *Bingo!* A smile of accomplishment took over his tired face, and a plan of attack was beginning to take shape in his mind. He moved his mouse cursor arrow to the print icon, clicked on it and out spit the necessary info. He took the sheet with this treasured phone number and address on it from the printer, folded it up and tucked it safely away in his bathrobe pocket. Two hours had just flown by. At 6:30 a.m. he felt a tug on his bathrobe hanging off to the side of the chair.

"Daddy, I'm thirsty. I can't find any juice in the fridge." Phillip looked down at P.T. He was holding a small scrap of his trusty "night night" blanket which he refused to give up.

"Morning there, little man. Did you and your 'night night' sleep well? Let's go see if we can find you something to drink." Phillip shut the computer down and he and P.T. headed for the kitchen. Phillip started a pot of coffee and poured P.T. some juice. As Phillip studied the freezer for something easy to heat up for breakfast, Kassy dragged in. She shuffled up to Phillip, stood on her tiptoes, and kissed him on the neck.

"Have you come up with a game plan on what you are going to do yet?" Kassy asked sleepily.

"Yeah, I think so. First I want to go see John Robinson."

"Wait a minute. Did we not elect your buddy John to the House in Washington, D.C. last November? You're saying you're going to Washington? Why not just call him?"

"This is too important! I have to walk this through if I expect to get heard. Anyway, John is going to need to see what evidence I have. The pictures and my records. I'm going to call Jack and Cindy up this morning and see if they will work doubles at the store till I get back. Can you handle P.T.? Maybe call in at the hospital for some time off or see if my Mom can help out?"

"Whatever. We'll do what we have to do." With that, Kassy threw her hands into the air, shook her head and started to the bedroom to pack Phillip a bag.

"Dad, I want to go to Washington with you!" P.T. begged, sliding over to catch Phillip's hand.

"Sorry, son, this is real important business, I won't have time to do any sight-seeing."

CHAPTER THIRTEEN

AFTER A TEN-HOUR DRIVE, Phillip's pickup truck crossed the Potomac River. He landed smack dab in the middle of Washington. He was more than a little awestruck since he had never been to D.C. before. It was getting close to dark so he drove around some to get his bearings. He felt a childlike excitement as he pulled past several of the places he had always wanted to see as a child. Stopping at a traffic light adjacent to the Lincoln Memorial, he craned his neck to get a better look. He gazed up at what appeared to be about a million steps to the Parthenon-like, white marble structure. Inside the promenade, he could just make out the statue of Abraham Lincoln sitting on his throne viewing his Washington D.C. kingdom laid out before him. Phillip thought, *Wow, I never knew it was so big. That damn thing must have cost a bundle of taxpayers' dollars!* Phillip also saw a sign for The Wall, the Vietnam War Memorial, but he couldn't see it from the street. The light changed and he moved on. He pulled over to the curb adjacent to the Washington Monument and looked across the green lawn, scanning skyward to the top of the solid white tip of the spire. He smiled, thinking back to twenty-five years ago and how Gum had described this as an upside down white spike. "Hmm, Gum, you were right," Phillip mumbled to himself.

He threaded his way back out into traffic and on down by the Smithsonian, where he pulled over to the side of the street and stopped once more. He looked past the antique carousel spinning its magic for a group of school kids. He smiled at the sounds of laughter and squeals of delight filling the air. As he took in the view of the red brick gothic and unique architectural structure, he thought, *Now there. That's where I would like to spend a day, or more like a month.* The Smithsonian had always been the place he wanted to see. He noticed the city metamorphosing as darkness fell. All the tourists were being replaced by Washington's creatures of the night. Phillip thought, *Yeah, all the freaks come up at night. Time to get a room.* He began his hunt for a hotel. As he rounded a corner, there stood the Watergate complex. *Perfect.*

Phillip awoke early the next morning. He took a shuttle bus over to the Capitol building since he had been forewarned about the parking situation in Washington. The desk clerk at the Watergate simply stated, "There is no parking in D.C. You better take the bus!" He wanted to find John early, maybe even catch some lunch with him.

By afternoon Phillip finally located Representative Robinson's office. It was in the basement of the House of Representatives' building down a long marble hall. This was more of the typical Washington protocol. The newer members of the House got the worst offices. It was like a game of musical offices. When one senior member moved up, the other junior members would move up too. That was why Phillip had such a hard time finding John, who had already moved three times since November.

He entered the outer office of Georgia Representative John Robinson. A very pretty secretary looked up from her desk. She assessed Phillip's attire. With bright red alligator golf shirt, Levi blue jeans, and Rockport hiking boots, he hardly looked the part of a visiting dignitary.

"Yes, Sir, how may I help you?"

"I'm looking for John."

"John? John who, Sir?"

"Oh, I'm sorry. John Robinson, my representative."

"And do you have an appointment with Representative Robinson, Sir?"

"No, just ring him up on that little box you got there on your desk. Tell him that the record holder for the biggest large mouth bass ever caught on Stroud Lake wants to see him." Phillip winked at the secretary. "I'm a very close friend of his."

She smiled. "Oh, you had me going there for a minute. I hope you're telling the truth. This might cost me my job." She held down the intercom button. "Sir, excuse me, but there is a gentleman out here who says to inform you that he holds the record for some type of fish caught on Stroud Lake."

"Is that so? Ask that bozo how much did it weigh?" John Robinson was a quick study and had already guessed who was waiting to see him.

Phillip, overhearing this, leaned over the desk and spoke into the box. "Fourteen pounds, seven ounces. That would make that bad boy exactly one ounce bigger than the one you caught that day!"

"One ounce my foot! If you hadn't cheated, you rat, and stuffed two ounces of fishing lead down your bass's throat, I would hold that record! Phillip, you dog, get in here."

Ms. Presley smiled in relief and wiped her brow. She stood and showed Phillip the door to the Representative's office. John, in his standard-issued three-piece dark blue suit with matching yellow and blue striped power neck tie and dark brown wing tipped shoes, was waiting just inside the door with a hearty handshake.

"Phillip, what brings you up here?"

"Good to see you, John. I need your help." Then he spotted John's bass. "Oh, I see you brought your puny fish with you."

Phillip pointed to the wall behind John's desk where the huge mounted, almost-a-record large mouth bass was hanging with the crank bait it was caught on dangling from its mouth.

Chuckling, John responded, "Yeah, I got your puny right here." He walked over to the fish and gave the crank bait a flick with his finger. He turned and offered Phillip a chair, the red and silver crank bait still swinging back and forth behind him. "Have a seat. How can I help you, Phillip?"

Phillip sat down and dragged the chair up close to the front of John's desk. He took a deep breath, reached into his pocket and pulled out a large overstuffed envelope. He began his tale. As he told the story of Gum, Chu, and Danworth, he laid out what little evidence he had accumulated. A few photos, some notes he had written at the time, and the newspaper article from Memorial Day. Phillip found it hard to tell the story even though twenty-plus years had gone by. He stopped from time to time to gather himself and swallow a hard dry swallow. When he reached the end of his account, he looked up at John. He could tell that his friend had been truly moved by his story.

John cleared his throat. "God, Phillip, I have known you all these years. I never knew that happened to you. Hell, I never knew you had been to Vietnam. I knew you had been in the Air Force at that time, but you never said anything about being over there and all."

"It's just not something I felt like talking about or remembering. It's like when you were a kid up in a corner of the house doing something you know you weren't supposed to be doing. You know, like playing with your dad's cigarette lighter. In walks your mom. What do you do? You throw that lighter down and run to the farthest place that you can get, pretending it never happened. So, when I got out of that lunatic war, I ran like a bat out of hell! I never wanted to look back. Now it's looking back at me and I have to do something about it. Besides, it doesn't make for good fishing talk, if you catch my drift," Phillip replied.

"So why me, Phillip? Why are you here? What do you expect me to do about this?"

"I don't know exactly, John. I just thought maybe you could help me get some answers. I guess you being up here with the bigwigs, you might could ask around. I just want to know if Chu was even investigated on the shooting like Colonel Danworth told me and what the outcome was."

John leaned back in his overstuffed, worn red leather office chair. It creaked as he placed his left hand behind his neck and rubbed. He pointed his right index finger at Phillip. "Hmm, tell you what. I do have a close contact at the State Department. Let me call him, run this by him, see what he says. This may cost us a fishing trip down the road. Good ol' Sid eyes that 'puny Bass' every time he comes in here. Where are you staying? I'll give you a call later this evening if I can reach him."

"That would be great. You tell Sid there is always room for one more in my boat. I am over at the Watergate, room two-twelve."

"Watergate? That figures. Did you snoop around and see if you could scare up some of Nixon's old ghosts?"

Laughing, Phillip replied, "You know me well, John, old friend." Both stood and shook hands.

John turned to walk Phillip to the door and remarked, "I know you, yes, but not that well." He was referring to the conversation that had just taken place. "Good to see you, Phillip. Talk to you later on."

Phillip headed back to the hotel and went down to the lobby bar for happy hour. He had a couple of beers and headed back up to his room for the night. He ordered room service since he didn't want to leave the room and miss John's call. He phoned home to report in and check on P.T. After dinner he watched a couple of old movies on the super station, falling asleep during the middle of "Ice Station Zebra," one of his and Howard Hughes's favorite flicks.

At 2:13 a.m. the phone rang. Dazed, Phillip reached over and knocked the receiver onto the floor.

"Phillip? Phillip? You there, buddy?" John squawked.

"Yes, John, I'm here. Damn, what time is it? You must have some good news for me."

"Sorry, the news is not good. I was just at this late night mixer and I saw Sid there. I gave him the rundown on your problem and told him what you had. Sid said you have to come up with a lot more evidence against this guy to get them to even look into it. I'm sorry, Phillip. I did try. If you can get me some more dirt on this bastard, I'll try again. OK?"

"I understand, John, and thanks. I'll stay in touch. Goodnight."

Phillip hung up the phone. He got up and went into the bathroom and got a drink of water. Looking into the mirror while rubbing the sleep from his eyes, he thought, *Well, that's that. My only hope now is Colonel Benjamin Danworth.* He walked over to the dresser, picked up his worn flight bag, opened it, and plundered through it. Finding what he was looking for, he took out the folded piece of paper with Colonel Danworth's phone number on it that he had printed on his computer. He lay back down on the bed and fell asleep grasping the folded paper.

At 6 a.m. Phillip awoke. Although he wanted to make the call immediately, he didn't want to wake anyone up. *No reason to start this off on the wrong foot,* he thought. So he showered and went down to the restaurant for coffee and a smoke. At 8 a.m. he couldn't wait any longer. So he returned to his room, took the paper from his pocket and dialed the phone number.

Ring, Ring, Ring, Ring, Ring. An eternity seemed to go by. Finally he heard a click.

"Hello," An elderly woman's voice spoke.

"Ma'am, uh, is this Colonel Benjamin Danworth's residence? Ma'am?"

"Yes, this is Colonel Danworth's residence. This is Lillian Danworth speaking. Who is this please?"

"This is Phillip Turner, Sergeant Turner, ma'am. I knew the Colonel a long time ago. May I speak with the Colonel please?"

"No, I don't think I can let you can speak with the Colonel. You see, he has been seriously ill as of late and I don't want to disturb him. I will tell him you called though." Phillip could hear a distant gravelly voice muttering in the background. "What, Dear?" Phillip could tell she was holding the phone to her chest to muffle it. "Yes, Dear, the man said his name was Sergeant Phillip Turner. You do? Well, if you feel up to it then." She raised the phone back to her ear.

"Sergeant Turner, hold on just one second. The Colonel remembers you and wants to have a word with you. Now don't talk too long and wear him down. Here's the Colonel."

Coughing, a weak, gruff voice came on the line. "Turner, is that you? My old crew chief Turner?" Danworth's voice was crackling with gurgles of sputum.

"Yes, Sir. It's me. How are you, Sir? Good to hear your voice!"

"Drop the small talk, Turner." Danworth coughed, "What's your business?"

"Sir, I don't really know how to say this, but, I need to talk to you about Colonel Chu. Please don't hang up on me, Sir; you're my only hope to find out what happened."

A long pause ensued. Phillip grew anxious waiting for this most important answer. He could hear the Colonel on the other end of the line taking shallow, labored breaths.

"Sir?"

Finally, a response. "Son, can you come here to see me? I live in Lexington, Kentucky. I think the time has come for you and me to talk. Oh, and, son, if you're coming you better hurry. I'm not sure how much time I have left on this earth."

"Sir, thank you. I'm in Washington, D.C., but if I leave now I can make it there by dark."

"OK. Come to six seventeen Falcon Drive. I'll be waiting for you. Oh, and one more thing. Cut the sir and Colonel crap. That ended a long time ago. Just call me Ben."

Phillip hung up the phone. He raced to gather his belongings and check out of the hotel.

He gassed up his truck, popped a Jimmy Buffet cassette into the player, turned the volume up and headed west back across the Potomac River and out of town. On the drive he lost himself in daydreams of fond memories. He thought of the first time he saw Kassy in the check-out line at the commissary. He visualized P.T.'s first birthday party and how he threw the cake on the floor. Kassy had worked on that cake for a good two days and it only lasted about thirty seconds after it was presented to P.T. They didn't even have time to take a picture of it. Kassy cried till she started to laugh.

Phillip smiled. He remembered Gum's first bike ride and the look of pride and joy he had on his face. Gum's glee then faded to that last look of fear and of being lost. Phillip started to tear up; he snorted in his runny nose and rubbed the tears from his eyes. The smile on Phillip's face changed to the determined look of a man on a mission. The truck rolled on, westward bound.

CHAPTER FOURTEEN

PHILLIP ARRIVED IN LEXINGTON at around 8 p.m. Eastern Standard Time. Just inside the city limits he stopped and gassed up the truck.

It was a good time for a leg stretch and a chance to shake off the road wearies. He bought a bottle of Pepsi, a small bag of salted peanuts and a city map. He set up a command post on the hood of his truck. He tore the bag of peanuts open and dumped them into the Pepsi. With his thumb securely stuffed in the neck of the bottle, he gave it a good shake. As the fizz inside the drink bubbled up, pushing at the thumb cork, he released the cocktail into his mouth. He gulped and chewed with great satisfaction.

Setting the concoction temporarily aside, Phillip unfolded the map. He smoothed it down on the hood of the truck, then searched for his destination.

Near Falcon Drive he checked into a motel for a quick shower and to call the Danworth residence.

"Hello." The now familiar, elderly female voice answered.

"This is Sergeant Phillip Turner, ma'am. May I speak with the Colonel, please?"

"Yes, Sergeant Turner, you may. He has been expecting your call. I must say I don't think this is such a good idea. But hold on one sec. I will get him for you."

Danworth took the phone. He was coughing out of control. Phillip held the phone back from his ear. "Phillip, where are you? Are you going to make it tonight?"

"Yes, Sir, um, Ben. I'm just down the street from you at the Lexington Inn. I know it's getting late. Would you rather wait till morning to talk?"

"No, hell no. I want to get this done. Come on over!" Danworth hung the phone up.

Phillip pulled his truck into the driveway at 617 Falcon Drive. The neighborhood appeared to be middle class, clean and quiet. The house was a rather small, red brick, ranch style home with a neat little yard, not at all what he had expected a retired Colonel to be living in. Phillip noticed a handicapped wheelchair ramp near the front door. He rang the doorbell and Lillian Danworth greeted him.

"Good evening, young man. Come right in. Ben is in the rest room and will meet you on the screen porch." She showed Phillip the way.

He took a seat on the one bench at the picnic table in the middle of the porch. He tapped his fingers on the red wood planks and surveyed the various items on the table. He saw a stack of photographs. The only one he could make out was the picture on top of the stack. It was a photo of several aluminum coffins sitting in a warehouse. Phillip thought, *These look just like the ones we used to haul back and forth from Nam.* Also on the table were a stack of documents, some maps, and that little gray-top spiral notebook that went everywhere with the Colonel.

Phillip heard the sound of huffing and puffing and the squeaking of a wheel. He looked up to see what once was a healthy hulk of a man reduced to a pathetic, shriveled-up, very sick man, old beyond his years. Ben came rolling in, riding in his wheelchair, oxygen tube hooked around his ears and passing under his nose. Phillip hardly recognized the man he used to think was bigger than life. His once invincible "John Wayne" had fallen. The one thing the Colonel still possessed from the past that Phillip did recognize was the perfect pencil-thin moustache. But even the moustache had turned to the dingy yellow of sickness. Phillip felt uncomfortable and didn't know quite how to react to what he saw. One part of him was telling him to take the easy way out. Just leave. Drop it. Don't bother this pathetic creature. The other part told him that if he did, it would hurt the Colonel's feelings and he should stay to get his answers.

Ben wheeled up to the empty side of the picnic table. He coughed. Yellow sputum slung out and stuck to the hand he was raising to cover his mouth. Ben gave an embarrassed smile and wiped the sputum on his pants' lap. He locked the handbrakes on the chair and reached across the table, offering his freshly wiped hand in friendship.

"Good to see you, Phillip. You did say Phillip, right? You will have to bear with me, son. The old memory has been playing some tricks on me lately. The morphine patch doesn't help much either."

Phillip stood and leaned across the table and took Danworth's hand.

"Yes, Sir, it's Phillip. Good to see you, Sir, Ben. Sorry."

The night was warm and sticky. Ben hollered out, "Lillian! Lillian! Could you come in here for a minute?" Lillian poked her head in the doorway. "Ah, could you turn this ceiling fan on and get Phillip a beer and me one, too."

"Now, Dear, the doctor wouldn't like that. No alcohol remember?"

"Just get the damn beers, Lillian! What difference does it make if I live two more days or two more weeks? I'm still dead in two weeks. Sorry, Phillip." The old Colonel managed to muster up a little of the old fire. Lillian gasped, shook her head, and stomped to the kitchen.

"Ben, I didn't realize you were that sick. Anything I can do?"

"Yeah, you can drink a beer with me. We can talk this out. And don't send flowers to my funeral." He coughed, wheezed, and chuckled. "Hell, that old mean-as-a-snake doctor has been condemning me to death for almost three years now. Hasn't got it right yet. This time I think he has a chance, though. He tells me that this lung cancer has just about done its work on me."

Lillian returned, dragging a playmate cooler full of beer and ice. "Here you go, sweetheart. I hope you enjoy your last night on earth. I'm going to bed now. Sergeant Turner, when you and the Colonel are done, would you mind letting yourself out? Goodnight."

Phillip stood and smiled warmly. "It was nice to have met you, Ma'am. Goodnight." Lillian left.

"Hand me one of those beers, Phillip, and tell me what got you on this Colonel Chu kick."

Phillip reached into the cooler and cracked open the pop-top. He took out a copy of the newspaper article that started his saga, unfolded it, turned it so Ben could read it, and handed both beer and paper over to him.

Ben took a sip of beer and set the can down. He dropped his eyes to the bottom part of his trifocal glasses and read the page. When he finished, he looked up at Phillip. Coughing, he said, "Yeah, now you want me to tell you what?"

Pointing a shaking index finger of condemnation at Chu's picture, Phillip responded, "Sir, I want you to tell me how some son of a bitch like that is living here. I want you to tell me what happened about the investigation you told me you had started when he shot that little boy. Sir, I want you to tell me you had nothing to do with letting that bastard get away with cold-blooded murder."

A remorseful look took over Ben Danworth's face. "Calm down, Sergeant. We're in for a long night here, so take it easy and hear me out." He paused to spit some sputum in a cup. "Now, first of all, I agree with you that Chu is a real piece of work. He is as ruthless as they come. You and I are the only two witnesses who saw him shoot the boy that day. I saw it just as clear as you did. Hell, I did have a bird's eye view from the cockpit. Everyone else assumed the sniper that shot you in the leg was the same shooter that hit the boy. So when Chu shot the sniper, well, hell, he got a medal. The dink son of a bitch got a medal for shooting his own damn man. Now don't that beat all."

Confused, Phillip took a big gulp of beer. "So, why didn't you turn him in?"

"Well, Phillip, there is more to this story than that. I couldn't turn Chu in. He was one of my partners. We were involved in a drug smuggling ring. It worked quite well. Chu would supply and pack. I would transport. And a fellow by the name of Geevers would take care of distribution once the stuff got to the States. So if I turned in Chu for shooting the boy. Well, hell, you can figure that out for yourself."

Ben took a wheezing breath and a sip of beer. He unlocked the brakes to his wheel chair and repositioned it. He strained as he reached over and flipped the first two photos toward Phillip. The pictures spun to a stop and Phillip picked them up. Picture one was the picture Phillip first saw of the aluminum coffins. Picture two was the same as picture one except it showed Chu packing one of the coffins with tightly wrapped bundles. Those bundles, according to Danworth, were processed opium ready for delivery to the States.

"This is where it would all start," Ben continued, pointing his bent index finger toward the photographs. "Chu was in charge of the Bien Hoa morgue. So he had no problem coming up with all the necessary shipping containers, so to speak, that we would need. His sources would deliver whatever Geevers ordered. Hash, black opium, heroin, you name it, Chu would have it there ready to be shipped. Hell, if Geevers wanted a hundred pounds of 'gook eyeballs,' I'm sure Chu would have gotten those too if there was a buck in it for him."

He made a sick chuckle, hacked and coughed, spit more sputum in the cup. "Chu would then have some of his men pack the special orders into the transfer cases. After the pack-up he would cover the stuff with butchered water buffalo parts, blood, and some guts for good measure. After you skinned them, they would look just like human arms and legs. Sometimes, though, I still think ol' Chu would throw in some real human parts. Probably someone who was giving him some trouble back there. I knew better than to ask too many questions."

Ben flipped the next photograph at Phillip. This one showed an open coffin with what appeared to be various bloody human body parts.

"Damn, Ben, these do look like the real thing. You bastards didn't care, did you?"

"Yeah, Phillip, we cared. We cared for money and not a damn thing else! Back to the story." After coughing, gagging, and gurgling, he hocked more sputum in his spit cup, then took a gulp of beer. "Damn. Sorry. OK, let's see now. Oh, Chu was good. He would handle the delivery of the caskets to the plane. If the Vietnamese inspectors came on board, he would orchestrate the sniper attacks. Remember those? Oh, by the way, you getting shot was pure accident. I guess the poor trigger man paid the price for that miss or hit, didn't he?"

He chuckled again, tossed another photo to Phillip. This one showed the plane C5a Balls12 on the ground at Travis AFB, California. The aft cargo doors were open, and a forklift was taking a pallet of caskets off the plane. Standing off in the distance was a US customs inspector with his German shepherd drug-sniffing dog at the sit position beside him.

"Now, you see that customs inspector back there with his dog? Well, that stupid SOB is Dobb. Dobb was very superstitious or stupidstitious, you could say. All we had to do was put one of these body parts stickers on the coffins." Ben leaned forward and sorted through the pile on the picnic table. He found one of the stickers and flipped it to Phillip. "We always made sure to have our boxes loaded last so Dobb would see them first. He would take one look at the coffins and turn real pale. His eyes would swim in his head. Beads of sweat would pop out on his forehead and he would turn tail and run. He would sign the whole load off as being checked just so he could get the hell out of there. And it worked every time. I would always schedule our arrivals to coincide with Dobb's shift."

Ben flipped the last photo down in front of Phillip. Phillip picked it up and began to study it. This picture showed a man who seemed to be taking inventory of stacked bundles. The bundles looked exactly like the ones Chu was shown packing in the previous pictures. The man was holding a clipboard, staring straight into the camera with a startled look on his face. But it wasn't the face that stood out; it was his solid white hair, unusual for someone who appeared to be in his early thirties. Just as the thought about the hair crossed Phillip's mind, he locked onto the man's eyes. In the black and white photo they had an eerie-grayish white look to them, with just black pinpricks for pupils.

"Now, this is my old buddy Bill Geevers," Ben said.

"Is he blind?" Phillip questioned, referring to the strange

appearance of his eyes.

"No, quite the contrary. That snake can see in the pitch black dark, I believe. I almost got caught taking that picture." Ben gave a gurgling chuckle. "Those eyes are spooky looking, ain't they? I saw him once in the dark, and I swear those damn eyes were lit up glowing at me, this kinda bluish-gray glow. Gave me the creeps. Anyway, Bill was the mastermind behind this whole setup. He was the one that introduced me to Chu. He was always a civilian. Hell, I don't really know what the hell he was. He was just over there with the CIA working on the Air America deal out of Bien Hoa. You remember anything about that CIA-run covert activity? Bill was pretty young to have made the connections he had. He was a real smart-ass, too. A real smart-ass!! OK, check the corner of that bundle, the second one from the bottom. See those numbers and that marking?" Ben pointed to a magnifying glass lying on the table. Phillip picked it up and examined the photo more closely.

"Yes, I see them. So?" Phillip answered.

"Hang on. Now, go back and look at the second picture I gave you and see if you can find a match to that bundle." Ben instructed.

Phillip obliged. "Yeah, OK. I found the matching bundle. So, what does this mean?"

"Well, my boy, that means I have just tied Bill Geevers to Colonel Chu. Now if I needed some type of insurance to keep these two off my back, this might help. I guess what I am really trying to say is, it's time to cash in this insurance policy."

Phillip looked deep into Ben's eyes. "What do you mean? I'm confused here."

Ben coughed. "I want you to take this information, all of it, back to Washington. You did say you had a friend in the House who can help you, right? I want you to get Chu and Geevers anyway you can. Take me down with them if you have to. It doesn't matter; I just can't live with this crap on me anymore. Two things I want you to know. I stopped doing my part of the smuggling when the little boy got shot. I knew Chu was getting out of hand. And it broke my heart to see a child pay the ultimate price for nothing at all. It really pissed Chu off when I broke it to him that I was out of the circle. He and Geevers even tried to have me wasted, I think. You remember 'Operation Baby Lift'?"

"I remember reading about it in the paper. That was when that C-5 went down during the orphan evacuation."

"That C-5 was Balls Twelve.

"Balls Twelve? You're shitting me? It was some type of mechanical failure on the aft cargo doors, right?"

"I don't know. You tell me. You were the maintenance crew chief. Ever heard of massive decompression from a leaking door seal? Enough inner pressure to blow those big-ass doors open without some help?"

Phillip thought back for a minute. He ran over in his mind the redundant safety latches on the doors and how it would be impossible for them to fail. He came to the only possible conclusion. "You're saying it was sabotage? So why weren't you on board? Wait a minute. That would mean Toomes, Reynolds, Captain Erin, Captain Benson, Major Stewart and the rest of the guys. They were all killed. They're all dead? Everyone on board was killed, I remember that much."

"No, thank the good lord, they were all with me. This is what happened. We were scheduled to fly Balls Twelve out of Tan Son Nhut airfield that day, but we were switched at the last minute. Seems we had run out of flying hours for the week. Hours didn't really ever matter except this time the Top Brass didn't want us on such a high profile mission. So, they sent us over to Bien Hoa and Balls Fifteen. The poor son of a bitches on Balls Fifteen were put on Balls Twelve."

The shock and horror was quite evident on Phillip's face.

"Look, I'm not saying for sure it was sabotage and that Chu and Geevers had anything to do with it. I just got the worst feeling about that so-called accident. It has haunted me to this day. They grounded all of the C-5s because of it, and all operations on C-5s to Nam were halted for a long time. I went ahead and took my early retirement and tried to fade away. Oh, and one other thing I feel is important for you to know, Phillip. I have never spent one dime of the 1.8 million dollars I made during the drug smuggling operations. I put it in a trust fund for war orphans and it will be activated upon my death. Well, that's not altogether true, either. You remember the envelope full of money I tried to give you at Travis?"

"Yes, Ben, I remember."

Ben rubbed his eyebrows. "That was a foolish thing to have done. I guess I was just trying to ease my conscience some. And when I found it in my locker, I just knew you had started to put some of this shit together for yourself."

"No, Ben, I didn't have a clue until tonight."

"That day. That day I watched a young boy become a hero and a man in the same second."

"That day? What are you talking about?" Phillip thought Ben was starting to lose some of his train of thought.

"It was extraordinary what you did for that little girl. What was her name? Sue Ling, wasn't it?"

"Extraordinarily stupid. I could have found a better way to have handled that." Phillip was now cued in on what Ben was referring to.

"No, what you did was calculated and correct. Even if I hadn't showed up, that guard would have let you in. I could see it written on his face. You had him. He was so scared and flustered. I was so very proud of you, son." Ben was almost in tears.

"Anyway, I took that part of the money and I bought the little girl a prosthetic leg with it. It took some doing and several measurements but she got the best leg money could buy. I got a doc in San Francisco to build it for me. It made her real happy, Phillip, and I felt you would have done that for her if you had had the opportunity."

Phillip's eyes welled with tears as he thought of pretty Sue Ling and how he had found her after she had been maimed by the land mine. He smiled at the news of now knowing she lived through the ordeal. "Thank you, Ben. Thank you for doing that."

Ben reached over and picked up the gray-top spiral notebook. He flipped through it one more time, then tossed it in the air to Phillip. Phillip caught it in midair. "So, Sergeant Turner, will you help me make some type of atonement for my actions?"

"Colonel, all I really care about is that bastard Chu. If that means hurting this Geevers fellow and dragging you in the dirt, too, so be it."

The night had passed into early morning. Phillip's eyes were blurry. He could tell that the long session had worn down the Colonel, who grew weaker by the minute. Phillip stood and stretched out his arms, yawned, and threw his head back. "Let me get this straight, Sir. You are giving me all this information to do with what I will?"

With trembling hands, Ben unlocked the handbrakes and rolled his wheelchair slowly back from the table. A coughing fit overtook him. Phillip rushed to the old man's side, leaning down to offer what assistance he could.

"Sir?"

"Yes, damn it. Take all of it."

"No, Sir, I was asking if you were going to be alright, Sir?"

Choking and clutching his chest, Ben squeaked out, "Probably not. Get this stuff together and take off, Phillip. I am going to see if I can make it to the bedroom. Oh, good luck on your mission. I really do hope you can get that Chu bastard. Goodnight."

Ben turned his wheel chair and rolled out the door. Phillip sat back down at the picnic table to take a minute to absorb all that had just taken place. After gathering his thoughts, he piled all the documents and photos in a neat stack. He placed the little gray notebook in his back pocket. He then hooked his arm under the pile and hoisted it up under his arm. As silent as a mouse, he crept toward the front door, turning off the lights as he went. He double-checked the front door to make sure it was latched securely behind him.

After sleeping only a few hours, Phillip arose early to go through all the stuff Ben had given him. He decided that he had at least enough damning evidence to start an investigation into Chu's actions. Packing up in a hurry, he departed once again for Washington D.C.

The long drive back and the lack of sleep over the past several days began to take their toll. Phillip's head nodded down, then jerked back up. In an attempt to stay awake, he popped in an Eagles tape and turned the volume up extra loud. He rolled down the windows and turned his air conditioner on high. Just as his head was about to drop for the final and fatal time, and as his truck slowly veered off to the shoulder of the interstate, his cellular phone rang out. The foreign sound was just enough to bring him back to a semi-state of consciousness.

He realized his plight and jerked the steering wheel sharply back to the left, just missing the guardrail by inches. Shaking his head violently, he pulled back into the emergency lane and skidded the truck safely to a stop.

The phone was still ringing. Phillip reached down, picked it up off the floor and switched it on. His heart was pounding, and he was unable to catch his breath long enough to ask who had just saved his life.

"Phillip? Phillip Turner, is that you? Phillip?" Kassy was on the other end, trying to get him to respond.

"Hi, baby, thanks for calling!" He didn't go into why he was so glad she called.

"Where are you? Why do you sound so strange? I haven't heard from you in over a day now. I take it you are either on I-95 south or I-20 west headed home. That is right, isn't it?" Kassy's voice was leading and anxious to hear the answers she wanted to hear.

"Well, not exactly. You see, I got in touch with Colonel Danworth. And…." A long pause. "I drove over to see him in Lexington, Kentucky, yesterday. And…."

"And nothing. Drove over? Lexington, Kentucky? Phillip, have you lost your mind? That's half way across the country, and you're making it sound like it's just down the street." Kassy was pissed. "So now you are on your way back home and you will be here when?"

Phillip took a long pause, trying to think of just how to put his next statement. "Well, no, baby. I can't come home just yet. You see I am on my way back to Washington. Kassy, look, the Colonel gave me all I need to get Chu! And I want to give it to John as soon as I can!"

"Oh, Phillip. Just what am I going to do with you? Look, sweetheart, Jack and Cindy are getting tired of working doubles. I need to tell them something. So just how much longer do you think this is going to take? And how much is all this running all over the countryside costing us? I just can't wait to see the Master Card bill next month!"

Phillip thought to himself, figuring a time schedule. "Just tell them I will give them a bonus when I get back. I should be home the day after tomorrow, or the next, OK?"

"Alright. Just be careful, will you? P.T. misses his dad, and I miss you, too. And try not to spend too much money. Bye."

"I miss you two with all my heart. Bye."

Phillip switched off the phone and pulled back onto the interstate. He headed for the first motel he saw to get some much-needed rest.

CHAPTER FIFTEEN

EARLY THE NEXT MORNING he was back on the road feeling refreshed and making good time. Phillip called John Robinson from his cell-phone.

"Good morning, Representative Robinson's office. How may I direct your call?"

"This is Phillip Turner. Could I speak to John, please? Make that Representative Robinson, please. I need to set up a meeting with him later this afternoon. You do remember me, don't you?"

"The fishing buddy. How could I ever forget you? Hold please, and I will tell the Representative you are on the phone." After a long pause, Ms. Presley came back on. "The Representative would like to know if he might meet with you later this evening? He says he will be tied up in committee meetings the rest of the afternoon."

"Tell the Representative that will be Hunky Dory and..." Phillip was now trying to get her goat.

Ms. Presley interrupted, "Hunky what?"

"Never mind. Just tell the Representative that I called ahead and made reservations at the Ramada Inn in Alexandria, Virginia. It's the Ramada adjacent to the Iwo Jima Memorial. Tell him I am still on the road, and I will call him back when I get there to give him the room number."

"Hold, please." Another long pause. "Sir, the Representative has instructed me to inform you that he will meet with you at six p.m. this evening at your hotel. And, Sir, no need for you to call back. I will be more than able to obtain the correct room number for the Representative."

"Roger that, Ms. Presley."

"Sir?"

"That will be fine, miss. Tell John, the Representative, I look forward to seeing him this evening. Oh, and thanks for all your help, Ms. Presley."

After checking into his room, Phillip headed out to look over The Iwo Jima Memorial. He could see it just outside his room window and couldn't resist a closer inspection. He stopped and bought a Pepsi on the way through the hotel lobby, but was unable to find one measly little bag of salted peanuts in the whole house. He left the cool climate controlled confines of the hotel lobby and stepped out into the Virginia July heat.

Approaching the monument, he began a deliberate pace to an unheard military cadence around the enormous bronze sculpture. As he took his last sip of Pepsi, a feeling of patriotism began to swell up in his heart. He gazed upward at the cluster of a half dozen pairs of hands reaching out in unison to erect the American flag on top of Mount Suribachi. The six huge, bronze soldiers strained against the wind to fulcrum the flagpole into a pile of rocks in order to swing the flag upright and let it fly in triumph and glory. Shielding his eyes from the blazing late afternoon sun, he pondered, as so many had before: *Is this what war was all about? The placing of just a flag on the high ground? A piece of cloth? How many good people had to give up their lives in order for this scene to take place?*

He lowered his head and looked to the base of the sculpture. There in the light gray, rough Swedish granite base burnished in gold, he saw listed the names and dates of every principal Marine Corps engagement since the Corp was founded in 1775. He read each one and tried to envision the places where these battles took place. After circling the monument, he paused at the words of Chester W. Nimitz, the Fleet Admiral of the Pacific at the time. Phillip crouched down on his haunches to get a better look. He reached out with his right hand and traced the golden letters with his fingers. Of the fighting heroes of Iwo Jima, the Admiral had simply written: "Uncommon Valor was a Common Virtue."

A perfect little red and black spotted ladybug had crawled onto Phillip's outstretched hand. He smiled and brought his hand closer to view. The ladybug made its climb all the way to the top of his middle knuckle. When its tiny wings opened, Phillip gave a gentle puff of breath to the insect and off it sailed in the unpredictable breezes. He clasped his hands and bowed his head.

In a low whisper Phillip prayed, "God? God? Are you here, God? I know it's been awhile. Like, maybe, twenty-five years. I think Kassy may have put it right for me a couple of days ago. She was trying to explain the meaning of need to me. Now I know what she meant. I am going to need your help, God. I can't say that I would blame you if you didn't help. I gave up on you the day Gum got shot, and here I am needing your help and guidance. But I see things like this statue and it makes me yearn for answers. I know the reason that flag had to go up on top of that mountain. If we hadn't gotten that job done then, so many other good people would have had to give up their lives, many more than it took to erect our flag on that mountain so far away. I know this. I was just wondering why we have to do this trade-off to begin with? It's not a perfect world, is it, God? So I guess we just try to make it a little better when given a chance. And I take it you are giving me that chance, right?"

He paused and thought about the newspaper article that started all this. He remembered how he had checked his local paper when he got home and no picture of Chu at the wall was in that paper. Phillip bit at his bottom lip, chewing lightly. "You know, if I hadn't been in Hickory that day and picked up that paper, I wouldn't be here, right? Thanks for my answer. And, God, hang close to me on this one, OK? In Jesus' name, Amen."

He stood and faced his flag. He snapped to attention and gave a crisp salute. Pride swelled inside him. He turned and walked in a determined stride back toward his hotel.

At 6 p.m. sharp there was a knock on Phillip's empty hotel room door. John Robinson had arrived. John pulled back the left sleeve of his dark blue suit to check the time on his watch. He knocked on the door a little harder. "Phillip, are you in there?" He knocked one more round and double-checked the time once more. As John was turning to leave, he spied Phillip lumbering down the hallway toward him. At least it appeared to be Phillip. It was hard to tell since the person was carrying a stack of papers clear up past his nose.

"Phillip, is that you?"

"John? Hey, yeah, it's me. Here, can you lend a hand and unlock the door?"

John reached down under the stack of papers and took the dangling hotel key from Phillip's hand and unlocked the door.

"Thanks. Sorry I'm a little late. Had a hard time finding a copy machine around here. I had to go to a Kinko's down the street. Come on in. We have lots to talk about." Phillip entered the room first and proceeded to unload his papers into separate stacks on the bed.

"Have a seat and we'll get right on this." Phillip continued his work while motioning John to the two chairs and table set up by the window.

"You must have some new information for me on this Chu fellow. And by your excitement it must be some good stuff."

"I think so. I went to see Colonel Danworth while I was gone. You remember me telling you about him. And this is all the information he gave me. It was real strange — that meeting. It was like the Colonel had been waiting to give this to me. Anyway, I think this should be more than enough for your friend Sid Langham to go and get that bastard Chu and make him answer some of the questions these documents will bring up."

"Let's see what you got."

The two men sat down at the table and went into a long drawn-out pow-wow. About 9 p.m. John leaned back in his chair. Rocking back so that the two front legs came up off the floor, he stretched and yawned.

"Wow, looks like somebody has been doing his homework. Got anything else?" John asked.

"Nope, that's a wrap. Here, I made you two copies of everything. I even copied this little gray notebook. All the photos are there, too. I figured you might want to keep a copy. One is for you to give Sid."

"OK, real good. This should get results. I'm afraid it will take some time, though. So, why don't you head home in the morning and I'll call you there? I think someone back home is anxious to see you."

"Wait a minute. Have you talked to Kassy?"

"Yeah, she called late today. I told her you were fine and that we were meeting tonight. She made me promise to get your butt back on the road home as soon as I could. Anyway, this really is going to take some time. There's no sense in you hanging out in a hotel room for days on end. I'll get on this and stay on it. Now get your butt home. *Comprende, amigo?*"

Phillip laughed and shook his head. "No speak *espanol, amigo el Juano.*"

At the door, Phillip gave John a pat on the back. "*Hasta la vista,* John, and thanks again for all your help. Without you I would be truly lost on this."

"Save that thanks until we get something done about this monster. Take care, and have a safe trip back home. I'll call you as soon as I find anything out. *Hasta la vista* to you, *amigo.*"

The next morning after a good night's rest Phillip left for home. He had slept hard with a sound feeling that the wheels of justice were finally turning in his favor.

He made good time and arrived home in the early evening. Making the last crook in his driveway, Phillip spotted P.T. torturing a frog out in the front yard. When P.T. saw his dad pull up, he leaped to his feet and ran to the truck. The frog made a safe getaway. Zeke, the golden retriever, tried to take up where P.T. had left off, but the frog was nowhere to be found. Zeke sniffed and dug around in vain.

"Dad! Dad! You're home. Great! Mom! Hey, Mom, Dad's home! Come out, Mom! What'd ya bring me, Dad?"

Phillip flipped the seat back forward, reached behind it, pulled out a paper sack and handed it to P.T. P.T. squealed with glee, ripped the bag open, and out fell a Washington Redskins' cap. He reached down, grabbed the cap and put it on.

"Cool! Thanks, Dad. I love the Redskins. Now where did that frog get off to?" P.T. scurried away.

"Welcome home, sweetheart." Kassy came out the front door, walked up to Phillip, wrapped her arms around him, and planted a big wet one on him.

"Glad to see someone missed me," Phillip said, pointing over at P.T. and rolling his eyes back. P.T. and Zeke continued to search for the escaped frog; the team was on a mission.

"Don't take it personally. You know how important frogs are to little boys and dogs. Now, what did you bring me?"

"Bring you? I didn't know you wanted something. Hold on. Let me look back here one more time and see if I can find something for Me Lady. Ah, here we go. How's this?" He pulled out a crusty old sweat sock that was probably left by one of the assembly line workers when the truck was built.

"Forget it! If that's what you think of me, then I suggest you go out for dinner 'cause there ain't going to be anything here for you to eat."

"Good suggestion. I think we will all go out to eat tonight. After all, it is your birthday, sweetheart." Phillip laughed. "Hold on, hold on. I grabbed that sock by mistake. Here, this is what I was trying to retrieve." He now produced another sack and offered it to Kassy. "Happy birthday, Kassy."

Kassy opened it to find a small box inside wrapped in gold paper. She hurriedly tore the gold paper and opened a black velvet box. Inside, was a gold locket and chain. She opened the locket to find a tiny picture of P.T. and his dad inside. On the other side of the picture the inscription read, "Without you, we are nothing."

"Oh, Phillip, this is so sweet. You shouldn't have. Yes, you should. When did you have time to do all this?"

"I do have my ways. Hope you like it."

"Thank you. I will always treasure this." She gave him a big hug and gently patted his back.

The next few days went well. Phillip seemed to be returning to his old self. He anticipated the news from Washington would come any time. One evening after dinner the phone rang.

"Hello? Yes, hi, John. How are you?" Kassy said, looking excitedly at Phillip. "Yes, he's right here. He hardly ever gets more than ten feet from the phone. Here he is now." Kassy handed Phillip the phone.

"*Hola* there, *ole amigo*. What you got good to tell me?" Phillip sat down on the couch to listen.

"Well, what a tangled web we weave. You and this Chu fellow have a lot of heads turning up here. I got all of the information to Sid Langham the other day. He was very impressed with the content. After briefly looking over it in my presence, he seemed more than sure we were on the right track. Man, talk about what a difference a day makes. Well, Sid calls back the next morning and asks me if I have any more copies of the all the stuff. I thought that was strange. I mean, if he needed copies, why not have his secretary run some off, right? Anyway, I tell Sid yes, I do have one more set of copies. And I do ask him why. He then gives me some mumbo jumbo about how he must have misplaced them or they got lost. I asked him if he had gotten to do any more research into the matter before he misplaced the stuff. He started hedging on that question, too. I mean he was being very vague about the whole deal. This didn't at all seem like the Sid I knew. This guy was always taking the bull by the horns. He pitty-pats around a little more and then said he had another call coming in and had to go. Said he would be in touch. Practically hung the damn phone up on me.

"Soon after I get off the phone with Sid, some cat barges into my front office. This guy puts the fear of God into poor little Ms. Presley. After he gets through scaring her half to death with all of his government bullshit, he storms back to make my acquaintance. He shoves an impressive looking badge in front of my face and introduces himself as a Bill Geevers. Ring any bells? Phillip, this is one freaky looking *hombre*. I have never seen a 'suit' in Washington that looked like this dude. He had long solid white hair tied in a ponytail down the back of his tailored gray pin-stripped Brook's Brothers suit. His clean-shaven face was a deep dark tan. Hard to tell but he appeared to be in his early sixties. But you would never know that by his build. Even under the suit you could tell he was built like a brick shithouse. Last, but not least, this cat had these eyes. Man, those eyes! You know what a star sapphire looks like?" John took a breath and waited.

Phillip stood nervously and walked to the stacked stone fireplace. Holding the phone to his right ear, he propped his left arm up on the rough-sawn cedar mantel. "Yeah, sure I do. It's P.T.'s birthstone. Its a blue polished stone with a cloudy white star that floats around in the middle of it. And no matter which way you turn it, the star will look back at you."

"Bingo! Give that man a prize. Phillip, I know I am carrying on about the way this dude looks. But, it's just one of those times you see someone that makes that kind of impression, you remember every detail about them. It's like your mind telling you to beware and to remember."

Phillip nodded to himself and pictured the first time he laid eyes on Chu. He could visualize every last detail.

"Well, it turns out that your Mr. Geevers and this Mr. Geevers are one and the same. Man, you really know how to pick 'em, don't you? He is some high-ranking dude, near the top in the CIA. Geevers gives me the spiel about national security being threatened. You know the routine. Then he demands I turn over all documents pertaining to your friend Chu. Now, I just wonder how in the world did he know about this? Ah, good ol' Sid. Anyway, I told him I wouldn't do it. He then told me he had the power to hold me in contempt under the National Security Act. And if I didn't give him what he wanted, he was going to arrest me on the spot. Well, I am now ashamed to say I gave him the copies. He told me to forget I ever heard his name and the name Chu and to forward the same message to you."

Phillip, speechless, finally responded. "Damn, John. Sorry I got you involved. I guess we should just let this go, huh?" He knew deep inside he would never be able to stop.

"Listen, there's more. After my heated meeting with Mr. Spooky Eyes Geevers, and after I was able to calm down a bit, I got pissed, I mean real pissed that I, a duly elected member of the House of Representatives, allowed such foolishness to take place in my office. So, what did I do? I went and told on Mr. Geevers to my big brother, so to speak. I went to see Senator Winslow R. Pettagrew. You know, the Man. Well, our gracious senior Senator from Georgia was more than receptive to my problem. He said he would teach Mr. Geevers, CIA or no CIA, not to play around with any good ol' Georgia boys. But here's the kicker. I told him all I could remember from the files. The good Senator said he would be more than happy to help on that front, too. He instructed me to tell you to send more sets of copies of all you have for me to give him. But you are also going to have to produce Colonel Danworth in person to back all these records up. He will have to be interviewed extensively, and under oath. He said without the Colonel, we can stop right now. We have nothing. Do you understand, Phillip? Can you produce Colonel Danworth here in person? Will he come here and testify?"

Phillip shifted the receiver to his other ear. "He'll come. We may have to make some special provisions for him. He's pretty sick right now. But, I know the Colonel, and he will do everything in his power to help on this. Thanks for everything. I'll call you as soon as I have confirmation from the Colonel on when we can meet in Washington."

Phillip immediately pulled out his wallet to get Ben Danworth's phone number. He hastily dialed the digits. The phone rang and Lillian Danworth answered.

"Hello, Danworth's residence."

"Mrs. Danworth? Hi, I hope it's not too late. This is Phillip Turner. Do you remember my visit not too long ago? May I speak with the Colonel, please? I mean if he hasn't already turned in for the night?"

"Yes, son, I remember you. I wish I could let you speak with Ben, but..." She broke down and cried quietly, sniffled and came back on. "But the Colonel, Ben, passed away day before yesterday. We had his funeral service this morning." She cried some more.

Phillip dropped his head in despair. His emotions were torn between the loss of the Colonel and the lost feeling of "where do I go from here?" He put his personal frets aside and tried to comfort Mrs. Danworth. "Oh, ma'am, I am so sorry to hear that. Is there anything I can do for you?"

"No, there is nothing anyone can do now. It is in the hands of the Lord. But I do want to thank you."

"Thank me?" Phillip was puzzled.

"Yes, thank you. Ever since your visit here with Ben, he seemed to be more at peace with himself. It was like you had lifted a heavy burden from him. I feel that he was finally ready to meet his maker. And for that, you have my never-ending gratitude. Now that I have pulled myself together a little better, was there something I could help you with in Ben's place?"

"No, ma'am, it was strictly something for the Colonel. It was just some minor information I was looking for. If you ever are in need of something from me, though, please feel free to call or write." He gave Lillian his phone number and home address. "Take care of yourself, Mrs. Danworth. Again, please accept my sincere condolences. Good bye."

Kassy noticed the extreme highs and lows Phillip had just gone through over the past couple of hours with the two phone calls. She made some fresh coffee and poured a large mug for him.

"Here, baby, come sit down at the table and let's share a cup of Joe." Kassy winked, hoping to cheer him up a bit. He took a seat and stirred some sugar in his coffee. He had reached an extreme low point.

CHAPTER SIXTEEN

"KASSY, I just don't know what to think anymore. Every time I seem to be getting somewhere on this, another bomb blows up in my face. Did you hear Mrs. Danworth and me? The Colonel is dead, and, without him, John won't be able to help me."

Kassy moved behind Phillip and gently massaged his shoulders. She then gave each shoulder a pat. She tried to console him with the secret hope that maybe this quest was coming to an end.

"Well, at least you've tried, Phillip. At least you did do the right thing as far as you could go. And I'm very proud of you." She leaned down and gently caressed his neck.

Phillip reached back with both hands, placed them on Kassy's, and squeezed gently. "Thanks, sweetheart, I needed that."

Phillip pulled on Kassy's hand, leading her around to rest on his lap. He put his arms around her and held her tight. "Kassy, I need to tell you something. I want you to know why I have gone off the deep end with something that happened so long ago, why this is so important to me."

Kassy turned and looked into Phillips eyes. "You have nothing to explain to me. I know how you cared for the boy."

"No, that's not what I wanted to say. I mean, yes, I loved Gum just like a son. But it was the first time I saw him and his rag-tag band of culprits." A fond smile of remembrance overtook his frown. "I looked at those kids and I really got the feeling of 'there, but for the grace of God, go I.' I saw in Gum's little coal black eyes what could have been me. Just in another country. Just dealt a really bad hand. But, somehow, this kid was going to help me through my plight. Gum knew his part and help he did. He took away my fears of growing up and becoming a man. He gave me a reason for being over there. Vietnam was a scary place, Kassy. You could see it seared on the faces of the grunts we would ferry back to the 'world'. Every time I would learn we were flying back into that 'Black Hole,' part of me was terrified that this would be the last time for me. We would surely be shot down, and I would die in the crash or something else just as bad might happen. But knowing that little light, Gum, was sitting in the 'Black Hole' waiting for me, I could push my fears aside. He made me want to go back time and time again. He gave me courage beyond belief. Remember awhile back I mentioned a girl named Sue Ling?"

"Phillip, don't talk to me like I am some kind of outsider. You cut me off the last time you brought her name up. You didn't give me a chance to zero in on whom you were talking about. Of course I remember Sue Ling and how bad I felt about her stepping on the land mine."

Still seated on Phillip's lap, Kassy leaned over the kitchen table and grabbed her purse. Dragging it over, she began digging around inside until she retrieved her wallet. She opened it and sorted through the mess of dollar bills and store coupons, then flipped over to the checkbook side of the wallet. There in the back she found what she was searching for. She unfolded a tattered, yellowed photograph. It was a picture of Phillip, Gum and Sue Ling standing side by side, holding a shredded vinyl kite. Each had a grin as wide as Texas, as if they were holding the crown jewels of England. Kassy smiled and handed the photo to Phillip.

Staring at the picture Kassy had carried all those years, a feeling of guilt overtook Phillip. He realized that Kassy had been with him every step of the way, and he owed her respect for her deep understanding and loyalty. "I know you remember, Kassy. I'm sorry."

"Now what did you want to say about Sue Ling?"

"It really isn't about Sue Ling, it's more about Gum. By the way, Colonel Danworth did tell me he saw to it that she got a prosthetic leg and that she was doing well the last time he saw her."

Kassy smiled.

"What I wanted to tell you was that the day after Sue Ling was hurt, I went looking for Gum. I wanted to tell him how she was doing and make sure he wasn't in too much trouble from Sue Ling's family for helping me kidnap her to the hospital. I went into town and found Gum in his favorite spot. It's a place he would go when he wanted to be alone and think. What his special place had once been was a park in the center of town. The park had long since disappeared, and the jungle had taken back over. It was really kind of neat, though. Ten feet inside, and under the thick jungle canopy, you felt you were all alone and a million miles away. I spotted Gum in a small clearing. He was perched, half-squatting, on a large rock, shredding the leaves of a banana plant. He looked just like a little monkey working the day away. Just as Gum caught sight of me, a huge cloudburst came up and dumped out buckets of rain. I was running around looking for some type of cover. I must have looked like a chicken with his head cut off. Gum fell off the rock and began rolling around in the mud laughing his butt off at me. I can hear him now, jabbering away in that broken pidgin English. 'What a matter, Turner? You fraid you get wet? You already wet, Turner! You already wet! You stop running now.'"

Phillip smiled and continued.

"I looked over at Gum and said, 'Oh yeah, I may be wet, but I can take you on.' We started a mud-wrestling match that should have been on TV. We rolled and tussled and slapped mud on each other. Finally exhausted, we flipped over on our backs in the middle of this mud puddle. We hadn't noticed that the rain had stopped. The sun was already beaming through the trees and reflecting off the steam that was slowly rising up from the hot ground. We both lay there trying to catch our breath.

"It was so peaceful and beautiful for just that instant. There was a devout holiness in that jungle cathedral. Gum felt it, too. I couldn't help myself, Kassy, I began to weep. I was weeping for Sue Ling. It was like Gum was reading my mind. He sat up in the mud and looked down at me. This is what he told me. He said, 'Turner, you have God. I have Buddha. They both the same, I think. You pray to God, I chant to Buddha. We both ask same thing. I think if my Buddha and your God could tell us, they would say they no want war. But they have to let us make own mistakes and then live with mistakes. It not their part to make things work right; we must work things right way. Yes?'

"What he was saying was don't waste time blaming God and yourself for things, but use that time for learning, growing, and change. If only I could do just that. That little seven-year-old kid was so damn smart. Can you imagine what he might have become if he had been given a chance? Oh, Kassy, he meant so much to me, and I feel I owe so much to him. And, damn it all, I just can't find the way to pay him back. No matter how hard I try, I just can't find the way."

Kassy leaned over, knocked her head to his, and cried out loud with him. She stroked his hair and cuddled him as a mother would. "I love you, Phillip Turner. And, I know if anyone in this world is able to find his way to do anything at all, then that someone is you. Remember, your dad would always say, 'Rome wasn't built in a day, boy.' And what did you always answer?"

"'Yeah, but Rome was built, wasn't it, Dad?'" Phillip smiled, sniffled a little. He hugged Kassy and burrowed deep into her chest. "One other thing about Gum you should know, sweetheart. If it wasn't for him, I don't think you and I would have ever gotten together." Phillip thought back to that day in the commissary, the first time he and Kassy met and what had brought the two to that point.

"Really? You want to explain that to me?" Kassy remarked, somewhat puzzled.

"That's a whole 'nother story. Some day I'll tell you all about it." Phillip smiled and his mood lightened more as he remembered how Gum saved him from the grips of the "Saigon drip."

Kassy changed the subject. "I need to go pick P.T. up at the skating rink. Want to ride along?"

"Sure, I'll go. Thanks again for hearing me out."

"Hey, that's what best friends are for."

Several days passed before the next bomb dropped. The weather was starting to cool a bit. The long hot humid days of a Georgia summer were getting a little shorter and were slowly giving way to some cooler mornings.

Phillip made his daily run to the post office. As he was pulling out the tightly packed bundle of mainly junk mail from the under-sized post office box, a small pale green registered mail card fell to the floor. He bent down to pick it up and read the to and from on the card as he straightened his back. It was from Lillian Danworth. He wondered what this meant as he went to the postal counter to sign for the letter.

The postmaster handed Phillip a large manila envelope. When he got to his truck he tossed the other mail onto the passenger seat and tore into the parcel. He pulled out another large sealed mani-la envelope with a note stapled to the outside. The note read:

"Dear Mr. Turner,

I found this on Ben's desk the other day. He had left me a note with it. He wrote if you were ever to call or come by, then I was to give this to you. I hope that maybe this contains the help you were looking for when you called. Again I wish to thank you for whatever you did for Ben. You made acceptance of his death much easier for me, knowing he had resolved some of his inner turmoil. If you are ever in Lexington, please feel free to call or come by.

Sincerely,
Lillian Danworth"

Phillip pulled the letter from the staples and flipped it on the dashboard. He then took a deep breath and opened the sealed envelope. He pulled out a folder. This, too, had a letter stapled to it. This one was from the Colonel:

"Sergeant Turner, Phillip, sorry, (old habits are hard to break; just ask my doc. and undertaker):
Greetings from the grave! ~Boo~ (pardon my pun)"

Phillip smiled and read on.

"Since you are reading this, that means I have gone on to the great blue yonder. Don't grieve for me. And I hope Miss Lillian isn't grieving too much either. I take it you have called, looking for some more help. That is why Miss Lillian has gotten this to you. Well, I can't help you find that SOB and, believe you me, I tried real hard to locate Chu. But if and when you do find him, I want you to have this last bit of ammo to make him come clean. In this folder you will find several pictures with negatives. (You know how I love photos). All of these pics are of our man Chu doing the wild thing. He is doing this love dance with none other than his wife's sister. He was doing it then, and 5 will get you 10, he is still doing it now. Now the important part. Seems like Chu's wife has always suspected this and several times, when I knew them, said if she ever caught them, she would cut all that dangles off of him. And, buddy, she would too. She used to scare the shit out of me when she would go into her jealous rages. You show these pictures to Chu when you catch up with him. And, well, whatever justice you want will be yours.

Good luck, Phillip!
Colonel Ben Danworth USAF ret.

P.S. Tell Chu I will see him in hell!!"

Phillip scrutinized the photos inside the folder. The yearning to get Chu boiled down in his gut. When he got back home, he showed Kassy what the mailman had delivered. One particular photo showed Chu in nothing but cowboy boots and a cowboy hat. He was on his knees behind his partner with her on all fours.

Kassy exclaimed, "Yeehaw, ride-em, Cowboy!!"

They both had a good laugh at that.

Phillip neatly stacked the photos and returned them to the folder.

"Well, I guess I'll put this with the rest of my conglomeration."

He headed to the bedroom closet to get out his flight bag. He stuffed the folder in for safekeeping. Staring down at the bag, he conjured up the old Grimms' fairy tale, "Hansel and Gretel." He smiled and muttered, "I guess this is just another bread crumb waiting to be eaten up by some bird." Phillip felt that maybe he had come to a turning point, and it might be time to give up on Chu and get on with his own life. He tried to resolve this in his mind, but it was to no avail. He gritted his teeth and clenched his fists in defiance. Out loud he pronounced, "I think maybe I'll hold on to this bag of crumbs awhile longer. I'm going to find your Ginger-Bread House, Chu, you bastard. You'll see!"

CHAPTER SEVENTEEN

MONTHS PASSED. P.T. entered the third grade. He was growing up quickly. That year he chose to go trick-or-treating as a hobo, a sure sign that probably the next year he wouldn't even want to go anymore. Claiming that dressing up was for little kids, not him, he would just stay home and help give out the candy to "the little kids."

Thanksgiving came, and it was time for the annual family trip to Saint Simon's Island. Phillip and Kassy had been going down to the island since just before they were married. And Phillip had come here with his folks ever since he was a kid. This had always been their favorite place. "One day we're going to live down here." Phillip said it every time they arrived.

The island was a quaint place that had not yet fallen victim to the 'tack-y-ization' of the other nearby resorts, such as Hilton Head and, the tackiest of the tacky, Myrtle Beach. In fact, it had regressed more than progressed. Access was by a lone one-lane toll bridge. The main drag of commerce, often referred to as the Village, offered several small gift shops, a few really good restaurants, one pool hall (have to have a pool hall at the beach), and, of course, the fishing pier, a pier you could really catch fish from. The main sources of recreation here were fishing, sunbathing in the mild ocean breezes, or riding bikes all over the flat, easy-to-navigate island.

The Turner family spent lots of time riding their bikes along the trails of history on the island. The sun was dropping low on the horizon on their first day. Phillip, with his bike propped between his legs, smiled and turned to Kassy.

"Hey, lady, you up for a ride to the bluff? I saw in the paper that low tide is right at sundown."

"No, thanks, I'm a little beat. I think I'll head back to the hotel and finish unpacking."

"Suit yourself. Well, P.T., you in or out for the ride?"

"Count me in, Dad; I'm with you. Okay, Mom?"

"Okay, sweetie. You guys have fun." Kassy turned her bike around and headed off.

Phillip took the point with P.T. close behind. They wound along the bike path adjacent to Demere Road. They pulled up at the monument to the battle of Bloody Marsh. Phillip dismounted, dropped the kickstand, and walked over to the bronze plaque. Pointing out from the overlook, he instructed, "Now here, P.T., a battle was fought back in 1742. It was a fight between the British troops of General Oglethorpe and some Spanish troops pushing north from Florida. The battle was so brutal and bloody that the marsh here turned crimson for days after the fight was over. And you know what else?"

"Yeah, Dad, I know, I know. If the British had lost that day we would be talking in Spanish and not English." P.T. had heard this before and was anxious to continue their ride without the history lesson.

"Ah, very good, Grasshopper. You learn well."

"You tell me this story every time we stop here, Dad."

The two modern day explorers remounted their mechanical steeds of sprockets, chains and wheels, and eased off down the winding dirt bike trail toward the sea. Breaking out from the mix of palms and oaks, they arrived at the bluff. It was a small clearing that jutted out into the marsh. They stood only seven feet above sea level, but this was all that was needed to be in total command of the view. The duo propped their bikes against a lone Palmetto tree and squatted down on their heels. P.T. fished around with his hands, picking up oyster shells to skip out into the foamy tide below. With the brightly polished golden rays of the warm setting autumn sun to their backs and the yellow tipped marsh outstretched to the ocean in front, they weren't quite able to make out just where the land ended and the mighty Atlantic began.

The gentle breezes whistled through the reeds as they blew in waves across the marsh plains and swirled around the wet black mud flats. The scent of the mud had a sweet, dirty, salty redolence to it, which lingered in the back of their throats and gave them a taste each time they swallowed. As the tide continued its relentless retreat to open waters, more and more of the new land came to life. The mud perked and popped as tiny fiddler crabs by the zillions raced around in schools, making whole patches of earth appear to be moving in various directions. Phillip closed his eyes and drew in a deep salty breath. He exhaled and smiled a contented smile.

Kassy had finished her unpacking and decided to go to the atrium lobby for some hot tea and a sweet roll. This was one of the few places they had ever stayed where the guests would really want to hang out in the lobby just to pass some time. It had a relaxed welcome, you-belong-here, kind of feeling. They always stayed here at the King and Prince Hotel, a wonderful Spanish colonial structure originally built back in the 1930s as a private club. The King and Prince had always managed to retain its unique intimacy of giving that members-only feeling all through its transitions into becoming a first class hotel, sort of an escape from reality for the every-day type of person, even if just for a day or two. The amenities were impeccable.

The sunset had caught Kassy's eye, so she sauntered outside onto the Oleander patio with cup and saucer in hand. She took a seat under a palm and continued her gaze out to sea. A funny looking, black ink spot floating way out in the sun-washed golden surf had grabbed her curiosity. As the ink spot got closer inland, it grew in size and began to shimmer. The sun caught hold and focused its rays of passionate purples, marmalade oranges, puckish pinks, and a dash of disco silver onto the shimmering spot. With this transformation, the spot appeared to be Christmas tree tinsel floating aimlessly out in the sea.

Wonder what that could be? Kassy thought to herself. As if to answer her question, a squadron of hungry seagulls swooped in and hovered above the spot. As they remained suspended in midair, their wings twisting and adjusting in the breezes to maintain position, they started cawing and screeching out attack signals. Then, they formed up and dove into the shinny tinsel, each gull reappearing with a small bait fish grasped firmly in its beak. The tinsel broke apart into several different small pods and then disappeared completely. Kassy grinned, having unraveled her mystery. She closed her eyes and took in a deep salty breath. She exhaled and smiled as she thought of the two loves of her life, her Lewis and Clark out on expedition on the other side of the island.

The magic of Saint Simon's had worked its charm on the Turner family. The extended Thanksgiving weekend had passed much too fast for each one of them.

On the eve of their departure for home, Phillip decided to do some last minute fishing and or drinking, as the case might be. The weather was incredibly warm for that time of year. In fact, it had been downright hot. That night was no exception. The sultry breeze was coming in from the southeast at three to five knots, and the temperature remained in the high seventies at 8 p.m. Phillip, taking full advantage of the rare heat wave, donned a t-shirt, cut-off blue jeans and flip-flops. He filled his extra large playmate cooler with ice and beer. He walked over to where Kassy was sitting watching TV, bent down, and kissed her cheek.

"You sure you and P.T. don't want to at least ride your bikes down to the pier with me?"

Kassy, with her feet propped up and eyes fixed on the TV set, reached back and stroked Phillip's beard. "No, you go ahead, sweetie. P.T. has already had his bath and I don't want him getting sweaty. And I am totally whipped from our bike ride this afternoon. Don't stay up and play too late. I want to leave pretty early in the morning. Oh, and stay out of that pool hall!"

Phillip reached into the closet and grabbed two fishing rods with reels and his tackle box, then headed out the door. After arranging all of his gear to balance on his bike just right, he rolled down the bike path toward the pier. He wobbled back and forth till he was able to gain enough speed to help balance the overloaded bike. He thought to himself, *God with this much crap now, I wonder how I am going to bring all the fish home?* Then he chuckled, conjuring his game plan for the evening: drinking all the beer up to facilitate fish transportation.

Arriving at the pier, he peddled half way out onto the five-hundred foot jetty, dismounted and began pushing his bike along. The slap-slap slapping of his flip flops against his bare heels and the tick-tick ticking of the gears on his bike seemed to be playing a little tune. He puckered his lips and began to whistle along with the new-found song. He picked up the tempo of his gait as he strutted down the long concrete slab. The heat of the day was still rising from the concrete. Phillip felt the warmth as it swirled around his bare legs and then escaped into the cool of the night.

When he got to end of the pier, he looked to the right and then to the left. Odd, he thought, that just he and a lone stranger were the only two out there to enjoy that wonderful night. Phillip eased down to within a few yards of the stranger. He set up shop, thinking that maybe the other angler had found the hot spot on the pier for fish. After he got all arranged and set up, he dug around in his cooler searching for his bait.

"Ah, crap!" he shouted, "I forgot my bait! Hey, buddy, do you mind watching my stuff while I run back to the King and Prince?" He never gave a thought to not trusting this total stranger in a situation like this.

"No need for you to go all the way back to your hotel, friend. I've got plenty of bait, that is, if you don't mind fishing with cut mullet."

"Hey, thanks, mullet is fine. That's what I was going to bring. Make a deal with you. I'll use your bait if you'll help me drink my beer."

"Deal."

Phillip started to move his gear closer to his new found friend. As he got a piece of bait and cast out his line into the surf, he asked, "Caught any tonight?"

"Just a few sheep-head and a whiting or two." The stranger pointed to his catch bucket.

"Shrimping been good this year?" Phillip continued the conversation.

"Yeah, man! Best year I've ever seen. And with this extended Indian summer we're having, we might even be catchin' em at Christmas. Every time I get to go, I cooler out. You know, forty-eight quarts worth, heads on. And I'm talking jumbo selects too, pal." The stranger extended his left arm and opened his palm, then made a chop with his right hand half way up his forearm, signifying the size of the shrimp.

"Man, oh man, I would like to get into some of that action," Phillip said in envy. "Wish we didn't have to leave in the morning." He flipped the top of his cooler open. " You from around here? I mean, you don't sound local."

"No. I'm one of them damn transplanted Yankees."

Phillip reached into the cooler and pulled out a bottle of ice cold Miller. A sliver of ice drizzled down to the bottom of the bottle and fell off. He twisted the hissing top off before he handed it over.

"Here you go, pal. So how did you end up here?"

"Well, back when I was in the Air Force, I had a buddy who used to talk about this place all the time. I did a stint at Warner Robbins AFB over in Macon. I drove down here one day to check the place out. All my buddy had told me about it was true. I love this island. So, after I got divorced a few years ago, well, my kids had grown up and flown the nest too—so I said 'what the heck' and moved here. I own the little seashell shop on the square over there. You may have been in it before."

"My wife loves that shop. You have made some cash off her, believe you me. So you were in the Air Force, too? I used to be a crew chief on C-5s, flew out of Travis mainly. Ever been there?"

"I've been there. I was a loadmaster on C-5s."

"For real? Damn, small world. When were you in?"

"70 to 74. And you?" he asked.

"About the same, 69 to 73. Hey, my primary plane was Balls 12. Ever flown on her?"

"Been on Balls 12 many a flight. Colonel Danworth was the C.O. on her."

An eerie "been-there-done-that" feeling crawled up the back of Phillip's neck. He scratched the top of his head under his ball cap and began to rub at the funny feeling in his neck. "You know, come to think of it, you do look and sound a little familiar. What's your name anyhow?"

"Me? Toomes, Bill."

Phillip jumped to his feet. "Sergeant Billy frigging Toomes. Holy moly puddin pie, kiss the girls and make 'em cry! I don't believe it! Toomes, it's me. Phillip Turner!"

Now Toomes was on his feet. "Phillip Turner, Jesus H. Christ! How are you?"

Both men hugged each other as if they were two lost brothers finally finding each other after years of searching. They did their DAP hand shake as if it was just yesterday they had performed the stylized ritual started by African-American troops when "In Country."

"Phillip, you're the reason I'm here. You're the buddy I was talking about that turned me on to this place. You know, I often wondered if I would ever run into you down here, that is, if you were even still alive. Damn, man, it's good to see you!"

Both men stepped back to get a better look at one another under the dim, bluish glow of the solitary street lamp located at the end of the pier. Phillip made his verbal assessment first.

"Damn, Billy, last time I saw you, you had a head full of hair and washboard stomach. Now look at you; you're bald as a bat and fat as a tick."

"Gee, thanks, you always did have a way with words. You ain't no Robert Redford yourself, you know. You got that beard covering up some ugly?"

With a chuckle of good humor, the two old buddies settled down into a long bull session. They went over the old days and the new days.

"Careful, looks like you got a bite there," Toomes cautioned.

Phillip squatted over his pole and gingerly took hold. Slowly he raised the rod tip and cranked in the slack on the line. Just at the right moment he jerked up the rod tip to set the hook. "Got'em! Feels like a good one, too. Probably a sheep-head." Phillip reeled in his catch, a nice sheep-head indeed.

"Good one, Phil!" Toomes congratulated.

Phillip re-baited his line and threw back out, and the guys resumed their conversation. Phillip told of his recent search for Colonel Chu and all that had led up to it.

"Sorry to hear about Colonel Danworth. And you say you got all this good stuff on that low-life Chu, but you can't find him, huh? Do you have a computer at home? You on the internet?"

"Yeah, yeah, I've tried all the searches possible on the net. It's good but not that good. It did help me locate Danworth though."

"Hold your horses. I didn't mean using the net the conventional way. Look, awhile back I ran into a guy out there on the net. This guy can get you any information you want any time. I mean this guy can get you whatever you need. I was in need of his services. I decline to say what for, but he came through. This guy ain't cheap though. He is, I guess you could say, a hacker for hire."

Phillip's interest drew keen. "Look, I think Chu is being protected somehow by the CIA or something."

"Doesn't matter. My guy can find him for you."

"OK, tell me more. How can I get in touch with this super-hacker?"

"This is how you do it, Phillip. You don't find him; he has to find you. Ever used Mirc on the net?"

"The internet relay chat thing? Yeah, I believe I'm running Mirc32. Don't use it much."

"That's going to change. You're going to use it a lot if you're going to connect with this guy. Now, after you have logged onto the net, turn on Mirc and log onto it through Undernet: EU, NO, Oslo or Undernet: EU, NL, Amsterdam. Now run a rooms list. You will usually get around two-to three-thousand rooms. Sound familiar?"

Phillip nodded.

"Now, weed through all the pervert rooms and look for anything with Warez in the name. Hackers love Warez. That's their code for hacking. You'll find a lot of Warez stuff out there too, so be patient. You'll have to go into a lot of rooms and start to chat. Tell some type of story of how you're in need of a 'locator'. Now he won't be in the room by this handle, but when he contacts you, he will be using the handle 'Dark Angel.' Oh, almost forgot. Before you do any looking, set up a private room with the name 'Angel's Lair.' Make it private with the access code number of 69698989xxx. When Dark Angel hits on you, tell him to go to this room to talk. This will really get his attention 'cause this is the room and access code he gives only to his prior clients, when they need to get in touch with him. Just tell him that 'Death Master' sent you and said it would be OK. Tell him 'Death Master' wanted to be sure the real 'Dark Angel' contacted you, and this was a way to be sure. Then, my boy, it is up to you to negotiate the deal. Remember, he ain't cheap. But he's real good. Did you get all that? Oh, and by the way, call me at the shop in the morning, and I'll give you my home phone. You probably won't remember half of this shit tomorrow anyway, and we can stay in touch."

"Wow, that is a lot to remember. OK, I'll call in the morning. So, how about another cold one?"

"Sure, thanks."

"So, Billy, you haven't mentioned Red."

"Red?" Billy asked.

"You know, Stan (Red) Reynolds. You guys were as thick as mud back in the good old days. Did you guys stay in touch or what?"

"I really don't like to talk about Reynolds. But since it's you and you did ask. Stan and I kept in touch after the Air Force. He would write these real bizarre letters to me. He would talk of demons and dragons. These letters would sometimes be up to one-hundred pages at a time. It really bothered me to read them, but I felt I owed it to him. He was in and out of the VA. I mean, he could have written a book on the different VAs across the country. Every time I got a letter, it was from a new place. I don't think those guys at the VA have got that post-traumatic syndrome thing figured out yet. Hell, it wasn't PTS that took Red down; it was that Agent Orange shit that got him. The docs took the easy way out and called it PTS. You know Red used to dip that crap out of barrels into quart mason jars. He would peddle it to his buddies back home as weed-killer. It was weed-killer all right. Killed people just as good; it just took longer.

"One day I got a letter from him and he was in the VA in Duluth. I didn't understand one word he had written, but he was just four blocks away from me at the time so I decided to go see him. God, I hate thinking about it now. It was pitiful, man. When I asked around after I got on campus, I was told that Stan Reynolds was lying under a big sycamore tree down by the psych building. As I walked up to Stan, I didn't even come close to recognizing him. All I saw was this drawn-up old man lying in a fetal position on his side. Stan had just turned thirty. He stunk, too, man, even from ten feet away. He had a bright yellow padded helmet on. He held a burning cigarette in each nicotine stained hand. All he would do is just lie there all day long, burning blades of grass and drool this green spit from his mouth. Each time a cigarette burned down he would begin to shake and quiver till he lit another. Then he would slam his head to the ground, pounding as hard as he could; thus the reason for the helmet.

"I walked a little closer holding my nose. When I finally got up the nerve to speak his name, I said very low, 'Stan, Red. It's me. It's Toomes. Billy. Remember me, Stan?' At that, you would have thought someone was shooting him out of a cannon. Stan rolled around in the dirt, frantically spitting and choking. He made it to his feet and starting screaming and running to the front door of the psych unit. An orderly came rushing out and grabbed Stan by his helmet and dragged him inside. That was the last time I saw Stan Reynolds. About seven or eight days later, I was relieved to read his obituary in the morning paper."

Phillip took his Atlanta Falcons hat off and rubbed his head. "Damn, Billy. Sorry I brought that up."

"No, it's OK, really. I think by finally getting to tell someone about Stan, I think I feel a little better about that whole deal."

Phillip checked his watch. To his surprise it was 3 a.m.

"I hate to wrap this fishing trip up, but it is really getting late, or early, depending on how you look at it."

Billy then looked at his watch and replied, "You got that right, brother! Guess we better call it a night."

Phillip studied the inside of his cooler. "Looks like we're out of cold beer anyhow. Kassy will have my butt out of bed at o-six-hundred. That gives me almost three fast hours of sleep before the drive home."

The two vets packed up their gear and headed back down the gangway of the pier. At the end of the pier, they paused and turned to each other. They did their DAP handshake, hugged, and patted each other on the back.

Phillip said, "It's been righteous, dude. Later on."

"Later on then, Phillip Turner. Been great seeing you again. Oh, and thanks one more time for turning me on to the island."

"You bet. Maybe one day we'll be neighbors down here. See ya."

With his mind full of new bread crumbs, Phillip stood up on his pedals and wobbled off toward the King and Prince.

Just like clockwork, at 6 a.m. Kassy sounded reveille. She had already been up for half an hour or so. The coffee was brewed and all the luggage packed. Phillip and P.T. dragged themselves out of bed and headed for their bathrooms. At 7 a.m. all was done, and The King and Prince Hotel disappeared from the rear view mirror of their Suburban.

On the way up I-95 north, the Chevy pushing more and more inland, Kassy looked over at Phillip with his head propped up against the side window. He was watching the transformation of tidal basin marshes into thick stands of Georgia pines, a depressing sight for someone so fond of the ocean.

"You're running a little off key this morning, baby. Rough night? What time did you get in from fishing anyway?"

Phillip slowly reached up and flipped open the vanity mirror cover on his windshield visor. He could see that P.T. had already gone back to sleep. A slight feeling of envy overtook Phillip's weary mind as he looked at his son sacked out in the back seat. He blinked off the bleary blur from his eyes and straightened himself in his seat.

"You're not going to believe this. Guess who I ran into last night on the pier?"

"Who?"

"Billy Toomes! Remember him from the Air Force?"

"That was one of your drinking buddies. He was on your flight crew, right?"

"Good memory."

"What was he doing on Saint Simons? Vacation?"

"Nope, he moved there. Lucky dog. He owns the little Sea Shell shop you like so much."

"Come to think of it, that guy in that shop did remind me of someone. Every time I went in there, I would get that deja-vu feeling. He sure has changed a lot. I guess you guys had plenty to talk about."

"Yeah, he gave me some good help on finding Colonel Chu. He told me about a guy I need to get in touch with on the internet. Toomes said this cat can run that bastard down for me."

"Hold it right there, Phillip Turner. Please! Please! Please, don't get this started back up now. Promise me you'll wait till after the holidays. Please, Phillip, you're just coming around again, and I don't want you back in that morbid state right now."

"This may be the break I've been looking for."

Kassy's voice was elevated. "Look, I'm just now getting the Master Card bill paid down from your stupid little jaunt to Washington and Kentucky back in the summer."

"Stupid? You think all this is stupid?" Phillip tried to restrain his anger. He looked in the visor mirror and could see P.T. stirring from the heated conversation. Kassy lowered her voice.

"I didn't mean the stupid part. God, the times I have told P.T. not to use that word. I just get frustrated with you sometimes, baby. I just think that if you start to pursue this again right now, you're being very selfish. Just put if off for about five weeks. Then, after P.T. has his Santa Claus and we have our annual New Year's Eve party, I'll help you all I can to track him down and whatever else you need to do. Promise me, Phillip, you will wait. Please?"

Phillip stared straight ahead down the interstate. He paused a long time. He began counting pine trees as they whizzed by. Finally he forced out a reply.

"OK, I'll try and wait."

"No, not try. Tell me you will wait."

Phillip made no reply. He went back to counting pine trees.

CHAPTER EIGHTEEN

AFTER THE FOUR-HOUR DRIVE HOME, Kassy continued to show no mercy. It was the Sunday after Thanksgiving and, come hell or high water, these Christmas decorations were going up. Every year Phillip fought this, stating that it got P.T. in a Christmas whirl way too early. And he was so hard to live with when every five minutes he asked how much longer till Santa came. And, as in every year prior, again Phillip lost his argument.

Trying to keep to his word, Phillip stayed away from searching for Chu until one day he could stand it no more. He gave Billy Toomes a call from the store. He thought to himself: *Hell, it won't hurt to just get the info on how to do the internet thing. Besides, I never promised I wouldn't. I just said I would try not to look for Chu. Therefore, if I do a little looking, I really won't be breaking my word, now will I?*

Still trying to make good on what had already become a half-promise to Kassy, Phillip held out. Not a day went by that Chu didn't enter his mind. Phillip refused to turn his computer on, afraid of what he might trigger. He would just go into his study and sit and stare at the blank black screen on his monitor. Sometimes he would even take out the sticky note he wrote Billy Toomes' instructions on and read them over and over again.

Finally, the search for Chu won out, and Phillip gave in. He had been lying beside Kassy with his mind racing for hours. While she slept, he fretted. He could stand it no more. He told himself he needed to check his e-mail. He hadn't done that in a while. There might be something important there, he lied to himself. With this false justification, he rolled out of bed and went to his study and fired up the computer.

He logged onto the internet and checked his e-mail. Then he surfed over to the new and hot web sites department. He looked at a couple of interesting web pages, trying to convince himself to go no further.

He turned on his Mirc32 internet relay chat program and logged on. First, he went into Mirc via Undernet:EU (for europe), NO. (for nothern) Oslo (for source city in Norway) Ping Pong. He was logged in. He then called up a list of channels and/or chat rooms. A total of 2854 rooms were listed. He took his mouse cursor and clicked on the scroll button to run down the long list of chat rooms. When he got to the W's, he slowed down the scroll. When he reached the Warez listings, he added them up with his finger pointing to each one on the screen to keep count: 28,29,30,31, *Damn*, he thought, *I wonder if there are always this many. The search to hook up with this Dark Angel might take forever.*

Phillip took a shot and picked a Warez chat room at random. He logged into a room called: *Warez Night Life* as "Caribbean Blue," a handle he used when he was on the net.

>Caribbean Blue has entered Warez Night Life:

>Caribbean Blue> says to> all> Hi all. New here looking for a little help.

Phillip typed in this lame greeting. Much to his surprise he got a response.

>Bandit>says to>Caribbean Blue>Welcome C.B. what kind of help are you looking for?

>Caribbean Blue>says to>Bandit> Well I was told I could find a locator around here. Know of any?

>Bandit>says to>Caribbean Blue>I don't quite know what you mean Blue. Could you be more clear?

>Caribbean Blue>says to>Bandit> I am in need of a person (hacker) that is capable of finding things others don't want them to find. If you catch my drift?

>Bandit>says to>Caribbean Blue> Oh, OK now I get it.*sly grin* Nope can't help you on that one C.B. Sorry :-(

Phillip thought, *damn, another rookie is here besides me.* Just then a message alert showed up.

>POLTERGEIST> wishes to establish a private chat with you. Do you accept? Yes[] or No[]

Phillip clicked on yes. A new private chat window opened up.

>Poltergeist>private to>Caribbean Blue> Howdy neighbor. I might be the locator you are looking for.

>Caribbean Blue>private to>Poltergeist>Hello to you. I am looking for a particular locator. I don't know if you are the one.

>Poltergeist>private to>Caribbean Blue> Look pal for a fee I can find you anything your heart desires. Now do you want to talk turkey or not?

>Caribbean Blue>private to>Poltergeist> I think I will pass this time. I need a certain type of angel. Thanks anyway, bud. Cya.....

CARIBBEAN BLUE has left the chat:

Phillip signed off Mirc. He logged off the net and shut his

computer down. He slid back in his chair and rubbed his eyes. Staring at the now blank screen, he thought, *Boy, oh Boy, this is going to really take some work. There has got to be a better way to build a railroad than this. I better give Ron a call in the morning and see if he can give me a hand at writing a program to speed this search up some.*

Phillip was no slouch when it came to the computer. But Ron was the whiz kid! Phillip referred to him as Master. Ron and Phillip went way back to high school days; they were on the golf team together until Phillip got into his hippie phase. The coach had no use for long hairs on his team, no matter how good they were. Phillip and Ron's friendship had remained intact for some thirty years. Ron was the one who talked Phillip into getting his first computer and had been showing him tricks on it ever since.

The two computer nerds got together at Ron's house after Jack relieved Phillip at the store. Phillip didn't want Kassy to get wind of what he was up to. He feared the grave consequences. The two hashed out just what needed to be done and came up with a flow chart. The program they came up with was designed to work whenever the computer was logged into Mirc. They built a cyber robot of sorts. First, it would automatically set up the Angel's Lair chat room with the secret pass code that Billy had given him. Then it would go in and call up all the Warez named chat rooms, sending a chat message every few minutes to each room. The message read:

>Caribbean Blue>says to all> In urgent need of an Angel. Seeking the Angel that travels by night. If you are that Angel, please go to your safe cloud. I will be there with your charge.

Then all Phillip would have to do was monitor the Angel's Lair chat room for a response.

"This is going to make things a lot easier on me, Ron. Thanks a lot. You know you're so good at this cyber stuff, why can't you do what I want this Dark Angel to do for me?"

"Simple answer, Phillip. I don't hack. As much as I love fooling around with this stuff. I figured in the beginning not to learn any of it and I wouldn't be tempted to try. So I can't even run an easy password crack. Don't know how and don't want to know. Besides if you get caught pulling off any of that crap, there are some serious penalties that go with it. So, be careful, my friend. You will be traveling in dangerous territory yourself. You may get into trouble, too."

"Yeah, I know. But don't worry, I'll be extra cautious. Besides, this is the only way I know to get what I want. Here, go ahead and copy the program on this floppy disc. I better hurry or Kassy will have too many questions for me to answer."

The search for Chu continued. For the next three weeks, every night, seven nights a week Phillip would wait till all was quiet in the house. Kassy and P.T. would be fast asleep. Then, like a phantom of the night, he returned to his quest. Each day that passed, Phillip felt more and more guilt. He knew he was not spending enough time with P.T., for every chance he got during the day he would try and steal a cat-nap. The cat-naps had become more important than a game of catch or a simple conversation with his son. Phillip felt the loss because it was always in those little talks with P.T. that the boy managed to tell his dad something profound, something Phillip would remember and cherish for the rest of his life. He tried to put his obsession off time and time again. He would lie in bed fighting with his mind, *take a night off, just one night.* When he could fight no longer, he would roll out of bed and creep stealthily into the study to begin his nightly search.

The program he and Ron had come up with worked flawlessly. But there was no response to his request for a meeting with Dark Angel. Phillip was even starting to have doubts if there was such a person as Dark Angel. The lack of sleep was really beginning to show on Phillip's face in the mornings, but Kassy never even questioned him about his blurry-looking eyes. She was all consumed by the Christmas season and was in her own tizzy, trying to get ready for the coming celebrations.

Friday morning at 3:30 a.m. the message finally came in. Phillip had gone to get a cup of coffee and had minimized the Mirc screen, just in case Kassy got up and came in. He didn't want her to see what was running. When he returned, the Mirc alert window down on his tool bar at the bottom of the screen was flashing bright blue, signifying a message had been received. Phillip could not believe his eyes. He rubbed at them hard and looked again. Quickly, he tried to move his cursor to the blue flashing box. For a second he was unable to control the position of the cursor. He was so excited his mouse was out of control. Finally, he was able to click on the box. The Mirc screen maximized to full screen. It read:

DARK ANGEL has entered the chat:
>Dark Angel>says to>Caribbean Blue> I hear you have been looking for me?
>Dark Angel>says to>Caribbean Blue>I guess you're not here. Next time then.

Phillip's heart sank and he panicked, *Oh God don't let me have screwed up and missed him. I've been trying so long to find this guy.* Then as fast as he could he type:
>Caribbean Blue>says to>Dark Angel>Wait please!! I need to talk to you!! I was away from the 'puter for just a minute. Are you still here?? Please be here!!!

There was a long pause that seemed to turn into days. Then a reply flashed up.
>Dark Angel>says to>Caribbean Blue>I'm still here. How did you get the information to set this room up with my codes?

Phillip breathed a sigh of relief. *Oh, thank you, God.* He adjusted his chair closer to his keyboard, typed back, and clicked "send."

>Caribbean Blue>says to>Dark Angel>Death Master told me to do this. He is a close friend of mine. He says you helped him once and you will be able to help me too.

>Dark Angel>says to>Caribbean Blue>Death Master sent you. *Hmmm* Well, he knows better than to give out such information as this room code. But if he thought it was that important, then I guess we will be able to do some business.

>Caribbean Blue>says to>Dark Angel>Good. Glad to hear it. I need you to find someone for me. His name is Colonel Chu.

>Dark Angel>says to>Caribbean Blue>Hang on there, pal. Let's get the preliminaries taken care of first. I do this as a business, not out of the goodness of my heart. First, before we can start, I need you to set up a cyber cash account. Or do you already have one set up?

>Caribbean Blue>says to Dark Angel>No, I don't have a cyber cash account. But I do know how to set one up.

>Dark Angel>says to>Caribbean Blue>Good. When you get the account set up, I want you to go to this address: http://www.offshore-accounts-swiss-bank.com... When you get there, I want you to access the deposits section. Then transfer five hundred dollars from your cyber cash account to this numbered account. Use this code:~3~%576~09~76-0000. Add C.B. to the end of the code and I will know it was you that made the deposit. If you get all that done before tomorrow night at this time, I will meet you back in here then. Do you understand?

>Caribbean Blue>says to>Dark Angel>Yes. Roger that, I understand. Death Master said you weren't cheap. I guess he was right. Are you sure you can deliver what I want?

DARK ANGEL has left the chat:

Phillip slumped back in his chair, *Ah, shit, I hope I didn't insult him.* He clicked on the save icon and then the print icon. His printer began to hum and whir. Out spat the entire chat session he had just had with Dark Angel. He took out the printed pages and stuck them underneath some magazines on his desk for concealment. He shut the computer down and quickly tip-toed back to bed and attempted to get a few hours of sleep.

On Saturday, Phillip was off and slept in. After he heard Kassy leave to drop P.T. off at the skating rink, he got up and went to the computer. He set up the cyber cash account and made the funds transfer as Dark Angel had instructed him to do. He took the five hundred out of his store account so Kassy couldn't get wind of the withdrawal until they did the books at the end of the month. Now all he had to do was wait. That was the hard part.

At 3 a.m. on Sunday morning he awoke from a light sleep and crept back to the computer. He started the Mirc program and waited the wait. At exactly 3:30 a.m. Dark Angel signed into the Angel's Lair chat room.

DARK ANGEL enters the chat:
>Dark Angel>says to>Caribbean Blue>Good evening, Blue. Nice to see that you have complied with the rules. I have received the funds.
>Caribbean Blue>says to>Dark Angel>Good evening to you, Sir.
>Dark Angel>says to>Caribbean Blue>Now that's better. I see you learn proper etiquette fast. So how now may I be a service to you, Blue? >Caribbean Blue>says to>Dark Angel>There is someone I need to find. I am unable to locate the individual by conventional means. Therefore, I am in need of your specialty.
>Dark Angel>says to>Caribbean Blue>I don't see any prob-

lem with your request. Tell me what you can about this individual.

>Caribbean Blue>says to>Dark Angel>His name is Colonel Chu, never got a first name on him. I do have a recent newspaper photo of him. I have a scanner and I can send it to you in a file if you want.

>Dark Angel>says to>Caribbean Blue>Ok, Mr. Blue, I have set my preferences to accept files from you. So go ahead and send the pic. But first a word of warning to you. If I detect one piece of a corrupt file or virus infected byte, I will shut you down. I will crash and wipe your hard drive so clean you will never be able to reformat it. All you can do is go buy new stuff. Clear?

>Caribbean Blue>says to>Dark Angel>Crystal Clear, Mr. Angel. The scan is just about complete and I will forward the file. Notify me when you have finished receiving it and if it came in clear enough for you.

>Dark Angel>says to>Caribbean Blue>I got it. Looks good. BRB(be right back).

There was a long pause in the exchange.

>Dark Angel>says to>Caribbean Blue>OK, I'm back. I was running a preliminary check on our boy Chu. You know that if you were an Asian and you wanted to blend in, then Chu would be the name of choice. It's as common as John Smith. Go figure. So is this an alias or not?

>Caribbean Blue>says to>Dark Angel>No alias. That's his original name. Having problems with this one?

>Dark Angel>says to>Caribbean Blue>Nothing I can't handle. It will just take a little time. See you back here tomorrow night. Same time, same channel. Oh, BTW (by the way), better be prepared to transfer more funds. It all depends on how secure this Chu fellow is and how much digging I have to do.

DARK ANGEL leaves the chat:

Phillip was once again left alone. He reached up and punched the power button. The computer shut off. He rolled his chair back, stretched, and scratched his head. He got up and went to bed, dazed by all that had just occurred.

CHAPTER NINETEEN

MONDAY MORNING at 3:15 a.m. Phillip again found himself seated and blurry-eyed in front of his computer. At 3:30 a.m. as promised:

DARK ANGEL enters the chat:

>Dark Angel>says to>Caribbean Blue>Fancy meeting you here!

>Caribbean Blue>says to>Dark Angel>Excuse me if I don't laugh at your humor but I am really burnt out. Did you get the information I seek?

>Dark Angel>says to>Caribbean Blue>Yes, Phillip Turner. I have all you could possibly need to locate your Colonel Chu. BTW, he is a retired General now. Didn't you even read your

newspaper article?

>Caribbean Blue>says to>Dark Angel>I read it and I knew he was a General. It must have slipped my mind. Just that I still think of the bastard as the way he was, not the way he is. Now how in the hell did you find out my name?

>Dark Angel>says to>Caribbean Blue>Not to worry. I knew who you were and where you were the first time I spoke with you in here. It's part of my profession, remember. A good lesson for you to learn. Don't ever think you are anonymous when you're out here on the net. Even just chatting, you can be traced real easily. Now back to business. Your man Chu is a slick one. He was extra hard to track down. I had to mess around in some government top secret files to get what I needed. So I will need you to transfer one thousand dollars to my account in order for us to complete our business.

>Caribbean Blue>says to>Dark Angel>One thousand what?? Are you nuts? No way, pal!

>Dark Angel>says to>Caribbean Blue>Hey, suit yourself. If you don't want the info, then don't pay the price. I will, however, keep the first five hundred you already paid for my troubles.

>Caribbean Blue>says to>Dark Angel>No wait! I do want the information! I just wasn't prepared for your high fee. I will need to transfer some more funds that's all. You are a bandit, you know.

>Dark Angel>says to>Caribbean Blue>Good. Glad you see things my way. I will wait here for you. It shouldn't take you more than about five minutes to do. Now hurry. General Chu is waiting. ;-) **smirk**

He minimized his chat screen and went into his cyber cash account. He made the necessary commands and began the funds transfer. He thought to himself, *If Kassy catches me doing this before I can pay the credit card back.... I just better not let her find out, that's all!*

>Caribbean Blue>says to>Dark Angel>Ok, I have sent the

money to you. Can we get on with this?

>Dark Angel>says to>Caribbean Blue>Yes, as soon as I get confirmation on the money's arrival. This part usually takes some time. So while we wait, you want to tell me why you want this Chu so bad? Keep in mind you don't have to answer. It has nothing to do with you getting all the information you just purchased. I am just curious. I don't make the connection with you two. You are a simple man of moderate means. Chu, on the other hand, is a serious case, a major player, CIA- connected, somewhat involved in the witness protection program. And last but not least, he has beaucoup bucks. So??????

Phillip told Dark Angel Gum's story. He went into great detail of how Chu took the life of his little friend. He told him of the dead ends he had run into in Washington. Phillip painted a picture of the revenge he sought against Chu. At the end of this long explanation, he waited for a response from Dark Angel.

>Caribbean Blue>says to>Dark Angel>Are you still with me?

Still there was more silence.

>Caribbean Blue>says to >Dark Angel>Are you still here or not?

After what seemed an eternity, Dark Angel responded.

>Dark Angel>says to>Caribbean Blue>Yes, I am right here. Just trying to comprehend all you just told me. For the first time in a long time I am completely taken aback.

Another very long pause.

>Dark Angel>says to>Caribbean Blue>I just refused your last deposit and I have sent your other five hundred back to your cyber cash account.

>Caribbean Blue>says to>Dark Angel>Hey, wait a minute. What the hell is going on here? Does this mean you're not going to send me my information?

Nothing. Phillip's heart was pounding. He had no idea what to type next. He just sat and stared at a dormant screen. Then up popped an alert.

DARK ANGEL WISHES TO SEND YOU A FILE DO YOU ACCEPT? Yes[]or No[].

Immediately he clicked yes. Phillip fell back in his chair as the file was being sent. His mind was spinning, not knowing what to expect next.

>Dark Angel>says to>Caribbean Blue>This one is on the house, Phillip. I have a two-year-old boy and seven-year-old girl. All I want from you as payment for my services is… I want you to go out there and get that son-of-bitch. Then I want you to get back home to your little boy as fast as you can. Deal?

>Caribbean Blue>says to>Dark Angel>Deal! And thanks so much!

>Dark Angel>says to>Caribbean Blue>You're welcome. Look over the file well. It should contain all you need. But if there is something else you see that you need, you will be able to reach me at:D.Angel@hotmail.com. This e-mail address will be active for three days and then it will be changed. My computer checks it every ten minutes so it won't take me long to get back to you. This is the procedure I offer all my clients. After three days, then you will have to track me down the same way you did before. Good luck, Phillip Turner, and Godspeed.

DARK ANGEL leaves the chat:

Once again Phillip was left stunned and sitting alone. He rubbed his eyes, then jotted down the e-mail address on a sticky note. He taped it next to the power button on his PC. He then went into his Windows Explorer, found the file Dark Angel had just downloaded, and opened it. Up popped more information than he had hoped for. *Damn, this guy is good!*

Contained in the file was the following information:

Chu, Pak Thung Retired General South Vietnamese Army. Regular.

Born March 10,1929 in Danc Ku province Laos.

Crossed border into South Vietnam in 1949.

Joined the South Vietnamese army in 1950.

Chu, Pak Thung changed name legally to Chu, Thomas Perry when entered U.S.A. April 16,1975.

Also included were:

Chu's home phone number.

Chu's home fax number.

Chu's computer phone number.

Chu's e-mail address.

Chu's home address.

Chu's favorite country club and membership number.

Chu's club photo.

Chu's golf handicap.

Phillip printed several copies of the file. He wanted to make sure he didn't misplace any of this. He heard Kassy stirring and looked at his watch. "Damn, its already 6:30," he muttered as he quickly turned off the computer.

He crept pass the kitchen where Kassy was making coffee and headed to the shower. After a quick wet down, he donned his bathrobe and grabbed a towel. He entered the kitchen while toweling off his wet head, kissed Kassy on the back of her neck.

"Morning, sunshine. Sleep well?"

"As well as can be expected."

Phillip, puzzled, thought he had been made.

"Expected?" he asked.

"Just nerves. You know I always get this way when my parents come down for the holidays."

"Parents? Ah, that's right. They're due in today. I had forgotten. Do I need to pick them up at the airport?"

"No, where's your mind at? They never fly. You know Mom's phobias."

Phillip retreated to get dressed, relieved that he had gotten away with being up all night again. Now all he had to do was stay awake the rest of the day.

After his shift at the store he returned home to find that the in-laws had arrived. A note was left on the dining room table stating that Kassy, P.T., P.T.'s Grandma and Pa Pa had all gone to the mall to see Santa. Phillip raced for the bed to take advantage of his luck. He belly flopped in bed and tried in vain to get some precious sleep. He tossed and turned but just couldn't get Chu off of his mind.

Then he did something really stupid. He got up and went to his computer. He just couldn't help himself. He took out the printed file on Chu. He picked up the phone and dialed the Palm Springs area code. He then punched in Chu's home phone number. On the second ring the phone on the other end was answered.

"Mr. and Mrs. Thomas Chu's residence. May I help you?"

"Yes, uh, Mrs. Chu?"

"No, this is the Chu's housekeeper. How may I help you?"

"Uh, may I speak with Colonel Chu, please?"

"And who may I say is calling?"

Phillip hesitated. Then came stupid number two.

"Uh, tell the Colonel that Colonel Ben Danworth is calling."

Phillip thought, *God, why did I do that?* He listened in the background to the maid telling someone what was going on.

"Gentleman on the phone says he wants to talk to a Colonel Chu. He says he is Colonel Danworth."

"Hang up!" A gruff heavy Vietnamese accent could be heard in the background. Then the phone clicked off.

Phillip dropped his head. He knew he had just blown it. *Why? Why? Why did I just do that?* Distraught, he went back to the bedroom and laid back down. He drifted off to sleep.

"Phillip, we're home. Mom and Dad are here. You want to get up and say hello?"

Phillip groggily got up and tried to shake the weariness off. He staggered into the living room and put on his best jovial show. After what he thought had been a nice long chat, he begged off saying he had some important business to finish up in his study.

Kassy was miffed by this. She hopped up and caught Phillip in the hall. Blocking his way, she faced him, staring dead into his eyes. "Don't you think that was just a little bit rude of you?"

"What? I thought we had a real nice visit."

"Visit, my ass! You weren't in there for more than five minutes. This is the first time you have seen Mom and Dad since last Christmas."

Afraid Kassy might figure out that he was up to something, he took the sheepish way out.

"I'm sorry. I didn't realize it was just five minutes. I'll hurry this up and we can spend the rest of the evening together. Okay, sweetheart?" Phillip smiled and reached around Kassy to give her a love pat on the butt.

Kassy caught the love pat in mid-swing and shoved it back. "Save it, buster! I don't mean like a rain-check either!" Kassy turned and stormed back toward the living room.

With guilt riding on his shoulders, Phillip entered his study. He closed and locked the door behind him. He picked up the phone and once again dialed Chu's home phone number. *Ring, ring, ring.* The phone picked up. Phillip felt relief replace the guilt. He reached to hang up, then a familiar tone of beeps came on. "The number you have reached has been disconnected."

The recording confirmed what Phillip was dreading. He immediately turned his computer on and fired off an e-mail to Dark Angel.

To: DAngel@hotmail.com:

From:CBlue@fmmail.com:

Dark Angel,

I have a problem. I made contact with our prey by phone. Bad move! I am sorry and will not make the same mistake again. However, the current home phone number has been changed due to my indiscretion. Can you help? I will wait for your response. Thank you.

C. Blue

Phillip sent the e-mail and then quickly returned to his guests, hoping Kassy had calmed down. After dinner and a few drinks, they all sat down to view *It's A Wonderful Life* on TBS. Phillip tried to figure out if this had become an annual ritual or an annual ordeal.

Once all had bedded down for the night and the house grew quiet, he returned to his study to check his e-mail. Once logged onto the net, his Netscape browser showed an exclamation point beside an icon of a small envelope in the lower right hand corner of the screen, signaling incoming mail. Phillip clicked his cursor on the mail icon. The screen maximized to the e-mail screen. He checked the subjects and clicked on :re-DAngel. A reply from Dark Angel had come in.

To:CBlue@fmmail.com.

From:DAngel@hotmail.com.

Caribbean Blue, here is the information you requested. (The phone number followed.)

All else with our prey has not changed as of yet. Keep in mind that you will probably want to set your trap as soon as possible. Rabbits do not stay in the same briar patch very long after the thorns have been rustled.

Dark Angel

Phillip knew what Dark Angel was trying to get across. It was now or never to make his move. He slid his chair back away from the computer. He stretched out his legs and crossed them at the ankles. He put both hands behind his head and interlocked his fingers. He rolled his eyes to the back of his head and closed them. He took a deep breath. On the exhale he had made his decision. He would go for it. The next night he would leave to track his man down and make Colonel Pak Thung Chu pay the price.

CHAPTER TWENTY

IT WAS DECEMBER 20. Phillip called Jack into work early. He broke the news that Jack and Cindy would have to work doubles again for a couple of days. That didn't sit well with Jack, this close to Christmas, and he told Phillip so. An argument ensued. After several minutes of heated conversation, Phillip began pacing, his face had turned beet red and the big vein in his neck was pulsing.

"Look, Jack, if you and Cindy can't work this out, just call Kassy, let her know what you're doing, and just lock the damn doors. Go home, do what you have to do, and don't worry anymore about it! OK?"

Jack, in all the years of working for Phillip had never heard him say, "Just lock the doors." Jack could see real pain on Phillip's face and detected a relentless determination in his voice.

Jack felt a funny kind of fear for Phillip's well-being and realized how important it was to lend a helping hand to his friend and boss, so he calmed down and tried to put Phillip's mind at ease.

"OK, buddy, we'll do our part. You go do whatever the hell you need to do. Don't worry, the store will be here for you when you return. OK, boss?"

Jack held out his right hand. Phillip took it and gave it a shake.

"Thanks, Jack. I'll try and make this up to you when I get back. I'm going to be doing a lot of making up after this is all over. Oh, and if you talk to Kassy before I get out of here, not a word of this."

Phillip returned home at 4:30 p.m. He knew that Kassy, P.T. and the in-laws were out doing some last-minute holiday shopping. He figured that should give him enough time to take care of his business. He went to the bedroom closet and took out a carry-on style clothes bag. He also retrieved his old flight bag that had been with him all those years. He rummaged through it, making sure the photos of Chu were still in it. Taking the clothes bag into the bathroom, he piled in the necessities: toothbrush, toothpaste, razor, and deodorant. He searched under the sink cabinet until he found the box of surgical gloves Kassy had brought home from the hospital. He jammed three pairs into the bag.

He quickly went to his study, turned on the computer, and scanned the photos of Chu and his love queen onto the hard drive. He composed an e-mail for Colonel Chu. It read:

Yippee Yi Oh Kai Aiee, you bastard! Does your wife like westerns? If not, I suggest you hit star sixtynine on your telephone, pardner, and call me back.

Phillip attached the cowboy photo of Chu and the sister-in-law to the end of the short message. It would come up as a file and auto open when Chu read the message. He then clicked on the send later command, and saved the e-mail to another program where he would be able to call from another phone and send it remotely.

He moved to the closet in the study. Inside the cramped space he crouched down and pulled the carpet back to reveal a small floor safe. He dialed the combination, reached in, and pulled out a heavy, bulky burlap sack. Inside the sack were several smaller white cotton sacks, the type banks gave out for carrying large amounts of coins and paper money. Each cotton sack contained a separate handgun with ammo for that gun. He stopped untying strings and examining guns when he came to the weapon he was looking for. It was a Glock 19, a 9mm semi-automatic military type weapon. Holding seventeen rounds when fully loaded, it was very accurate and lethal. One other important feature, which earned it the name the "highjacker's gun," was that seventy-five percent of its make-up was plastic, making it very hard for metal detectors to pick it up at airports. He double-checked to make sure that this was the Glock he was looking for. He owned two of these weapons, one a registered legal model, and this one. He grinned as he turned the gun over on its side to reveal that the serial numbers had been ground off. It was one of many unclaimed guns he had taken in on pawn at the store. When Phillip first got it, he and a cop friend had raised the numbers with acid. After the gun showed up as a 'no tracer,' Phillip reground the numbers so they could not be raised again. He put the rest of the gun sacks back into the burlap bag and set it aside.

He set the Glock on the floor and dug around in the safe until he felt a couple of bundles of money. He pulled one out that was wrapped with masking tape and had 5,000 written on the tape with magic marker. He looked down with regret at the bundle of money resting in the palm of his hand. Phillip had been pinching money from the cash register at the store ever since the day P.T. had been born. His secret plan was to take P.T. on his sixteenth birthday straight from the DMV when he got his driver's license to any car lot in town. He would say, "Son, pick her out. Whatever you want, you can have it." He hoped he wouldn't have to make an alternate secret plan, but in the interim he would have to use the money towards a greater cause. He packed the gun and the money away in his flight bag.

He returned to the safe for one more dig. This time he retrieved a stack of various IDs tightly wrapped with a rubber band. It was surprising what people would leave as collateral for a six-pack of beer or even a pack of cigarettes. Some of these IDs came into Phillip's possession when the customer owed less than a dollar and never came back to pay up and retrieve the ID. He snapped the rubber band and it broke. The IDs fell to the floor. Phillip sifted through them until he spotted an Indiana driver's license looking up at him. He checked the expiration date first and it was still current.

He looked closely at the photograph. *Hmm*, he thought, *I guess if I cut my beard down to a Fu-Man-Chu mustache like this guy has, and I use my reading glasses, I might pass. Thirty-five? I don't know. Glad he's had a rough-looking thirty-five years. Yeah, you'll do just fine, Mr. Alton Scarborough.* Phillip gathered everything back up and reloaded the safe.

Back at the computer, he logged onto the net, rang his cyber cash account up, and made a new account in the name of Alton Scarborough. The transfer of funds from one cyber account to the other, gave Alton fifteen hundred dollars to go traveling with. After checking the airline web pages, he booked a flight for Alton Scarborough with Delta, from Atlanta to Los Angeles, paying with cyber cash. The ticket would be waiting to be picked up at the Delta desk in Atlanta.

Now he had to do what he had been dreading. He had to write Kassy a note trying to explain just what he had undertaken.

Kassy, My Dearest and Best Friend,

I don't know how to begin this or how I am going to end this. So just let me say a few things. I love you with all my heart. I have no excuse or reason that you would understand as to why I am doing this, this way. I just know that I have to do it, Kassy. It is like the pursuit for Chu now has complete control over me and I just act as a puppet. You already know what I am going to do. If all works, if God willing and you and P.T. will forgive me, I will see you by Christmas Day. Kassy, I am so sorry that I have to do it now, but I see no other way or time.

Remember, a promise made should always be a promise kept. Let me be true to myself and keep my promise. This will allow me to stay true to you. Take care and kiss P.T. for me.

Please try to understand.

With undying love,
Phillip

Not satisfied with the note, but also realizing he would never get it right, he printed it out, signed it, then went back to the bedroom and packed a minimum amount of clothes. He took the two bags out to his truck and placed them behind the seat to hide them from view.

The rest of the evening was agonizing. Phillip tried to maintain his composure throughout the night. When he went to tuck P.T. in and tell him goodnight, he had to fight back the tears. He knew the next few days might not go as planned and he might never see his son again. As Phillip reached to switch the light off, P.T. said. "Dad, you're the best."

Phillip slowly turned back to face P.T. He smiled warmly and lowered his head. "Thanks, Son. I'm not the best yet, but I'm trying real hard. I love you, P.T. Goodnight."

CHAPTER TWENTY-ONE

AT 2:30 THE NEXT MORNING, December 21, Phillip slowly eased the front door open, and stepped out into the cold, crisp morning. Zeke raced up from his bedroom under the steps and licked his hand. Phillip patted Zeke's head, kneeled down to give him a good neck rub and a kiss on his cold wet nose.

He could see his breath in the cold air as he whispered, "Now, you take good care of your people in there, Zeke ol' buddy. When I get back, I'll see that you're rewarded with a nice big soup bone. OK, boy?"

He started his truck and turned it around to head out of the driveway. About half way down the long drive he stopped. He turned his head and wiped the frosty condensation from the back glass. As he took one last look, he saw through the rising vapor of his exhaust a safe home with its trusty guard sitting in the middle of the drive, tail wagging, beckoning for him to return to the safety and warmth. This was his one last chance to call it all off and return to his secure life. It would had been so easy for him to just turn the truck around and go back to bed. He drew in a deep breath; a feeling of "things-are-going-to-be-all-right" over-took him. He smiled, faced forward, and put the truck back into gear. He slowly rolled the rest of the way out of the drive. Zeke trotted behind and stopped at the end of the drive. He gave one loud bark as his master's truck disappeared from sight.

After Phillip got on I-20 west heading to Atlanta, he started going over in his head what he would need to have accomplished before arriving in Palm Springs, California. Planning his wardrobe to suit a night meeting with Chu, he decided he would need to make a stop to do some shopping before getting to the Atlanta airport. He checked his watch and realized his arrival in Atlanta would be much too early for any shopping. He drove on toward his mission, switching on his windshield wipers when a cold drizzle started. He turned up the heat in the cab of the truck.

As the sun started to break the dark of night, he came to the Hartsfield International Airport exit. He spotted a Stockade Storage facility just off the exit and decided this would be a good idea. He didn't want his truck spotted in the airport parking lot, just in case someone came looking for him. He pulled up to the locked gate and honked his horn. A sleepy-eyed custodian pulled up the venetian blinds on a window overlooking the drive. Phillip motioned for him to open the gate. The custodian opened the window instead.

The custodian yawned and rubbed his eyes. "Go away! Don't you know it is only 6 a.m., buddy?"

Phillip rolled his window down. "I'm real sorry to wake you up, but do you think I could rent a small garage-size compartment for a month? One with a roll up garage door?"

"Lucky for you, it's been a slow month. Yeah, come on in and fill out the paper work. I'll start a pot of coffee."

"Sounds good. Thanks." Phillip turned the truck off and went inside.

After paying for a month's rent, Phillip had the custodian call him a cab. He pulled his truck into the assigned garage, got his bags, and waited at the gate for his short ride to the airport.

The custodian thought what Phillip was doing was a little odd, so he came back out and questioned him about it. Phillip put his mind at ease by telling him he was going to be away for about a month, and that this was cheaper than the airport parking lot, and a lot more secure. The custodian accepted the explanation. In fact, he thought it was such a good idea, he thanked Phillip, and told him he was going to advertise it as a new service, saying that if it took off, he might even offer a free shuttle to the airport.

When the taxi arrived, Phillip climbed into the back seat with his bags. He checked his watch. It was 7 a.m. He rolled his head back and thought of Kassy. He feared she was awake by then and had probably found his note. He wondered how she was handling the news. He hoped for the best. His emotions had hit a low point.

"Here we are. Hartsfield International Airport. That'll be five dollars and eighty-five cents."

The cab driver's remarks brought Phillip back to the present. He shook off the bad feelings as he dug in his wallet and pulled out a ten dollar bill.

Upon entering the huge main lobby of the already-bustling airport, he checked the overhead monitors for flight information. He spied his Delta flight number 476 leaving for LAX at 8 a.m. on schedule. *Perfect*, he thought. *But I'm going to have to get on the good foot to make it.* He jogged to the Delta concourse and rushed into the men's restroom. Hastily reaching into his front pocket, he snatched out a disposable razor and his reading glasses. He tossed the glasses up on the stainless steel shelf under the mirror. Frenziedly slapping soap and water on his face, he dragged the razor across his beard in a fury. Finally he was satisfied that the mustache would match the one on Alton Scarborough's driver's license. Running toward the Delta counter, he skidded to a stop. "Damn! The glasses!" He ran back to the restroom, retrieved the glasses, and sped back out onto the concourse. Careening around the corner, he came to a halt and changed his gait to a fast walk as he approached the ticket agent at the Delta counter. Out of breath, he puffed up.

"Hi, I'm Phi.….Phil.…I'm freezing in here. Sorry, I mean I am Alton Scarborough. Do I still have enough time to make your flight 476 to LAX? You should have a ticket here for me."

The ticket agent looked up and raised an eyebrow, then looked back down at her keyboard. With a blur of fingers on the keys clacking, she looked back up. "I think we can still get you on that flight. I will need some sort of picture ID please."

Phillip had already placed the driver's license on the counter. He had his thumb conveniently covering the photo. The ticket agent reached up and slid the ID out from under Phillip's grasping thumb. She placed it on her keyboard so that she could read from it. More lightning-fast clacking of the keys. She then handed the license back to Phillip. "Thank you, Mr. Scarborough. You will be departing Hartsfield International Airport at 8 a.m. Eastern Standard Time, arriving at Los Angeles International at 10:50 a.m. local Pacific time."

"Just under three hours. Boy, what a fast flight. How do ya'll do that?" Phillip just couldn't resist the joke.

"We can only work that magic when you're going west. Now to get back here, it will take you 7 hours and 10 minutes for the same flight." The ticket agent laughed. "Better hurry, Sir. Will you be wanting a window or aisle seat?"

"Doesn't matter."

"I see this ticket is a one-way. Did you wish to upgrade that to a round trip?"

Phillip took a dry swallow. "Better keep it one way. I'm not sure how long I will be out there."

The two went through the rest of the ticketing procedure. Phillip checked both bags, betting that being as late as he was they probably wouldn't even be x-rayed.

"Here is your ticket, Mr. Scarborough. If you will just sign right here." She gestured and handed Phillip a pen. She tore her copy from the ticket packet. "Your L-10-11 is boarding at this time at gate three, concourse B. You'd better hurry, Sir. Have a nice flight and thank you for flying Delta."

Phillip made a beeline for his flight and barely made it. As the plane left its gate and taxied out to wait in line for takeoff, Phillip slumped back in his seat. He took out a pair of headphones from the seat-back pouch in front of him; he unwrapped the plastic covering and put them on. He switched channels on the dial located on the armrest. When he came to a Crosby Stills and Nash tune, he settled back. He fell into a deep sleep and didn't even wake when the jumbo jet made its takeoff roll and lumbered into the cold, rainy morning sky.

Five hours into the flight a stewardess reached down to flip the lever on Phillip's armrest. As the seat eased back to its upright position, Phillip groggily regained consciousness.

"Sorry, Sir. But we will be on final approach soon, and I needed to do that."

"We're here already?" Phillip squinted and focused one eye on his watch. "Guess we are, aren't we."

The big jet made a smooth-as-silk landing. Phillip departed the aircraft and found his way to the baggage check conveyor. After retrieving his bags, he went over to the Thrifty Car rental counter. He had noticed on the back of his ticket folder their advertisement for rapid check in. "Just hand the rental car agent your ticket and we will handle the rest," the ad read. He figured that was just what Alton Scarborough was looking for.

Phillip handed his ticket over. "Good morning. I need to rent a cheap ride, please. Whatcha got on special today?"

"Well, let's see. Ah, here we go. Yes, I think this is right up your alley. It's a late model GEO. Two door economy with air. We call it our roller skate special. That will be $49.95 per day. Need insurance?"

"$49.95? Back home that car goes for $19.95. What's the deal here?"

"Welcome to L.A." The rental agent smirked.

"I'll take it. I have my own insurance, thank you."

"Okie Dokie. I hope you have all the special riders on your insurance policy though. Remember you're in L.A. now."

"Fine, fine, fine. Write the damn insurance too."

"Very good. That will be $79.95 per day for everything. Don't forget to refill the tank when you return the vehicle."

Phillip shook his head in disgust and snatched the keys off the counter. He turned to ask for some simple directions to I-10 east, then changed his mind, deciding that the guy didn't like him very much and would probably steer him off on a wild goose chase.

After a very long Easter egg hunt in the rental car parking lot, Phillip found his golden egg. The world famous L.A. smog had made it difficult to see as well as breathe. The yellowish-brown haze made his eyes water and his lungs burn.

Phillip had trouble negotiating his long, lanky frame into the tight confines of the sub-compact. He didn't notice the foul stench waiting for him inside until he was able to clear some of the outside smog from his lungs. Holding his nose tightly and cupping his mouth, he quickly rolled down all the windows, figuring the smog had to be safer than that stink. He started up the little car, headed out of the parking lot and pulled into the first filling station he saw to ask for directions.

A plump Mexican man with a hairy belly button peering out from beneath an undersized t-shirt approached his car. "Filler up,

Senor?"

The Mexican stuck his head inside the window and then snapped it back. He backed away, holding his nose with one hand and fanning the invisible stench with the other. "You okay in there, *Senor*. Need I call an ambulance?"

"Just some directions, please. I need to know how to get to I-10 east."

The Mexican told him the quickest and most direct way to go. Not wanting to have to smell that again, he reached inside the pay booth and took out one of those hang-from-the-rear-view-mirror car deodorizers.

"Here, *Senor*, a free gift for you. Have a nice trip, *Senor*."

"Thanks, *amigo*, I needed that." Phillip took the gift, promptly lost his grip, and it dropped it to the floorboard of the passenger's side. When he reached down to retrieve it, the stench grew worse. He spied a Burger King bag wadded up and stuffed under the seat. With a strong tug he freed the bag. *God, this thing must weigh three pounds or more what the hell is it?* He carefully opened the bag to find a fully loaded Pampers. He held the tightly wrapped softball sized pamper out the window. "Hey, *amigo*, I think I found the problemo," he called out.

"*Si, senor*. That must have been a *enorme bebe*'," the Mexican replied.

"Here, catch!" Phillip chuckled as the Mexican jumped back. He flipped the lethal softball into a nearby trashcan. He gave a wave goodbye, and drove away with the pine-tree-on-a-rope swinging freely from the mirror. He took I-405 north through Culver City then jumped on I-10 east. After clearing most of Los Angeles proper and feeling safe about where he was heading, he exited at Ontario where he had spotted a mall off to the right.

He headed inside to do some shopping. He first located a Pic and Pay shoe store. There he bought a pair of solid black tennis shoes and a pair of black shoelaces to replace the white ones that came with the shoes. Next he located a sporting goods store. There he got a solid black cotton jogging suit and a pair of black socks. At the Spencer's novelty store he purchased a tin of black-face Halloween make up. As luck would have it, located right beside the Spencer's was a Surf and Ski shop. He plundered through all the ski hats and masks he could find, but not one would fill his requirement. He asked for assistance from a sales clerk, telling her he was going to be in extremely cold conditions and needed one of the old style masks that would completely cover his face, the kind that had holes cut out just for your mouth and eyes. The clerk told him she would check in the back. She returned with three, one red, one blue, and one black. Phillip smiled and picked the black one.

He now had all he had come for, except for one item. He searched the mall in vain for a box of black Rit dye. Remembering he had seen a K-mart across the street from the mall, he headed that way. Upon entering K-mart, he was over-come by the smell of fresh popped corn. He hurried to the candy counter and purchased a large bag. He found his Rit dye and decided to make one more stop. In the household goods section he picked up a can of odor killer guaranteed to eliminate odor of any kind.

He put the single can back and took a case of four down from the top shelf. With his supplies in one hand, he began flipping popcorn puffs into the air and catching them in his mouth as he strolled across the parking lot.

Back on I-10 he drove east. He passed through Beaumont, Banning, Cabazon, and through the San Gorgonio Pass. He exit-ed on state road 111 south and drove into Palm Springs at around 3 p.m. He got some late lunch and a city map. With the map sprawled across the hood of the rental car, and a dripping sub-sandwich in one hand, Phillip navigated his free index finger along the grid. He figured out that Chu lived down in Rancho

Mirage, a suburb of Palm Springs. He spent the rest of his afternoon checking out the territory and the lay of the land.

He found Chu's country club and golf course. Chu lived in an exclusive neighborhood connected to the club course. There was a guardhouse located at the entrance to the residential part of the complex. Phillip pulled over to the side of the road and switched the car off. It spit and sputtered, shook and coughed, until finally the engine gave up. Rubbing his forehead, he pondered how to get past the guards. He needed to get inside the neighborhood and get a close look at Chu's house.

Bingo! He remembered a Domino's Pizza located at the six-point traffic circle just down the road. He cranked the car; it shuddered to life. He spun around and headed back down Frank Sinatra Drive to Thompson Road and the traffic circle. He pulled around back and stopped at a dempster dumpster behind Domino's. Climbing inside, he gathered up several discarded pizza boxes. Then he really lucked out. There, under some rubble, he found a Domino's delivery cone, the kind they stuck on the antenna to help identify the car. It was a little torn up, but nothing tape wouldn't fix. With his gold strike in hand, Phillip crawled out of the dumpster and back into his car. He neatly stacked the pizza boxes beside him in the passenger seat and taped the cone onto the car antenna.

He took a deep breath, trying to muster up some extra self-confidence. Off he drove right back up to the guardhouse. The guard was sitting outside having a smoke and soaking up the golden warm rays of the desert sun. Shielding his eyes, he glanced up at Phillip's car. When he spotted the Domino's cone, he waved Phillip through. He didn't even stop him to ask where he was going to make his delivery.

"Yes, yes, yes!" Phillip said, slapping the steering wheel with glee.

He now had free rein in the posh neighborhood. After cruising past numerous lavish estates, he finally located the address Dark Angel had given him. Chu's house was an enormous three-story structure, the biggest one on the block.

The mansion had a forbidding appeal. The walls were constructed of oversized solid white marble blocks that had been painstakingly hand-chiseled, cut to fit, and stacked perfectly. The matching marble piers at each end of the cobblestone circular drive supported huge ornate wrought iron gates. The automatic gates were locked securely to prevent any intrusion. Topiary lions guarded the contrasting polished peach colored marble steps that led to two ancient, far-eastern, hand-carved dragons, in the arched and very rare ko-koa-ba' double doors located at the entrance to the house. Phillip studied the small windows on the second and third floors. He was unable to see past the English ivy that had been allowed to grow rampant, covering the glass as if to hide some evil that lurked inside. Phillip slowly eased the car past the mansion, taking in all that he could, trying not to look too suspicious. He pulled on down the street and came to a cul-de-sac at the end of the road. A new house was under construction there. He stopped the car to think awhile.

A construction worker approached the car. He slapped his sweat-drenched gloved palm on Phillip's arm that was propped up, out the window.

"Hey, pal, got an extra pizza in there?"

Phillip, startled, jerked out of his concentrated state.

"Say what? Oh, no. Sorry, these are all spoken for. Maybe next time. OK?" Phillip reached over and patted the pizza boxes.

"Sure, whatever. I just thought sometimes you guys can't find an address. I would take the spare pizza off your hands. I'm about to starve, man!" That gave Phillip an idea; he would stop and pick up a pizza later to drop off for the gate guard. That should help sell the pizza scam even better.

"Next time, bud, I will try to look out for you."

Phillip wiped the sweat off his brow as he drove away. He decided to check into a motel room and wait until dark. Then he would try to get back into the subdivision again to get a better look at Chu's house after dark.

As dusk started to fall, he returned. Approaching the guard-house, he applied the brakes and slowed down. The guard was sitting inside with his feet propped up on a desk, watching TV. The guard peered over at Phillip's approaching car from under the brim of his cap. He held up his right hand and waved Phillip through. He drove directly to Chu's house and parked just outside the gates. He had a clear view of the front of the house. There was a pearl-colored Rolls Royce parked in the middle of the well-lit circular drive. After about five minutes one side of the massive ko-koa-ba'double front doors swung open. Out stepped General Chu and two ladies. They all seemed to be in a jovial chatting mood. Phillip recognized one of the ladies. She was quite a bit older, but he recognized her as the sister-in-law in the pictures Colonel Danworth had furnished. He figured the other lady to be Chu's wife. They all got into the Rolls. The automatic gates cycled open and the car pulled out past Phillip's car. Phillip ducked down behind the steering wheel to hide from view and took note of the time.

He cranked up the little car and pulled down to the end of the cul-de-sac. Stowing the six empty pizza boxes in the trunk, he left his bait pizza on the front seat beside him. He pulled up to the guardhouse and rolled down the window. When he gave a little toot on the horn to get the guard's attention, the guard walked around to see about the toot.

"Evening, do you like pepperoni?"

"Say what?"

"Do you like pepperoni? Extra pepperoni, that is."

"Yeah, I guess so. Why?"

Phillip reached over and picked the pizza box up and shoved

it out the window. "Here, this one is on the house. It was my last delivery and no one was home."

"No one home? I can call for you to make sure."

"Do you really want to do that? Wouldn't you rather have the pizza for yourself?" Phillip gave a sly grin and a wink. "If they call back, we will just send another pizza out. The company will pay for it."

"Thanks, buddy." The guard took the bait. Phillip waved, put the car in gear, and took off. He now had a partner in crime.

He returned to his motel room and fell spread eagle flat on his bed. A deep exhausted sleep overtook him. He would not wake until late the next morning.

CHAPTER TWENTY-TWO

DECEMBER 22, 1:00 p.m. Eastern Standard Time. More than 24 hours had passed since Kassy awoke to the disturbing note Phillip had left her. She grew more frantic by the moment. She hadn't slept and didn't know what to do. She picked up the phone and called John Robinson's office in Washington. She had found the number in Phillip's Rolodex on his desk, while she was tearing his study apart trying to find out any type of information on what exactly he was doing. The direct line to John's office rang. A female voice answered giving a recorded holiday greeting and explaining the office closure during the holidays. Kassy slowly pulled the receiver away from her ear, began to weep, and hung up the phone. No sooner had she done that, her phone began to ring.

"Hello! Phillip?" Kassy screamed into the receiver.

"No, Kassy, this is John Robinson. Hi, I was calling to talk to

Phillip, but I can tell he isn't there. Is he?"

"Oh, John, hi, I just tried to call you in Washington." Kassy sighed. "I'm sorry, I'm a nervous wreck. Phillip has taken off on this damn Chu thing. I don't know where he is. I don't even know if he is still alive. Can you help me, John? Please, say you know where he is. John? John?"

"Calm down Kassy. Phillip is the most resourceful person I know. Hell, he can do anything. Apparently he has located this Chu fellow. We couldn't do that in Washington for him. He's fine, I'm sure of that. How long has he been gone?"

"I don't know. A little over a day, I think. John, from the note he left I'm afraid." There was a very long pause. "I'm afraid that when he gets this Colonel Chu alone... well, I'm afraid..." She inhaled a deep, shaking breath. "No, I know Phillip is going to kill him! John?"

Kassy broke down crying into the phone.

"Oh, Kassy. I am so sorry. I have no idea how to find Phillip. I guess we can start at the airports. But I know Phillip. You're not going to find him unless he wants you to."

"Whatever you can do, please, please, do it." Kassy sniffled, trying to gather herself.

"I'll do my best, Kassy. Look, maybe you're just reading the note wrong and Phillip will call you soon. Would you feel better if I had Mary (John's wife) come over to stay with you some? You know, maybe a little company might help take your mind off the situation."

"Thanks, but no thanks. I just sent Mom and Dad back to New York. They didn't like it, but having them underfoot just made me more nervous. P.T. is all I'm able to handle right now. John, anything you can do to find Phillip, anything, please, please, please do it!"

"I will. You try to stay as calm as you can for P.T.'s sake and yours. I'll call you back as soon as I can find anything out. Take care. Bye."

Phillip rolled over, still fully clothed from the night before. He squinted one eye shut to focus on the red LED readout on the bedside clock. *10:30?* He jumped to his feet and raced to the shower.

After cleaning up, he focused on his mission. He jumped into his car and headed out to see what was going on over at Chu's house. On the way he stopped by a Dunkin Donuts and picked up a large coffee and a half a dozen glazed.

There were two guards standing at the side of the guardhouse when he approached. It looked like they were going through some sort of shift change. The guard holding a clipboard signaled for Phillip to pull over. Phillip put the car into low gear and began to slow down. The second guard tapped the first one on the shoulder and said something. He turned toward Phillip's car, smiled, and gave a two finger cub scout salute indicating "go right on ahead." It was the same guard as the night before. Phillip gave a nod of thanks to his partner and drove on through the gate. He pulled the car to the curb just down the street from Chu's estate. No sooner had he turned off the ignition switch than a golf cart zoomed past. Chu was driving with golf clubs swinging behind. Phillip cranked back up to follow the cart. Chu made a sharp right onto a cart path and disappeared over a knoll of grass on the golf course, then came back into view as he headed up another hill. Phillip had learned the layout here, so he figured Chu was heading to the clubhouse. Sure enough, as Phillip pulled up in the front parking lot, Chu wheeled in over by the side entrance where all the other golf carts were parked.

Phillip shut off the car and just sat there. He stayed out in the parking lot for over an hour trying to decide what to do next. He finally determined a meeting with Chu should take place, so he got out of his little white car and walked straight up to the front door. When he sauntered into the entrance parlor, a pretty brunette receptionist seated at an oversized oak desk asked if she could be of service. Phillip told her he was looking for Thomas Chu. She pointed in the direction of the members' lounge down the hall.

When Phillip got to the arched doorway of the members' lounge, he was halted by the host guarding the door.

"Good afternoon," he said in a snobbish tone. "How may I be of service to you?"

"I would like to speak with one of your members in there. Thomas Chu. Please."

"I am sorry, but I can not allow you in there. Members only, don't you know? I may be able to get Mr. Chu a message from you."

The host extended his hand, nodded his head and winked at Phillip, signifying a little palm greasing was in order. Phillip reached around behind his back and pulled out his wallet. At the same time the little gray spiral notebook of Colonel Danworth's fell to the floor. It had been stuck to the wallet. Phillip pulled out a twenty and looked at the host for approval. The host nodded his head. Phillip held up one finger signifying for the host to wait for just a second. He went over and sat in one of the overstuffed, diamond pleated, red leather chairs arranged facing each other in the corner. He flipped through the notebook until he came to a page that read:

10/1/72
Chu received $100,000.00 cash.
Partial payment for load no.2
$300,000.00 due when delivered 10/18/72

Both Colonel Danworth and Colonel Chu had initialed the note at the bottom.

Phillip ripped out the note and scribbled on the back of it. "Recognize this, Colonel Chu? It is of the utmost importance that we talk." He stood and handed the note with the twenty to the host.

"I will be right back, Sir."

The host entered the room and sought out Chu. Phillip craned his neck to see around the corner where Chu was seated. The host bent down and handed the note over to Chu who read the front and turned the note over to the back. Chu's head bucked back and his face turned dark red with anger. He turned to get a view of who had sent the note. His cold black eyes locked on to Phillip's blue eyes. The stare-down seemed to go on for minutes. A chill crawled up Phillip's back. These were the same eyes of the devil he first locked on to so many years ago. Phillip began to tremble with anger. His heart froze a beat and turned into a lump of cold marble hanging heavily in his chest. All he wanted to do was to shoot Chu down in cold blood right at this very moment. He didn't care that he was in a club; he just wanted Chu dead right then.

Chu broke off the stare. He puffed on the cigar in his mouth like an old time steam engine. A bright red coal formed at the tip of the cigar. Taking the cigar out of his mouth, he burned a hole in the middle of the note. The note smoldered; the sparks fanned out, consuming the paper. Chu dropped the remnants of the note into the ashtray. He then motioned the host to bend back down. He slapped one hand on the host's shoulder and whispered into his ear. The host stood straight up and fast walked to the door.

"You're going to have to leave. Mr. Chu said.... no, I won't repeat what he said. You're just going to have to leave immediately, or I have been told to call security and have you thrown out. Is that clear?"

"Hey, no problem. I was just leaving anyway. Give Mr. Chu my regards."

"Yeah, right. Don't think so."

Phillip, stomping out of the club, muttered to himself, " I guess the old son-of-a-bitch wants to play some good ol' All-American hard ball. Fine. Batter up."

Phillip returned to his motel room. He was in the seventh inning stretch and was forming the lineup for the final innings. He began the process of assembling the tools for the job ahead. He took out the surgical gloves he had brought from home; he mixed up the Rit indelible black dye in the bathroom sink. He stretched his neck and smiled as he thought what Kassy would be saying to him if she were to see him at this moment: *Oh, Phillip, you are such a stickler for perfection. I guess it's just part of your disease.* He smiled, put on a pair of gloves and dipped them into the sink, dying each one black. He sat down and watched TV with the gloves on until they dried completely. He repeated the process until all three pairs had been dyed.

He arranged all of the items he had bought the day before on the bed. He inventoried each item, checking over it again and again, making sure nothing but black would be visible. He replaced the white shoelaces with the black ones and took some of the dye he had mixed up and colored the little white emblems on the sides of each of the tennis shoes. He now applied the black face makeup, and donned his outfit, turning and examining the dark silhouette he had created in the full-length mirror. He wanted to be nothing more than a shadow in the dark safety of night. Satisfied with his uniform, he stripped down to his underwear and quickly washed out the sink.

The onset of the evening sunset produced a reddish orange glow that filtered through the closed window blinds. Blurry lines of red and orange were projected onto the adjacent wall. Phillip got redressed in his new stealth outfit. He pulled up to the guardhouse and was signaled through. He idled down to the end of the road where the new house was being built. He turned off the ignition and adjusted his rear view mirror to see how to apply the black face makeup. That night would be just a test run and reconnaissance mission.

Phillip pulled the black ski mask down over his face. He double-checked in the mirror one more time before getting out of the car and locking the door behind him. He dropped down into a ditch and hiked back up the other side. He pushed through a thicket of briars in the direction of the golf course. He broke through the brush and found himself in the middle of a moonlit fairway. Gazing up at the bright moon, he noted to himself, *hmm, looks like that it's about a day away from being full. Good.* He would use the moonlight to his advantage the following night.

Phillip paced the entire golf course that night. He was lonely and missed his family very much. He thought of P.T. and the night chats they had in the front yard while stargazing. He wished P.T. could be with him there to share the beautiful desert sky. He thought of Kassy and the first time he ever saw her, standing behind him in the check-out line at the base commissary so very long ago. He started to feel some remorse for what he had planned, but he shook it off and continued his mission.

He came to Chu's back yard. Crouching down behind the stone bar-b-que pit, he could see Chu through the large floor-to-ceiling length windows in the game room downstairs that overlooked the course. Chu was watching a newscast on his big screen TV.

Phillip turned from Chu's house and continued to walk and learn the lay of the course. He spotted what he was looking for: a large green on top of a hill. It was two fairways away from Chu's house and would be easy to get to from where he parked his car. On the right side of the green was a big cottonwood tree with large overhanging branches. He crept up to the flagstick and unfurled the flag. It was hole number thirteen. "Sorry, Chu, guess your luck is about to run out," he murmured. "This flagstick number thirteen will be your grave-marker."

Phillip took another look around, gathering his bearings. He pulled back the sleeve on his pullover and looked down at a little compass on his watchband. He took note, he then turned and headed in the direction of his car, keeping count of every step. He got back to the car and quickly wiped the black face off. He wanted to get out of there as quickly as he could. He hoped the guard hadn't noticed how long he had been inside the housing complex. He pulled up to the gate and gave a light beep beep of his horn. All he could see was the guard's hand when he stuck it up to wave him through. The guard had fallen asleep with his head lying on the desk and didn't seem to care if Phillip had been in there all night long.

CHAPTER TWENTY-THREE

DECEMBER 23. Phillip got up and had a good breakfast. He was anxious to get the job done, but he knew he would have to be patient that day. During his few days of watching Chu's house, he had learned that the hired help--maids, gardeners and such--left at 5:00 p.m. sharp. At 5:30 p.m. Chu's wife and sister-in-law usually went out somewhere. He figured it was probably to dinner at the club. Chu had been home alone after 5:30 for the past few days.

After lunch, Phillip went to his motel room. He picked up the phone and dialed his dedicated computer line at home. The phone rang once and the modem picked up. Phillip punched in the numeric commands for the modem to turn his computer on.

Just when the computer turned on and beeped, Kassy was passing by the study's closed door, and she heard the beep. She burst through the door, hoping in vain to find Phillip seated in front of his beloved computer. Her eyes darted frantically around the lonely vacant room. She figured Phillip had left the computer on auto answer to receive his e-mail. He had always done this. She dropped her head, distraught, and started to cry. She slammed the door shut and ran to the safety of her bedroom.

Phillip finished punching up the commands to send the e-mail he had prepared for Chu. He instructed the computer not to send it until 2 p.m. Eastern Standard Time. He calculated that in heavy network traffic it might take the mail around thirty minutes to go through the pop servers and end up on Chu's browser, so Chu should receive it by 5:30 p.m. Pacific Time. He hung up the phone and turned on the weather channel to get the local forecast. Sunset was to be at 5:58, so it should be dark before 7 p.m. There was going to be a full moon that night. No rain was predicted, just a few cirrus clouds moving in.

Phillip paced the floor with anticipation. It was only just past noon. He took out his wardrobe, spread it out on the bed, and double-checked it. All appeared to be in order. He went to his other bag and got out the photos he would be carrying with him to show Chu. He laid the little gray notebook on top of the pictures. He then started to piece together his 9mm Glock 19. He had taken the gun apart and placed each piece in a different location in his bags. This was to throw off any metal detection at the airports. After carefully assembling the weapon, he "dry fired" it several times. All was working perfectly. Phillip then loaded his clip. The gun's clip was capable of holding up to seventeen rounds at a time. But he had only brought three bullets. Even if the situation somehow got out of hand, he could only see the need for three rounds. One for Chu, one for Phillip, and one extra. He always carried an extra in case of a misfire or in case one got lost. Phillip never missed.

He slid the clip into the open bottom of the gun and gave it a sharp slap with his right palm. The clip locked in. He didn't pull the breech slide back to load a bullet in the firing chamber. He set the gun down on top of the notebook.

He got up and paced the floor. It was going to be a long afternoon, the longest afternoon of Phillip Turner's life. He took inventory again. He grabbed his flight bag and dug around again. He wanted to make sure nothing had been forgotten. He took hold of the box of Bazooka bubble gum in the bottom of the bag and pulled it out. He smiled and sat down on the corner of the bed, holding the box of gum between both hands. He rolled it to each side, reading all of the ingredients and piece count. He flipped it over to see what was stamped on the back. He hadn't noticed it before, but written in pencil and just about worn to where it couldn't be read was:

June 22, 1973
To Gum,
My friend, I will never forget you.
Turner

Phillip's eyes swelled with tears. He didn't even remember writing it. He thought to himself, *That was the day Gum was killed. I must have written that to him before I got off the plane and met him downtown. So long ago.*

He set the box of gum on the bed. He picked up the flight bag and turned it inside out. A flashlight and his Purple Heart medal fell out. He reached down and picked up the flashlight. He switched it on and off several times, testing it. He then picked up the Purple Heart and placed it back into the bag. He repacked all of the other items on top of it. He felt around blindly inside the bag, learning the location of each item. He zipped the bag closed and set it on the floor beside the bed.

He was growing more and more restless. He was getting hungry, too, but he knew he couldn't eat a meal at that time. Too many butterflies flying around in his stomach to hold much food down. He went down to the vending machines for a few snacks to knock the edge off.

He stared at the clock beside the bed and watched the final countdown. 4:45, 4:50, 5:08, 5:15, 5:28, 5:30, 5:34, 5:35, 5:36. *That's it! Zero hour.* He could stand it no longer. He picked up the phone and called Chu's house.

On two rings, someone picked up the phone. It was Chu.

"Hello." There was a slight pause. Hearing Chu's voice brought back that feeling of the cold, hard, heavy, lump of marble sitting in Phillip's chest. He was so nervous his knees were rattling together.

"Howdy there, pardner. Now, don't you hang up. This is real important stuff for you."

Click. The phone disconnected.

Phillip called right back. *Ring, ring, ring, ring.* On the tenth ring the phone picked up again. Chu answered.

"Look, whoever this is, don't be messing with me. I can take you out, you see."

Click. The phone hung up.

Phillip dialed the number again. *Ring, ring, ring, ring, ring.* On about the twenty-first ring, Chu finally picked. But this time Phillip didn't give him time to say a word. He shouted, "Hey, you still screwing your sister-in-law? Did your wife ever find out about that?"

A very long pause. Phillip could hear Chu's breathing.

"Who is this?" Chu asked.

"Ah, I thought that would get your attention. I want you to go to your computer. I have sent you some e-mail. Look for the subject Chu Boy Rides High in the Saddle. Just give that a little click of the mouse. If you like what you see, or even if you don't like it, but would like to find out more, then hit star 69 on your phone and call me back. Happy trails."

Phillip hung up the phone. He began pacing a track in the motel room carpet. He wished he could see the look on Chu's face at that very moment. He visualized Chu seeing the twenty-five year old picture of him and "sis-in-law". Seconds turned into hours. Phillip paced.

When the phone finally rang, Phillip stopped pacing and stared at it. It was his turn to play, to make the phone ring and wait. Finally he picked up the receiver.

"Yep?"

"Who are you? How much is this going to cost me?"

"Chu, is that you? How are you? Good to hear from you. And so soon, too."

"What do you want with me?"

"Relax, Buddy. I'm driving this bus now. You just sit back and try to enjoy the ride. But please remember to have the exact change and your transfers ready at all times." Phillip could hear a frantic clicking noise coming over the phone line. "Chu?"

"Yes, I am here. I am waiting for you to tell me what you want from me."

"Now then, Colonel Chu. I can call you, Colonel, can't I? This is what I want you to do. First, tell me when your wife and sister-in-law will get home. Or should I call "sis-in-law" your squaw?"

"They went into Palm Springs for a play. I don't think they will be back till late. After midnight, I guess."

"Good, real good. Now around eight tonight… No, exactly at eight, I want you to get in that cute little golf cart of yours and go for a drive. I want you to go to the thirteenth green. You know the one?"

"I know the one. It has that damn tree, right?"

"Very good, grasshopper. That tree gives you problems on your approach I take it? Now when you get there, I want you to pull under your tree facing north."

"North?"

"Yes, north, cowboy. Make sure the tree is on your right and the flagstick is on your left. Simple enough?"

"Yes, how much money do you want me to bring?"

"Now, did I ever say anything about money? I told you I am driving this bus. You just ride. OK? You just bring your shovel-faced ass in that little golf cart out there where I told you to. I have some more pictures to show you, and we have a lot to talk about."

"OK, you're the boss. Eight. I will leave my house at eight. One thing, please. How do I delete the e-mail? I tried and it just stayed there locked up on the picture."

Phillip grinned. He had figured out what all that clicking in the background was. He could just see Chu clicking that poor little computer mouse till its tail fell off.

Phillip chuckled. "What, you don't like westerns? How un-American of you. The mail will delete automatically ten minutes after you opened it." Phillip checked his watch. "That should be right about now."

"It just deleted and a big yellow smiley face with 'have a nice day' showed up. How long will that be there?"

"Not long. Cute trick, huh? Oh, yeah, always be careful of the e-mail you open. When you opened mine, I put another little virus in there for you. It read your entire hard-drive and sent a copy of your files to my computer. Thanks. It should be some interesting reading when I get home."

Phillip knew the virus part wasn't true, but he thought he would give Chu one more thing to worry about.

"Make sure you leave your house at eight. And I guess you already know this is a private party. If I think you have brought some back-up or I think you have double-crossed me in any way, well, just imagine your wife going to your fax machine tomorrow. I bet she likes westerns. Or maybe the guys at the club would enjoy an old time western. Don't forget I got plenty more old movie classics to share."

Phillip hung up the phone.

※

At 7:00 p.m. Phillip arrived at the guardhouse. The guard was standing propped up against the opened door. Phillip gave a nonchalant wave. The guard signaled for him to pull over. He noticed it was not the same guard as before. His partner was not on duty. Phillip eased up to the guard and rolled down his window. The guard slowly walked up, surveying the car. He bent down and stuck his head inside the window. He eyed the stack of pizza boxes on the front seat.

"Looks like you got a busy run tonight?"

"What?" Phillip's nerves were taught. He saw that the guard was looking at the pizza boxes. "Yeah, got plenty to deliver this time. I sure hope the tips are good tonight."

"Look, the reason I stopped you is, I didn't get to eat dinner tonight. And if you make another run out here, you think you could throw a large sausage and mushroom in there for me?"

"You betcha, Captain. I'll make it a supreme. You want thick, thin or pan crust? I'll even see to it that it's on the house." Phillip gave a wink.

"Pan crust sounds good. But just keep it with sausage and mushrooms. The peppers and onions give me too much gas. Thanks."

"No prob, but I need to run. You know that damn thirty-minute guarantee. Most people don't know this, but if I'm late, hell, man, I have to pay for it! Not the store! That free pizza comes right out of my pocket."

"See you when you get back. Have a nice night."

"You too, Captain. Bye."

Phillip put the car back into gear and pulled away. He wiped the nervous sweat from his brow. Then he smirked to himself, a little pleased with how well he had just pulled that off.

He continued on till he reached his parking space at the end of the cul-de-sac. There he smeared his black face on and pulled the stocking cap down over his face. He took out two pairs of the surgical gloves and snapped them on. He reached into his flight bag and took out his 9mm. He slid the breech open and it loaded a bullet in the firing chamber. He clicked the catch and the breech slammed shut. He leaned forward so that he could insert the gun in his waistband holster at the small of his back. He zipped the flight bag shut and got out of the car. Leaving the keys in the ignition, he checked the handle, making sure the door was unlocked in case he needed to get out of there fast.

He broke through the thick underbrush and stepped out onto the fairway. He had been hearing strange sounds as he made his way through the brambles. *Chick, chick, chick, shhhhhh, chick, chick, chick, shhhhhh.* It became clear what he was hearing. The sprinkler system was running full steam. He started to jog to his destination, bobbing and weaving to avoid the barrage of water jets. The water cannons suddenly stopped their rapid fire and died down to a drizzle. Relieved, Phillip slowed to a fast walk.

When he looked up at the rising moon, he had to shield his eyes from the bright glare. He thought back to his home in Georgia. *Ah, a hunter's moon. Me and the boys could do some good coon huntin' on a night like this.* He closed his eyes for a second and could just make out the sounds of the coon dogs baying and running down their prey.

His tennis shoes were pretty well soaked through, and his feet got a little cold. He figured that was why he was beginning to shiver. *Certainly not because he was getting nervous.* He climbed the final hill and spotted the site he had chosen. He surveyed the area well. Standing in complete solitude at the edge of the green, he saw the long night shadow he was casting beside the shadow of the fluttering flag on its stick. The two shadows seemed to be waltzing on a carpet of diamonds that the moon and the water droplets had created on the flat-as-a-billiard table surface of the green. Even with all the stealth black he was wearing, he was unable to hide from the light of the hunter's moon. A shadow creating a shadow.

He climbed the cottonwood and positioned himself in a sniper mode, trying to relax as well as he could while he waited. He checked his watch. 7:45 p.m. Suddenly he could hear the low-tone drone of a gas-powered golf cart. He knew that Chu's cart was electric and didn't make that noise. Something caught his eye. He squinted and strained his vision as he focused down the fairway toward Chu's house. He could just make out the silhouette of a golf cart approaching. Phillip's mind was racing. *I told him to wait till eight o-clock sharp. Stupid prick. What if that's not him? I know that's a gas engine I hear. What if he double-crossed me?*

The moon shone brightly on the cart as it drew ever closer. He saw that it was red and not white like Chu's cart. Phillip reached around his back and grasped his weapon. He made himself ready.

The cart continued on its path. Phillip froze. The cart rolled onto the green and slowly started to circle. In full view, Phillip could see the emblem of the golf course on the side of the cart. It appeared to be a service cart with a large toolbox mounted on the back. The cart stopped. Phillip's heart was pounding.

The driver got out of the cart, went around back and opened the toolbox. He reached into the box. Phillip took dead aim at the stranger's head. The stranger took out a strange looking rod with an auger on the end. He paced off three separate ways on the green. When he found his mark, he plunged the auger into the green. He twisted down on the t-handle several times and pulled out a plug of dirt. He went back to the toolbox and retrieved a fresh ball cup and placed it in the hole he had just dug. He then moved the flag stick to the new hole. He finished re-plugging the other hole, got back into the cart and left.

Phillip gasped for air. He had been holding his breath the whole time the greenskeeper had been below him doing his job. He rested his weapon.

Phillip checked his watch. 8:11 p.m. He heard the whir of an electric golf cart motor behind him. He reeled around as Chu pulled up. Chu stopped, then repositioned the cart just as he had been told. He reached down and flipped the gear lever to neutral and turned the key switch off.

Phillip sat in the cottonwood right smack dab above Chu. If he were to fall out, he would land in Chu's lap. Phillip remained motionless in the tree. He wanted to watch Chu squirm for a few minutes. Also, he waited to see if any unannounced guests might arrive. Chu did get antsy and started to get out of the golf cart.

"Stay right where you are, Colonel," Phillip ordered. "Now, please place both hands on the steering wheel. That's a good boy."

Chu swung his head to and fro trying to figure out where the voice was coming from.

"Good evening, Colonel Chu. It is so nice to see you again. By the way, you have a big spider crawling up the back of your neck."

Chu instinctively reached around with his right hand and slapped at the back of his neck.

"Now freeze right there, Colonel! Let's leave your trigger hand back there on your neck. Very, very slowly I want you to take your left hand from the steering wheel. And with two fingers I want you to pick up that newspaper you have resting in your lap. Keep in mind, Colonel, I have a gun aimed dead at the back of your right ear."

Chu began to sweat uncontrollably in the cool of night. He

complied with his captor's wishes.

"Just let the newspaper fall. Very good, Colonel. Left hand back on the steering wheel. Right hand stays where it is. Good. Now don't move, or it may be your last move."

Phillip turned on his flashlight and shined it down onto Chu's lap.

"Colonel? Now just what am I ever going to do with you? Is that a 45 auto I see in your lap? Say it ain't so, Joe. Say it ain't so."

Chu remained frozen, scared down to his socks.

"Here's the game we're going to play, Colonel. It's called pick up the gun in your lap with your left hand and toss it out onto the green. I want you to use your thumb and index finger only. Keep the other fingers outstretched. You know, kinda like you're having a spot of tea. You win if you do it real slow and just right and if the game master doesn't get pissed. I hear he is in a really bad mood right now. So play fair. No cheating now. Ready, set, go!"

Chu was raining sweat. His left hand trembled as he ever so slowly lowered it to his lap. He took the two digits and pinched the barrel of the gun. He slowly raised his hand with the gun dangling between his fingers. He rocked it once and let it go. *Thump.* It landed about six feet in front of the cart.

Soon as the gun hit the dirt, Phillip swung down on the overhanging limb and dropped to his feet on the green. Pointing his gun dead at Chu's face, he walked over to the 45, bent down, never taking his eyes off Chu, and picked up the weapon. Phillip approached the cart. Still at a safe distance, he placed his 9mm Glock under his left armpit. He took Chu's 45 and pulled the breech back, springing one of the bullets into the air. He did this several times, and the bullets flew out in random directions. The breech locked in the open position, meaning the gun was empty. He took the Glock out from under his arm, leaving Chu's 45 in his left hand. Phillip walked over to the passenger side of the cart and threw the 45 into the dash cubbyhole. Still keeping the gun trained at Chu's head, he policed up the bullets and put them in his pocket.

Taking the seat beside Chu, he placed the flight bag on the floorboard between his legs. While keeping his gun trained at Chu's head, he took his free left hand and dug into the bag. His fingers found the photographs, and he slapped them onto Chu's lap. Chu jerked and straightened up. Phillip reached back down in the bag and took out the flashlight. He clicked it on and shined it on the top photo.

"Here are the pictures I promised. I particularly like the last one the best. It really shows the true you."

Chu, still frozen in his position, took a dry swallow. He creaked out a few weak words. "What is this all about? What did I do to you?"

"It's all about one little boy a long, long, long time ago."

"Little boy? What little boy?"

Phillip again reached down into his bag. This time he took out the small case of Bazooka bubble gum. He slammed it as hard as he could on top of Chu's crotch. Chu made a gasping groan from the pain.

"You don't remember? Think back to Vietnam. Bien Hoa airport. Drugs. Colonel Danworth and Bill Geevers. Ring any bells?"

"Sure, but what little boy?"

Phillip started to get aggravated. "The little boy on the bicycle. The little boy I bought this gum for, you moron piece of shit."

Chu shook his head.

"You don't remember killing a little boy in cold blood? Don't tell me you can't even have enough respect to carry that deed in your memory."

"Ah, you talking about the day of the typhoon?"

"Yes, damn it all, the day of the storm. Remember now?"

"Those eyes. Your eyes, I remember you now. You were that guy in the club yesterday, too, weren't you? When I saw you yesterday, I knew there was something real familiar. You are the Sergeant I saved that day of the storm. You should be grateful to me."

Phillip's rage was boiling. "Look, you low life son of a bitch, I don't know who you think you're fooling. But it ain't me. I was there. I was right there. I saw you kill my friend dead in front of my eyes. No mistake! You see, I see this happening over and over again. It has never left my mind. It was you, and you alone, who was the shooter. That poor bastard you rode around to the back of the plane and shot too, the so-called sniper you say you saved me from. Ha! He was just another one of your pawns. He was missing shots on purpose. I could tell. Hell, man, no one shoots that badly. I'll have to hand it to you, though. That was pretty quick thinking to get out of the jam you were in. And you would have stayed out of the jam except for me. Sorry, Chu, but I'm here to make you pay the fiddler."

"Pay? Yes, now you are talking, Sergeant. I will pay. I am rich beyond belief. Let me share my riches with you, Sergeant. Let my money take all those bad memories away from you."

"Look, Chu, I told you this ain't about money. This is about right and wrong. You lose."

"Sergeant, be reasonable. That happened so very long ago. This is a different life now. That boy, he was a necessary diversion. He served his purpose. It had to be done. Besides, I think that boy was one of how you Americans classify "blood kin." He was one of my sister's sons."

That did it. The fuse was lit and burning fast. Phillip was smoldering.

"Are you trying to tell me that the little boy was your nephew?" he finally asked.

"Nephew. Yes, that's it. You see, I had to shoot my own

nephew."

Phillip blew. "You didn't have to shoot a damn thing! You worthless piece of shit!"

Phillip hiked up his left leg and kicked Chu in the neck, hurling him out of the cart onto the green. As Chu rolled on the ground in a daze, Phillip stood up on the seat. With gun in hand he leaped spread eagle into the air and onto Chu. Chu fought for his life. A combat to the death ensued. Both men rolled back and forth, fighting, kicking, scratching, and biting.

Finally, Phillip gained control and rolled on top of Chu. Chu's right arm was locked behind his own back as he laid on it. Phillip had his left knee dug deeply into Chu's chest, causing him to wheeze and gasp for air. Phillip's right foot pinned Chu's left arm in the dirt. Chu had no way to move. He was completely at Phillip's mercy.

Phillip stopped and took several deep breaths. He gagged and spit off to the side. He glared down at the helpless Chu.

"You bastard! You have no idea how much I hate you!"

Fire was shooting from Phillip's eyes. He had a death mask on, and Chu feared what was coming next.

Phillip reared his head to the sky and let out a shrill scream, one that invoked demons and devils to come to the killing. He had transformed into something not of this earth. It was sheer madness.

Phillip reached down with his left hand. He grasped under Chu's chin and forced his thumb into the right side of Chu's cheek while pressing his remaining fingers with all his might into the left side of Chu's cheek. He was trying to pry Chu's tightly clenched mouth open.

"Open your mouth, Chu! If you don't, I will blow a hole in it for you right now. Open your damn mouth."

Chu closed his eyes. His eyelids were fluttering a million miles a second. His lips trembled and he shakily opened his mouth. Phillip worked the muzzle of the gun down his throat. Chu gagged and choked.

"Open your eyes, you shit head. I want you to look me in the eye when I do you. I want my eyes to be the last thing on God's good earth you see."

Chu, resigned to die, opened his eyes. Phillip stared deeply into those black holes. A vision of Gum's haunting, scared, lost, and begging-for-help eyes took their place. Phillip saw the vision as a sign to do the deed. He told his mind to send the message to his hand to pull the trigger. His trigger finger began to squeeze, then froze. He felt a strange warmth coming through the double layer of latex gloves and into his hand. It was as though someone was holding his hand, soothing him, trying to calm him.

Phillip shook this feeling off. He closed his eyes and again told his mind to send the message to his hand to pull the trigger. His hand still would not respond.

With his eyes closed tight, the vision of Gum's eyes faded and P.T.'s eyes took their place. He could see Kassy at the front door of their house calling the two stargazers in for the night. Once Phillip had gained total dominance and control of Chu, reason and consequences won the battle over compulsion.

Phillip began to weep. He was unable to do this. Furious with himself, he pulled the gun out of Chu's mouth. He got off his chest and pointed the gun right between Chu's eyes and tried to pull the trigger again. His hand would not respond.

"Get your ass back in the cart. And don't you say a damn word, Colonel. Just get in the fucking cart."

With tears, sweat, and dirt all mixing together to form several streams of muck running down his face, Chu righted himself and half crawled, half pulled himself to the cart. He grabbed the steering wheel and pulled with all the strength he had left until he was in the cart. He sat there as still as he could, gasping and wheezing, head bowed, arms in his lap as if he were praying.

Phillip began to pace in front of the golf cart. He was more confused than he had ever been in his life. His soaked tennis shoes made a squishing noise with each step. Every few paces he stopped and took aim at Chu's head. He then lowered his gun and paced back and forth some more.

He just couldn't work this out in his mind. *Why can't I finish what I've worked so hard for? I risked everything I hold dear to get here. Why can't I just go ahead and pull the damn trigger and get the hell out of here?*

Finally, after pacing a path in front of the golf cart, Phillip slowly walked to the passenger side of the cart. He squatted down on his haunches and looked off to the side. In a calm, church-like voice, he addressed Chu one last time.

"Colonel, I don't want you to say a word to me."

Crying quietly, he leaned over and reached into the cart. He picked up the still burning flashlight, switched it off and put it in the flight bag. With his gun still in his hand, he sniffled and wiped at the snot running from his nose. He picked up the flight bag.

"Colonel, I want to kill you and watch you die more than anything in this world right now. But for some reason I just can't do it." He sniffled and wiped again.

"I guess there is a higher power telling me you're not worth this. Maybe it's just that I've finally come to my own good senses. I want to see my wife and kid more than I want to spend one more second out here in this stupid fucking desert on this stupid fucking golf course with your stupid fucking ass. Don't worry, Colonel, you will never hear from me again. You can go on and live out your sick, pathetic life. I won't bother you anymore."

He began to weep once more. "So, Colonel, all that's left for me to do now so I can go on living out my life is…"

A long pause. All was completely still except for Phillip's weeping and heavy breathing and Chu's wheezing. Phillip bowed his head. He then rose and looked Chu straight in his eyes one last time.

"Colonel Chu, I forgive… Screw that. You will have to forgive your own self. That's not my job." He paused and took a dry swallow. "I forgive myself for sweet little Gum's death. It's over now. It's done."

With that one simple heartfelt statement, Phillip experienced a feeling he had never felt before. Chills ran up and down his body and he felt the lifting of intense invisible weight from his shoulders. A burden that he had never really acknowledged was there before, had gone forever.

Holding his weapon upright and pointed away from Chu's head, he released the magazine clip. It fell to the ground. He grasped the breech and yanked it open, sending the brass shell loaded in the pipe flying through the air. He caught the glint of the shell spinning through the air out of the corner of his eye. A black streak flashed across his line of vision between the shell and moon. He heard a low thud of something catching the shell in midair. At that exact same instant, he felt something cold and foreign pressing hard against the nape of his neck.

"Freeze right there, sucker!" a voice ordered.

Phillip's mind flashed. He knew what was pressing hard into the top of his spine was the barrel of a gun.

CHAPTER TWENTY-FOUR

"DON'T MOVE, don't breathe, don't think," the voice continued.

Phillip remained motionless. His hands were frozen on the breech of his gun in the same position as when he had ejected the bullet.

"Now then, I am going to count to three and I want you to release your weapon with both hands at the same time. Do you think you have enough sense to do that? No, don't answer. Now, one, two, nah nah nah you already did the one two three bit with the good Colonel. Let's try eeny-meenie-miney-moe instead. You drop on moe. Ready? Eeny-meenie-miney-moe."

Thunk. Phillip's gun hit the grass. Chu was frozen in position, still seated in the cart. He began to crack a slight smile as he believed he had figured out who the stranger might be.

"Good. Nice work." The stranger, maintaining pressure with

his weapon, took his toe and gave a kick to Phillip's gun. It spun over and out of the way about ten feet from the golf cart. The stranger patted Phillip down, checking for a back-up piece. He found none.

"What? No back up? The Company would not approve. Now move over there and take a seat next to your golfing buddy."

Phillip complied. The stranger, with gun trained on the occupants of the golf cart, slowly moved over, bent down to pick up Phillip's gun and clip. "Hmm, a Glock 19 just like mine. They are sweet little baby dolls, aren't they? Hey, you sure you never worked for the Company?"

He slipped the clip back into the bottom side of his new-found weapon. It locked in with a click. Taking his gun and returning it to his back holster, in the same motion, he quickly chambered a round into Phillip's gun. With moonlight shining, Phillip got his first full look at the man. It was the golf course maintenance man.

"Now then, let's see what we have here, Tweedle Dee and Tweedle Dum. Mr. Turner, Mr. Chu, nice to see you two here tonight." He reached up, tipping his maintenance uniform ball-cap in a how-do-you-do manner. Long flowing white hair cascaded down his shoulders, framing his dark, tanned face. He looked more like some nasty smelling "carney" than a CIA man.

Chu blurted out. "Geevers! Good! You have come to help me. Good!"

"Maybe, maybe not, Mr. Chu. You just sit over there like a good little boy and shut up."

Phillip couldn't resist. He looked into Geevers' eyes and, sure enough, they were glowing bluish gray back at him. Geevers transferred the gun to his left hand. He turned it on its side, pointing it in the direction of Phillip's head. With his right hand he reached into the left top pocket of his uniform coveralls and pulled out a small black box the size of a hard pack of Marlboro cigarettes. A thin wire attached to the box led to and disappeared underneath the left side of his flowing white hair. He gave a yank and a tiny earphone slung out. He swung the earphone in a tight circle like a pocket watch on a chain. It neatly coiled itself around the black box. He tucked the apparatus back into his top pocket and walked backwards over to the thirteenth green flagstick, maintaining vigilant guard on his two captives. He slid his hand down from the top of the pole, and when his hand stopped about midway down, he removed a tiny bugging device. With the bug pinched between his fingers, he showed it off to the audience.

He sniped, "Let me see if I can get some of your quotes right." He cleared his throat and made a big production. "Sorry, Chu ol' boy, but I'm here to make you pay the fiddler. And let's not forget my personal favorite. I forgive myself for sweet little Gum's death. That one almost brought tears to my eyes." Geevers was really tickled with himself. He looked once more at the tiny bug.

"I can't believe you didn't see me place this. Of course you were perched up there like some big dumb black crow." Geevers pointed up into the cottonwood tree. "Yeah, I saw you up there as soon as I topped the hill over there. So, Mr. Turner, just what are you supposed to be dressed up like on this festive night? Are you a super ninja or maybe the first all black spider-man? I mean, really."

Phillip did not offer an answer. He was not amused or impressed with Geevers' quick tongue. He remained motionless as he began to size up the situation and his new combatant. He stole a glance into the cubbyhole of the golf cart and saw Chu's 45 auto there. He filed the location away in his mind. He had noticed that Geevers had an uncontrollable tick. Every few seconds he jerked his head several times off to the right. Phillip silently counted the seconds between each jerk. One one-thousand, two one-thousand, three one-thousand, four one-thousand, five one-thousand, flinch. He took note.

"So, Geevers, how did you know to come here and help me?"

Chu just couldn't keep his mouth shut.

Geevers turned his head, showing a puzzled look. He lashed out at Chu. "Did I not tell you to shut up? That means you no talkie, talkie. Checky, Checky? Understand, you stupid gook?"

Chu bit his bottom lip. He looked perplexed. Why would his long-term cohort act in this hostile manner towards him?

Geevers changed tempo. "However, for Mr. Turner's sake, I will entertain that question. Well, it all started back last summer when a Mr. Phillip Turner from Podunk, Georgia, decided to turn over some smoldering coals. He should have just let 'em burn on out. But no, he had to go stir those coals into a hot little fire. Didn't you, Mr. Turner? Now you're about to get your ass burnt. It seems Mr. Turner went to look up an old pal of yours and mine, Chu. Ben Danworth. We should have wasted that prick when we had the chance. Mr. Turner put some kind of bug up old Ben's butt so Ben gave Mr. Turner all this really good shit on me and you, Chu. Oh, that had a little rhyme to it.

"Anyway, as luck would have it, the first person in Washington who knew what to do with this really neat shit Ben gave up is one of my pals, Sid Langham. Sid really had no idea what was going on. He just saw my name and thought I could handle it. Lucky Sid. He gets to live. I started to monitor Mr. Turner's e-mail, phone taps, etcetera, etcetera, the usual Company procedures. In the meantime, I hopped on over to pay our Colonel Danworth a visit. That shit-head up and died! I felt like digging him back up and pumping a couple of rounds into him just for good measure. Instead I had to settle for a healthy piss on the fresh dirt piled up on his grave."

Phillip tried to remain calm and calculating. He kept counting seconds: four one-thousand, five one-thousand, flinch.

Geevers continued his speech. He loved to hear himself talk. "Now here's the stupid part. After finding out about Ben's demise and returning to Washington, all seemed quiet. I kept an eye on

Mr. Turner but nothing was happening. So I did nothing more, that is, until you, Mr. Chu, call me in a panic, telling me Danworth had called. Hell, Danworth was dead, so who could it have been? It didn't take long, maybe an hour or so, and in came the answer from Mr. Turner's e-mail. I had stopped listening on the phone, it takes too much time. Bad move. Why did they ever have to make damn computers red-neck friendly? And who in the flying fuck is this Dark Angel? He is a cute one all right. I ran a trace on him or her. We are in the age of political correctness. That son of a bitch zapped me and fucked up half the computers in the office."

Phillip smiled to himself and continued to count. Chu just sat there, still trying to get his breathing back to normal. Geevers began to pace frantically around the golf cart, maintaining his aim at both men. Phillip feared that he might spot Chu's 45 in the cubbyhole.

"I'm tired of telling this tale. You should be able to figure the rest out from there, Mr. Turner. Will you please take that stupid looking ski mask off!? I am sick of the unknown wrestler look!"

Phillip reached up and pulled the mask off. He nonchalantly tossed it into the cubbyhole covering the 45. He breathed out a sigh of relief.

"Now then, to the business at hand." Geevers paused after circling the golf cart. He stood two feet in front of it and began to dig in his pocket. He took out a handful of small vials of crack-cocaine and a wad of money in various denominations. He scattered the assortment indiscriminately around.

"This is going to be a murder-suicide thing over money and drugs. Works every time. I just have to do Mr. Turner's part. More work for me, never any rest for the weary. Chu, you have become nothing more than a thorn in my side. Watch closely, Mr. Turner. This was what I was going to give you the pleasure of doing. It's a shame you are such a pussy. It's just like magic. Do you like

230 · RICK TURNBULL

magic? Abracadabra and Zim-zala-bim. Disappear, Chu!
POOF!"

BANG!

Geevers had pulled the trigger point blank less than six inches from Chu's forehead. The shot rang out, splitting the calm of night. Chu's head recoiled. The back of his bald head exploded into a red mist cloud. There was blood everywhere. Phillip was stunned, his heart was pounding and skipping, the adrenaline flowing straight to his brain, causing it to numb and buzz.

With a grin of satisfaction on his face, Geevers approached the lifeless body of Chu. "I should have at least let Chu bid us a good evening. How rude of me." Geevers laughed and looked at Phillip. "Now, see how easy that is? Just like magic, huh?"

Geevers pulled on Chu's limp torso, forcing his body to slump over the steering wheel. He looked like an inquisitive child as he peered into the gaping hole in the back of Chu's head. A warm, misty vapor was rising up through the bloody hole. The stench of blood, brains, and fresh-burnt gun powder clung to the inner walls of Phillip's nostrils.

Geevers, with right arm maintaining aim at Phillip's left temple, took his free hand and dipped two fingers into Chu's open head wound. He raised his bloodied fingertips to his lips for a taste. He licked it with his tongue. "Yep, one hundred percent Gook alright. Hmm. I always figured he had a little Jew in him, he was such a good moneymaker. Let's make sure."

With that, Geevers took all of his left-hand, worked it in and dug deeply into Chu's head, feeling around in the bloody muck. He gave Chu's gray matter a couple of squeezes as if he was a Saturday shopper at the local grocery store checking for the freshest loaf of bread. He pulled his hand back out. The motion made a sickening, sucking and slurping sound. "Nope, brain is too small to be a Jew." He slung the bloody residue onto the grass, then looked down at the pattern he made with the blood. "Looks

kinda Christmasy, don't you think? The bright greens and reds."
He knew Phillip couldn't see the spew.

Geevers had a definite flair for the macabre. His grotesque
theatrics had become his trademark throughout his career with
the Company. Phillip remembered Danworth had warned him
about Geevers.

Geevers moved back to the front of the golf cart. He continued wiping his bloodied glove on the pants leg of his coveralls.

"For your information, Mr. Turner, after I leave here tonight I
have made more travel plans, destination Podunk, Georgia. I figure I better go down, clean your computer out, and take care of
any other loose ends. I just hate loose ends, don't you?" He pointed at Chu. "So I guess I will probably need to go ahead and take
care of your little woman. They always know too much. Kassy?
That's her name, isn't it? But don't worry yourself now. I would-
n't feel right letting your kid, P.T., grow up as an orphan."

Hearing the names of his family and the threats, life returned
to Phillip's eyes and he resumed counting, as if a switch had been
thrown. His mind was seething with hate. Three one-thousand,
four one-thousand, five one-thousand, *flinch*. Phillip, with eyes
fixed on Geevers' flinching, quickly reached down with his left
hand and switched on the key to the golf cart. Geevers steadied
his head and noticed the change on Phillip's face. He took a step
back. Two one-thousand, three one-thousand, four one-thousand,
five one-thousand, *flinch*. In the exact same motion Phillip
reached down and flipped the gear lever to forward and moved his
left foot to rest on top of the throttle pedal.

Geevers brought his head back to steady. He sensed something and took another step back. He brought his gun up to a fir-
ing-range position and locked his arms. He gingerly squeezed the
"Safe-Action" trigger until it engaged. The three internal safeties
of the weapon were released. One more ounce of pressure from
his trigger finger and the gun would fire.

One one-thousand, two one-thousand, three one-thousand, four one-thousand, five one-thousand, *flinch*! Phillip dropped his foot hard onto the throttle peddle. The golf cart responded and lurched forward.

Geevers, still caught up in his flinch, didn't even see it coming. He bounced off the front of the cart and went sailing back on his heels. He dropped to his butt and slid through a puddle of water on the green.

Phillip snatched Chu's 45 out of the cubbyhole as he dove out of the cart. He rolled in Geevers' direction while frantically digging in his pocket for a cartridge. His fingers grasped a round. He loaded it into the pipe and flipped the lever, slamming the breech shut. He rolled up onto his knees and took aim at Geevers.

Geevers was sitting up, making an attempt to get to his feet. Suddenly, Geevers' eyes really did light up. Geevers gasped for air as he fell flat on his back and sprang out straight as a board. He started trembling, then began squirming and flipping as his body went through several contortions. Geevers looked as if he were having a Grand Mal seizure. Or was this a ploy?

Phillip took aim. Geevers continued to flip and flop like a fish that had been caught and thrown up on the bank. A bluish-white tint pierced through his tanned lips, as a frothy mixture of regurgitated sputum oozed from his bared, locked, and grinding teeth. Finally, Geevers went limp and still.

Remaining at dead aim, Phillip got slowly to his feet. Geevers' eyes were clenched shut. He remained motionless. Phillip took a step closer. Geevers' eyes popped back open and he reached out toward Phillip. Phillip jumped back and adjusted his aim. Geevers grabbed his chest and took in a deep wheezing breath. He squeaked out "help me, you fucker" and fell back limp.

Phillip stood at ready for several seconds, but he detected no movement. He cautiously approached, one step at a time.

Nothing. He kicked Geevers' gun out of harm's way. He nudged Geevers with his toe. Still nothing. Phillip bent down with his right hand held back and away, pistol still aimed at Geevers' head. He placed two fingers on Geevers' carotid artery to feel for a pulse.

Geevers was dead. The emotions of release flooded into Phillip's heart. It was over; it was really over.

Phillip didn't have a clue as to what had just killed Geevers. He just knew he needed to clear the scene fast and clear it the right way.

He stood and mustered his thoughts. He first retrieved his ski mask and flight bag. He picked up the case of bubble gum that had fallen out of the golf cart and put it back into his flight bag. He decided to leave the photographs for the police to find.

He quickly moved to the side of the golf cart where Chu lay. Crouching down and leaning in between the steering wheel and Chu's slumped-over corpse, he placed the 45 in Chu's lifeless right hand that was half-resting on the floorboard. Air escaping from Chu's lungs made a gurgling groan. A dribble of warm bloody goo dripped from Chu's open mouth onto Phillip's exposed right ear tip. The warm goo oozed down to the soft, sensitive part where the ear was connected to his skull. Nausea froze Phillip. His stomach knotted up. Acidic bile boiled up and burned in the back of his throat. Phillip jerked his head back while clenching his teeth tight, trying hard not to go into convulsions of puke. He stamped his feet and wiped violently at his ear tip as if a hornet had latched on with its stinger and he couldn't shake it free.

Finally, Phillip was able to shake off the grizzlies and resume the task at hand. He remembered that Geevers was armed with the same weapon as he was. He rolled Geevers over, removed the Glock from its holster. Sitting down on the wet green, he placed his flashlight in his mouth and aimed the beam at the two guns.

Quickly he disassembled both weapons. He swapped barrels so that Geevers' gun had the barrel with the serial numbers ground down. He took Geevers' gun and walked over to the sand trap in the front of the green and fired a round into the sand. He wanted Geevers' new barrel to have that fresh-fired scent to match the frame of the gun. He dropped down on both knees and dug like a dog to retrieve the slug. He found it and stuck it into his pocket with the spent shell casing. He grabbed the trap rake and smoothed the crystal white sand back out.

Phillip knew that time had become the rarest commodity in the world. If someone hadn't heard the first shot several minutes before, the second shot would surely bring notice. He returned to Geevers' body one last time. He rolled him over onto his back. He placed the Glock beside Geevers' outstretched arm to look like what he hoped was a natural drop.

He knelt down on one knee and, in a sarcastic whisper, said, "You deserved so much more, you evil bastard. Hope you and Chu have yourselves a big time down in Hell."

Phillip jumped to his feet, took one final survey of the scene to make sure he didn't forget anything. Like a bolt of lightning, he took off in a sprint for his car.

CHAPTER TWENTY-FIVE

DECEMBER 24, early Christmas Eve morning, Phillip was spread-eagled on his motel bed sleeping in a coma-like state. He was still wearing his black outfit. Wet tennis shoes remained on his feet.

The dream had returned. Phillip tried desperately to pull himself out of the dreaded dream and into consciousness. He was once again alone in the dome of darkness on the railroad tracks. Fog was rolling in.

He heard the cries in front him. But this time they were more familiar. He couldn't quite make them out, but he was sure they were human and he knew that sound. He turned around to face his fear and there it was, the demon freight train bearing down on him, lights flashing and horns blaring. He knew that this was his chance to get a glimpse of the figure caught on the tracks. He turned back to look down the tracks. He squinted and strained his eyes and the figure was exposed. His heart pounded. It was P.T.

He screamed, "P.T. run! Run! Get off the tracks now!" P.T. continued to struggle. Somehow, his foot was trapped underneath the rail. Phillip turned back to face the oncoming train. In his most defiant voice of rage he screamed, "No, no, no! You will not take him too! You cannot do this again! I won't let you! You bastard, stop! Damn it, stop! I will not jump off these tracks again! You will have to take me first! Come and get me, you son of bitch!"

At that instant Phillip found his legs were freed, no longer frozen in place. He turned and raced with all his strength toward P.T.

The train was gaining on him, but he would not give up and leave the tracks.

At the last second he lunged for P.T. and grabbed him by the shoulders. With one last ounce of energy, he ripped P.T.'s foot free from the stuck tennis shoe trapped beneath the rail. They both rolled over to the side of the tracks and slid down the gravel embankment. The train suddenly disappeared. All was calm and peaceful.

Phillip woke at 7 a.m. He rolled over and sat up on the corner of the bed. He looked down at the floor and saw the flight bag. He rubbed his eyes, clearing the cobwebs from his head. Phillip leaned down and grabbed the bag. He frantically unzipped it, looking for proof that last night really did happen. He reached in and pulled out the Glock gun barrel with the serial numbers engraved on it. It really did happen. Chu was dead and so was Geevers.

Wait a minute. He rubbed the back of his neck; something was different. Something had drastically changed inside Phillip. For the first time in a very long time he felt totally at peace with himself. There was no burning hatred and no guilt.

He remembered the dream completely. *I finally saw it through. Does this mean all is really behind me now?* The only mission he had now was to get back home as quickly as he could. He knelt down beside his bed and said a quiet prayer of thanks. He sprang from his knees, packed his belongings, and dashed into the shower.

Phillip arrived at the Palm Springs airport amid a heavy rush of holiday travelers. He went to the rental car booth and turned in his GEO. Hastily, he located an airline reservation courtesy counter and walked up. The agent was on the phone. Jim was on his nametag. Phillip blurted out, "Good morning, Jim. I need a one way ticket to Atlanta, Georgia, please."

Jim, an effeminate fellow with the phone cradled between his left shoulder and ear, stopped writing. He held up his right pinky finger with pencil clasped in his palm. Holding Phillip at bay, Jim smiled and went back to jotting down the information that was being given to him from the other end of the phone line. Jim hung up the phone.

With the hint of a fake lisp, Jim said, "Sorry, Sir. I was busy. How may I help you?"

"I need to get to Atlanta, Georgia, as soon as possible."

"Sir, you know it is Christmas Eve. Busy, busy. Booked, booked. However, that call I just got was a cancellation. It was a party of three connecting in LAX and going on to Ho Chi Minh City, Vietnam." Jim looked sheepishly from side to side and motioned with his right pinky finger for Phillip to come a little closer. Phillip leaned his head over the counter. Jim lowered his voice to a backyard-fence whisper. "Terrible, just terrible. That call, you know?" Jim pointed at the phone. "Well, that was the Rancho Mirage Police Department, homicide division. Seems there was a murder last night. Well, at least that was what I think it was. The detective didn't come right out and say it was a murder. Did say deceased, I distinctly heard deceased. You put homicide together with deceased, what have you got? Murder, that's right, honey. Murder. Now back to the good news. We now have three vacant seats going to LAX."

Phillip gave Jim a shocked oh-my-goodness look and thought to himself, *this guy is flaky as a batch of Martha White's store-bought biscuits.*

The clerk looked down at his keyboard and typed in some codes. He smiled and looked back up.

"Eureka! You will be able to pick up your connector in LAX for Atlanta with just a one-hour layover. I have two passengers seated over there on stand-by. They get the first two seats, and I guess it's your lucky day. Merry Christmas. Your plane leaves in one hour."

Phillip was ecstatic. He purchased his ticket, found a coffee shop, and got a cup of coffee and a doughnut. There was a TV monitor hanging above the counter tuned to the local morning newscast. Phillip spotted a pay phone in the corner of the coffee shop. He walked over to it and reached for the receiver. He took a deep breath, slowly took the receiver off the hook, and dialed his home phone number.

11:35 am Eastern Standard Time.

Kassy was lying in bed with her eyes wide open staring blankly at the ceiling. Sleep had become a thing of the past for her, but she couldn't make herself get out of bed. The phone was right beside her on the nightstand. She jerked when it started to ring. She was afraid to pick it up because she feared it would be some state patrol officer or a coroner somewhere telling her that they had found Phillip's body. The phone continued to ring. Kassy finally got the nerve to pick it up.

"Hello?" Kassy whispered timidly.

"Kassy? It's me. Phillip."

A long pause followed. Kassy's heart leaped and skipped a beat. "Thank God."

"Kassy, is P.T. okay? Go check on him now, please. I need to know how he is."

"P.T. is fine, Phillip. He's taking a nap right here beside me. He had a real bad nightmare early this morning and came and got in bed with me. He mumbled something about a train and that you had saved him. I wish you could see him right now. He has the most peaceful look on his face."

"I love you, Kassy!"

Kassy began to sob. "I love you too, Phillip Turner. Where are you? Are you alright?"

"I'm fine, sweetheart. I'm fine. I want to come home now. Can I come home, please?"

Another long pause. Kassy was trying to settle down. "You can come home only…" She took a breath. "And I mean this from the bottom of my heart. Only if you promise never, ever to do anything like this again."

"I promise. I will never do it again. It's over. Finished."

"Over? Finished? Phillip, you didn't?"

"No, I didn't."

"Thank God."

Kassy squeezed her eyes shut and a tear trickled out. She sniffled. "Come home, Phillip. Come home to me and P.T. now! We love you!"

"I'm on my way, darling. I'm on my way!"

Phillip began to tear up.

"Where can P.T. and I meet you. At an airport? Columbia? Atlanta? Augusta? Where?"

"Baby, in eight hours I want you and P.T. to meet me at a very special place."

"Where? Phillip, just name it. We're ready to go anywhere for you."

"In eight hours I want you and P.T. to be at the front door of our home. I'll see you then. I love you so much, Kassy. Kassy, let Zeke in the house. Give the dog a break, OK?"

Kassy shook her head and laughed and cried at the same time.

"Zeke? He hasn't left the house except to walk up the drive to look for you every day since you've been gone."

Phillip laughed, then paused. "Kassy, I want you to do one thing for me if you can."

"Okay, What is it?"

"I was wondering if maybe you could go out and pick up a white poinsettia for Christmas?"

"Does it have to be a white one? I already have some real pretty red ones here."

"White if you can do it. You see white was always Dad's favorite color. I guess it was because he was colorblind. He told me once when I was a kid that white he could count on, it always looked exactly the same to him. No variations. It always looked the same. I want to…no, I need to take it to the cemetery tomorrow. I think it's time I showed P.T. where his granddad is buried. Do you think it will be alright with P.T. if we went by there tomorrow?"

Kassy was overwhelmed with joy. She knew Phillip had come full circle, and all his ghosts had been banished. The Phillip Turner she fell in love with so long ago was finally coming home.

"Phillip, I think that's a wonderful idea. I know P.T. will be proud to go and see where his granddad is resting. I'll have the white poinsettia on the front porch for you when you get here."

"Thank you, sweetheart. It means a lot to me. See you in eight, OK? I love you."

"I love you, too. Be careful. Hurry home. Bye."

"Oh, Kassy? Merry Christmas."

"It will be merry when you get home."

Phillip hung up the phone. He walked over to the trash can at the end of the counter. It was the type that stood tall and had rocking doors on it. He finished his coffee and put the Styrofoam cup into the can. He set his flight bag on top of the can and unzipped it. He was close enough to hear the TV monitor above the counter. The morning news was still on. He reached into the bag and took out the photocopies he had of Chu. He tore them up and put them in the can. He took out all of the documents he had and tore them up as well. He found the negatives. Biting and tugging on them with his teeth till they ripped apart, he threw the pieces away. His fingers closed on the little spiral gray notebook. He ripped it in two and dropped it in.

Something on the newscast distracted him; he stepped back so that he could view the monitor.

The morning news anchor was setting up a remote broadcast. "We are now going to cut away on location. We are taking you to the hamlet of Rancho Mirage. To the exclusive Thunderbird golf club and community. Andrea? Are you there?"

A pretty young African-American reporter was shown with a microphone and a yellow legal pad clenched in one hand. She was trying to adjust her ear-piece with the other hand. There was helicopter noise in the background. The camera angle pulled back to show the reporter standing off to the side of a golf green with a blood-stained white golf cart in the background. There was crime scene yellow tape strewn everywhere.

"Yes, I'm here. Thank you, Bill. This is Andrea Johnston. I am standing at the scene of a most bizarre incident. This one will make the nationals for sure, Bill!"

Andrea pointed skyward, and the cameraman followed her cue. The helicopter circling above flew into view with a CNN logo emblazoned on its side. The camera panned back to Andrea.

"Bill, this story has murder, accidental suicide, drugs, money, suspected black mail, suspected extra marital relationships, and even a possible government connection with roots in Washington. Now this is what we know. Around eleven o'clock last night a gunshot rang out, piercing the serenity of this peaceful neighborhood. Soon after the first shot, a second shot was heard. When police arrived on the scene, they found vials of crack cocaine, money, pornographic photographs, and two adult males dead at the scene. One of the males has been identified as Retired General Thomas Perry Chu of the South Vietnamese Army. General Chu is the one classified as the victim of the murder. He received a single gunshot wound to the forehead. The other adult male's identification is being withheld. General Chu was quite an affluent and outstanding member of the community here at the Thunderbird. He was well-thought of and gave much of his wealth to good causes."

Phillip was spellbound by the newscast. Andrea took a look down at her notes and continued.

"The following information was given to us in an exclusive WKPS interview with an eyewitness who was here on the scene last night. At around midnight, relatives of General Chu were informed by one of their neighbors of the incident. His surviving wife of thirty-six years and her sister rushed here to the scene. The police had not yet removed the bodies and had just begun collecting and tagging evidence. Mrs. Chu broke through the security lines and rushed to her husband's side. As she was trying to comfort the already deceased General Chu, she noticed several photographs beside him. She picked one of the photographs up and screamed out something in her native Vietnamese tongue. She then spit on the photograph and on the body of General Chu. With photograph in hand, she raced toward and pounced on her sister. This is a direct quote from our witness: 'Man, one hell of a cat fight broke out. I have never seen two women go at it like that before, and these were some old bats, too! When the cops got those two apart, neither one of 'em had any hair left.' When asked, police refused to comment on this."

The TV screen went to a split screen configuration, the anchor on one side and Andrea on location on the other. "Andrea, what else can you tell us about the other male involved?"

"Well, Bill, here is the tricky part." Andrea walked over a few steps and pointed to the ground. The camera pulled back to show a chalk outline of a body drawn on the grass. "Now this is coming directly from an anonymous source inside the Rancho Mirage police department. Male number two, as we will now refer to him, was the alleged shooter and died from a suspected heart attack. Male number two, we are also told, has been identified as some type of government official from Washington, D.C. Now the heart attack was believed to have been triggered by a stun gun or a Taser, if you will."

"A Taser? A stun gun? Andrea?"

"Yes, Bill. As you can now see I am now holding in my hand one of these devices, similar to the one that it is believed male number two possessed."

Andrea clicked the side button on the stun gun and blue electrical sparks flew back and forth between two stainless steel electrodes mounted about three inches apart on top of the device.

"Its sole purpose is self-defense and it has become a quite popular non-lethal alternative to carrying a gun. Most of time non-lethal, I might add. What this device does is deliver a high voltage shock to the nervous system. The device is capable of delivering up to three-hundred-thousand volts per jolt. Yes, that was three-hundred-thousand volts, Bill. When hit with the electrical shock, an assailant is rendered helpless for up to fifteen minutes.

"What our confidential source is telling us, is that male number two had this stun gun in his back pocket. The police think that male number two somehow fell backwards into a shallow puddle of water here on this green. The stun gun self-fired due to pressure from the fall or by a malfunction. The device continued to shock the wet male number two until its batteries were depleted. The shock must have caused the heart attack, killing male number two."

A somewhat disgruntled looking man with a badge hanging out of the breast pocket of his dark suit approached Andrea. He placed his hand on her shoulder and whispered into her ear. Andrea with a cat-caught-eating-the-canary look on her face, reported back in.

"Um, Bill, we are going to send it back over to you in the studio for now. It seems some of our privileged information may be turning a few heads out here. This has been Andrea Johnston with an exclusive WKPS remote news report. Back to you, Bill."

The girl wiping down the stainless steel lunch counter and watching the newscast with Phillip said, "Wow! Did you get a load of all that? Kinda gives you the creeps, don't it?"

Phillip, caught up in the revelations about the night before, mumbled to himself. "So that's what happened to Geevers. A Taser."

Phillip returned to the trashcan where he had left his flight bag. He reached in, took out the case of Bazooka bubble gum and tossed it. He dug around in the almost empty flight bag until his fingers touched his Purple Heart. He closed his hand on it and felt something foreign with it. When he removed his hand, he could see what else he had been feeling. There was one piece of Bazooka bubble gum sitting beside the Purple Heart. Phillip smiled.

He set the Purple Heart on top of the fight bag. He unwrapped the bubble gum, wadded up and threw the outer wax paper wrapper away. He took the comic part and unfolded it, squinting his eyes into focus to read the comic. It was that same ad Gum had cherished, the one about a brand new Schwinn bicycle for only 15,000 comic wrappers. The drawing showed a red bike with basket and bell on it.

Phillip wiped a tear of remembrance from his eye and folded the comic in a little triangle just like Gum would had done. He closed his eyes and a vision of Gum entered his mind. First it was the haunting sight of those lonely black eyes. That vanished and was replaced by the memory of Gum riding his bike that glorious afternoon before the storm. Gum flying his bike in and out of the crowd, squeals of glee coming from his mouth, arms outstretched as if he were really flying.

"Turner, look at me. I fly, just like you do, Turner! Look at me fly! Wheeeee!"

Phillip opened his watery eyes. He took the little triangle he had made and tucked it under the clasp on the back of his Purple Heart. He raised the medal to his lips and kissed it goodbye. Eyes closed and head raised, he murmured, "Thanks, Gum, I owe you one."

After tossing the Purple Heart into the trash can, he stuffed the empty flight bag in after it. He now possessed all he would need, the memory of his friend and his bike.

Phillip turned to leave the coffee shop. He stopped halfway to the door and returned to the trashcan. He reached back in, thinking he would have to take the flight bag back out to get what he was after. His fingers searched for the handles of the bag but instead found what he had returned for, the Purple Heart with the triangle-shaped comic tucked under the clasp. It was just sitting there on top of the bag waiting to be retrieved.

Phillip pulled his arm back out of the trashcan. Smiling, he flipped the medal into the air like you would toss a coin. He caught it on the fly and said to himself, "I bet Mad Dog would like to have this. He can show it to Red Leader or was that Red Rover?"

He smiled warmly and chuckled to himself. He flicked at the comic tucked under the clasp with his finger.

The counter girl called out, "Did you find what you were looking for?"

Phillip turned toward the girl and gave a contented smile. "Yeah, yeah, I found everything I had been looking for."

"Good. You have a good trip, now. Where ya heading anyway?"

"I'm headed home. I'm going home."

"That's nice. Real nice. You have a Merry Christmas now."

"I will. And Merry Christmas to you, too."

Phillip Turner walked out of the coffee shop, turned left, and disappeared down the hall.